Jo Bainbridge is a media professional that has worked with politicians through to porn stars. She was also once a contestant hopeful on a cooking show, studied marine biology (with a severe allergy to crustaceans), a chandelier cleaner and an art historian wannabe. Always one to try anything – this has led to many adventures, awkward moments and occasional conversations with overseas law enforcement.

Jo currently works on a news desk, builds LEGO with her two toddlers and aspires to be part of the slow food movement with her husband. When trying to write, she is easily distracted by a robust red wine, vegan ice-cream, Australian football league and cute dogs.

Jo has spent most of her life daydreaming and searching for romance.

For my mother, Judy, who loved to read, often from a sunny spot in our garden with a cup of tea. This all began when you left us and writing this has taken me on such an unexpected journey.

Not forgetting my husband Adrian who was a supporter of mine crawling into bed late with bleary eyes and for always being incredibly positive. I couldn't have gotten this across the finishing line without you.

And to everyone who lives with grief and suffers from a broken heart—you are not alone. May you find sparks of joy around you and wonderful people that make you smile again.

Jo Bainbridge

THE RIGHT SEASON

AUSTIN MACAULEY PUBLISHERS™

LONDON * CAMBRIDGE * NEW YORK * SHARJAH

A CIP catalogue record for this title is available from the British Library.

ISBN 9781528926720 (Paperback)
ISBN 9781528927659 (ePub e-book)

www.austinmacauley.com

First Published 2023
Austin Macauley Publishers Ltd®
1 Canada Square
Canary Wharf
London
E14 5AA

Thank you to Imelda Cribbin and AJ Collins, for your guidance, knowledge and brilliance. This novel found the right path because of you both.

To the team at Austin Macauley Publishers for taking a chance on my debut novel and for being as excited as I am to see this published.

Table of Contents

Chapter 1

The elevator doors open on the second floor. Medical students and hospital staff rush in, trying to claim a spot. Michael offers them a weak smile. As he's pushed further back into the elevator, he tries to breathe slowly, ignoring his rapidly beating heart and the sweat building up on the back of his neck. The doors open again.

"Sir?" A robust nurse next to him says. "Isn't this your floor?"

Michael jumps at the sound of her voice, nods his thanks and rushes out, almost knocking over other people. Never having been to an intensive care unit, he grows even more uncomfortable when the woman at the front desk ignores him. He looks past her shoulder and down a hall to where a nurse and a doctor have come out of a patient's room. They're locked in heavy conversation while flipping through medical records. Chances are it could be Ari's room.

He looks back at the woman at the desk. Her head still busy in paperwork. He clears his throat. "Umm, hi. I'm looking for a patient here. Ari...I mean Ariane Hennigan."

The woman looks up with a small frown. "It's a family area only, sir. Are you a family member?"

"Yeaaah...Yes, yes, I am."

She looks him over briefly. "Room 402 in the private wing."

Michael sheepishly smiles and walks off in a hurry before he can be called back to answer more questions.

He finds the right door and hesitates. His heart is hammering, and his palms are growing sweatier by the second. One more breath in and out. He raises his hand and knocks. He doesn't hear anything, so he opens the door. Three faces turn to him.

One of them, an older well-dressed man, looks confused and casts his eye over Michael's attire. "Young man, this is the private wing. I don't think you're in the right area."

"Errr, I think this is the right room. Is this Ari's room?"

Behind them, Michael can make out Ari lying on the bed, her features starting to come back to him: flawless fair skin, cute button nose, and long ash-blonde hair cascading around her shoulders. Her beauty has taken a back seat to the medical equipment surrounding her in the large room.

"I don't understand who you are or what you're doing here?" The man adds.

Michael guesses him to be Ari's dad. His silver-white hair is perfectly groomed and brushed back off his tanned face. A steel grey sports jacket matches the eyes staring at him.

"I'm Michael Wilson."

"We're Ariane's parents, and I've never heard of you." The man looks confused.

"I'm…" Michael stutters, then finds the confidence to keep talking. "I'm Macy's…father?"

Their faces are aghast in response.

"How dare you show your face in here!" Ari's mum says, a thumb and forefinger tightly pinching one of the pearls around her neck. She's a replica older version of Ari and immaculately dressed in an emerald pantsuit, not a hair out of place on her short bob, despite the harrowing situation.

The other person—a younger woman with golden-brown skin and chestnut curly hair—places a hand on Ari's mum's shoulder. "Winnie, it's my fault. I sent him a message about the car accident. I…I wasn't expecting him to respond, let alone show up."

Michael shifts from one foot to the other. "You're, Chloe, right? When I didn't hear back from you, I just had to come to the hospital."

"As you can see, this isn't a good time." Chloe narrows her bloodshot eyes.

"I didn't know what other option I had. I thought…this would be the right thing to do."

"You want to do the right thing?" Winnie raises her eyebrows. "It's a bit late for that now, don't you think?"

"No, no! That's why I'm here. I didn't know about any of this! I just met Ari…it was just one night and…sorry, that didn't come out as well as I had hoped," Michael says.

"This is my fault. I'll talk to him," Chloe says, looking at Ari's parents, then Michael. "You can buy me a coffee." She leans over Ari's bed and kisses her on the forehead.

Michael glances back at Ari's parents. "I'm sorry we had to meet like this."

They don't respond, so Chloe promptly ushers Michael out of the room. They walk awkwardly side by side down the hallway.

"Please, Chloe, I need to know. What you said in that message…it's really true? I'm a father?"

Chloe stops abruptly and faces him. "Let's get one thing straight. I know for a fact that you already knew about Macy. So, save the act."

"But that's why I'm here. I haven't spoken to Ari since that night we were together."

"How dare you!" Chloe throws her hands up. "This game you're playing with me. Don't."

"I swear, honestly, it's not a game."

"I can't believe you would turn up now and act as if this is all some big surprise."

"Honestly, until I saw your message, I didn't even know Ari was pregnant."

Chloe rolls her eyes. "Seriously? Look…Harold and Winnie can't deal with this right now. And I don't want to talk to you for a second longer. So, just leave." She starts to walk away.

Michael lightly catches her arm. "Please."

Chloe recoils and glares.

Michael holds up his hands, steps back, takes a breath and eyes Chloe. Is that contempt he sees? Perhaps. He looks up and down the empty corridor, then back at her. It's now or never. "Please, Chloe. Even if you don't believe me. I don't know what I should do now."

"Look, Michael. If that's even your real name. I've been Ari's best friend since we were kids. We've never lied or kept any secrets from each other. Especially, nothing as important as this. She told me that you wanted nothing to do with her or the baby. Given that she can't speak for herself right now, I'm guessing she wouldn't want you here."

Chloe's words sting.

"I would never say that." Michael takes a breath. "Look…I have to ask—are you sure the baby is even mine?"

"What? I can't believe you're still trying to worm your way out of your responsibilities. You disgust me," she hisses.

Michael clenches and unclenches a fist, trying to release his frustration. "I'm going to try and not react to what you just said. Look, you don't know anything about me, okay?"

"I know enough…and to answer the question. Yes, Macy is yours. You were the only one in a long time…she certainly hit rock bottom with you." She shakes her head and stalks off.

Michael calls after her. "If you hated me this whole time, why message me now? Why didn't you tell me when Macy was born?"

She turns to yell back. "It was never up to me. And now…I had to…she may not make it." Her eyes well up, and she disappears around the corner.

Michael rubs his hands over his face. "God dammit."

A few strangers turn to stare. Michael apologises as they look away and rush off. He goes back to the front desk to find the same nurse from earlier.

"Excuse me?"

"Did you find the room?" she asks.

"Yes, I did. But I was hoping you could help me find another patient?"

"Yes?"

"Macy. Macy Hennigan."

"The baby?"

"Yes."

"And you're the…?"

"The fa…father." Michael shuffles uncomfortably. *Doesn't get any easier to say.*

"Ah, I see. Okay. Well, down on Level 3, Paediatrics."

Michael finds his way to the room where they're keeping Macy. She's sleeping with small tubes coming out of her nose and wires attached to a heart monitor.

A nurse walks past, smiling. "You, the daddy?"

"Yes."

"She's doing really well."

"Can I…touch her?"

"Sure, you can, honey. You can give her a cuddle if you like. She's probably wondering where her mummy and daddy went." The nurse gives him a sympathetic look. She picks Macy up and gently places her into his hands.

"Umm, how do I hold her exactly?"

"Don't worry too much about the attachments to the machine. Just hold her how you would normally."

"Yeah, right. How I normally would," he mutters and looks down at Macy. "Will she be okay?"

"She's doing really well, given the circumstances. It was a pretty bad crash from the sound of it. Luckily, she was secured in her baby seat properly."

Michael nods and tunes out slightly as he looks down at this baby moving in his arms. Her eyes flicker open a little. Michael touches her small delicate hand, and she opens her lashes wider, then closes them again. He looks up at the hospital chart—she is indeed Macy Maree Hennigan, and she's just over three months old. He reads other details—size and weight—but none of that means much to him.

The nurse coughs, getting his attention. "I just need to check her vitals. Do you mind if I take her off your hands?"

"Sure, of course. Umm, when can I come back?"

"Any time. You're her daddy."

"Yeah, right, of course."

He leaves the hospital and heads to the nearest bar. The enormity of today's events swirl in his head. It had begun as a regular day: bench-press session, producing his latest sports podcast, then onto his actual paying job role—chasing a lead for his next article. But several hours later, he'd received a message about his supposed child, who he never knew existed.

With a Samuel Adams Boston Lager in hand, he finds a quiet corner with his phone and searches the family name. Ari had never mentioned her family that night. Maybe she didn't like talking about them to strangers, or perhaps, she just assumed he already knew she was from one of the wealthiest families in Massachusetts.

Chapter 2

Beth leans back in her office chair, taking a quick break from preparing a new client contract. As she finishes her Veranda Roast Grande and half-eaten bagel, her mind drifts back to last night—another failed attempt to do something different: yoga and speed dating combined. It started off well—one guy on her left was a 'light artist' and was quite interesting until they got to the tree pose. Beth's lack of balance meant that her foot came down hard on his toes, killing the conversation and any connection they might have had.

As she picks up her phone and deletes the dating app, she senses a familiar masculine figure in the doorway. "Good morning, Jordan."

Her secretary is right on time, as usual. His facial features and hair style is reminiscent of James Franco, and today, he's dressed in a tailored burgundy suit with crisp white shirt and navy tie.

"Morning!" He beams. "So, how was last night?"

"Don't ask," she mutters.

"Really, that bad?" He chuckles. "Sorry, but I do get a kick out of your stories."

"I'm glad they have some benefit for someone. I suppose it did make me leave work on time and do something that wasn't work related."

"See? Progress! Coffee?" He offers.

"No, but thanks. I'm dropping in to see Michael before my ten o'clock."

"Is your brother okay? You mentioned things were a bit rough for him right now."

"Ah, yeah, sort of." She frowns and looks down at her screen. "He will be…I think."

Jordan seems to sense her need for privacy on the issue and turns to leave. She calls after him. "Hold up. Didn't you have a date last night?"

"I sure did!"

"And?"

"It shows potential." His eyes twinkle.

"Yesss. That's exciting. At least one of us is having some luck. I want details later. But in the meantime, send flowers. No one ever sends flowers anymore. And make them blue."

"Will do…wait, blue flowers? Sounds depressing."

"No, the opposite. It stands for longing, a strong connection and desire."

"Huh. I never knew that."

"I used to date a guy who was writing a thesis on the Early Romanticism Movement. Ironically, he never bought me any flowers." Beth laughs.

"Really? How many signals does he need?"

"Right?"

"Well, it's only been one date. And we aren't at that stage yet."

"But imagine though, so romantic…" She looks away, daydreaming for a moment.

"Ah, are you sure you don't want me to fix you up with my cousin, Freddy? Remember? He isn't that bad."

"He wasn't that good either. Didn't he throw up in the elevator at our Christmas party last year? It still has an aroma in there." Beth pulls a disgusted face.

"He swears he's allergic to shrimp."

"Either way, he isn't my type."

"Not even a little?"

"Let's just say, he doesn't tick enough boxes."

"And just how many of these boxes are there?"

"I may have also created more after meeting him. But truth be told…I don't even know what I'm looking for anymore." Beth's phone beeps a reminder. "Dammit, I need to go already."

She grabs her things and rushes for the door. "Don't forget, flowers or send a cute lunch pack."

"You got it, boss." He grins as she rushes past.

*

Beth fights traffic in a summer downpour of rain and lashing winds. The frustration of the weather matches her mood. In the back of the Uber, Beth digs in her bag and pulls out her phone to check her makeup and lipstick are holding despite the rain drops that have made their way onto her perfectly made-up face. Success! Something going right.

Pressing the buzzer to Michael's apartment a few times, she finally hears the security door click. Her heels tap loudly on the cement as she climbs the stairs. She regrets not taking the elevator, but this will be her only exercise today.

"Bit early for a visit, isn't it?" Michael's voice calls out as Beth enters the apartment.

"Oh, I'm sorry. Did you have company last night?"

She finds him in the kitchen and kisses him on the cheek. He barely flinches, his head buried in a bowl of cereal.

"Yes, right you are! I find out that I have a love child, and all I can think about is sleeping with more women." He scoops another mouthful of cereal with a bent spoon.

Beth raises her eyebrows. "Good to see you still have your sense of humour."

"It's fading rapidly."

"Is the coffee on?" She doesn't wait for an answer but makes her way to the coffee machine.

"What on earth are those shoes you're wearing?" he asks.

"These little things?" She kicks up one foot slightly to admire. "Spectacular, aren't they?"

"So weird. You know, you're walking on what looks to be a sculpture of balls, not an actual heel?"

"Ah huh." She pours a coffee.

"Looks like something Jeff Koons would create if he made shoes. I don't know how you walk in those things."

Beth's back stiffens in response. "I don't know how you watch endless hours of sport, then watch highlights, then the replay, and then there's a big discussion about the game..."

"Yeah okay, we've had this argument before. Anyway, aren't you meant to be at work?" he asks.

"I'm on my way to a meeting. I just came to see how you are."

"You don't need to keep doing this. You've been here every day the last week."

"What else would I be doing?" She shrugs.

Beth takes a seat next to Michael at the kitchen bench.

He looks up and crinkles his forehead. "I like how you're worried about me. Do you even sleep anymore?"

"I look that good, do I? Thanks very much." She smacks him lightly on the shoulder. "Like you can talk. You're in desperate need of a shower. I don't even want to know what that smell is trying to escape your pores right now, and…this place is starting to look like a dump." She motions around the house.

"I've had a lot of stuff on my mind, as you know."

"Obviously. But surely, you can still think about this while tidying up? And maybe it's time to let go off this bachelor pizza apartment style, and be…"

"A bit more, fatherly-like?"

"Hmm…perhaps, more mature. We aren't getting any younger, you know."

"I'm sorry my youthful decor is offending you. I know you're more mature than me. That's what happens when you're the older sibling."

"I'm just trying to be helpful. One day, you'll have a woman stay here for longer than five minutes, and she might appreciate the effort."

Michael lifts his eyebrows. "I can go longer than five minutes."

Beth scrunches her nose. "Ewww, I don't need to know that."

"You brought it up. Why are you extra wound up today, anyway?"

Beth huffs. "Sorry. I went out last night for the first time in a while, and…let's just say, it was a wasted effort. Then I stayed up to do some work, which I could've finished earlier had I not gone out in the first place."

"Do you really need to keep putting in so many hours? I'm sure you'll be made partner by the end of the month. Regardless of what happens now. You've done all the hard work. And surely, the firm can see what a dick your competition is?"

"But James is only like that with me. And, unfortunately, the clients love him. He's practically unbeatable."

"Everyone has a weak spot."

"He protects his closely."

"So, what now?"

"I just can't fail. That's my solution. I've put so much time and energy into expanding my clientele list for the firm…if I get side-lined, I'll have to start again somewhere else. I can't even think about that for more than a second without breaking out in hives." She scratches her arms. "See?"

Michael chuckles. "You don't get hives."

"I do! Hey, I made you laugh today."

"Good play."

"You didn't answer my message this morning."

He nods. "I guess, I can't avoid talking about it." Michael finishes with his cereal bowl and places it in the sink with a thud. "It's been almost a week now, and I'm getting nowhere and still struggling to make sense of this."

"I wish I could somehow make this easier for you."

"I wish you could too. I don't even know what I'm meant to be doing. Am I just meant to accept that I'm a dad now?" He drags his feet back over to Beth at the bench. She reaches out and gives his arm a gentle squeeze.

"Most people get nine months to prepare for this. And even then, it's natural to freak out. So, I give you permission to be losing your mind about this. It's life changing."

"Glad to hear you think I'm losing my mind already." He manages a small smirk.

Beth holds up her hands. "I'm just saying whatever emotions you have right now—it's completely understandable."

"But I need to show Ari's parents that I'm responsible."

"I get that they think you knew about the baby. But as we both know, it's news to us. Stop trying to impress them and just be yourself."

"But 'me' is a single guy who likes to drink, eat pizza and watch and play a shit load of sport. I mean it's nothing ground-breaking. I need to be more than that."

"And you will."

"But how do I show them I'm father material when I don't even know how to look after myself properly? I'm thirty-one and still can't seem to manage that."

"Ok, but I'm thirty-three, and I still don't know either."

"Liar; you have a great job, an awesome apartment in the best area of the city, lots of prospects…"

"I currently have a job that pays well. But…I have no life, no time for friends or family. Certainly, no time for anyone else. I barely go out, and when I do, it's for work or it's a disaster. And I don't even remember the last time I made myself a meal. I usually just east pre-made meals from the freezer at one in the morning when I get home from work. So, I stick by my earlier statement."

"You're so competitive, even on who's having the shittiest time right now," Michael remarks.

"I am not! I just think sometimes you see my life through rose-tinted glasses. And that's just not how it is. Come on, Mr Reporter, it's your job to look past the gloss."

"Yeah, yeah. I know. But still."

"So, how is work going?"

"Err, it's going. Slowly. Sort of finding it hard to write at the moment."

"It's just stress. It will pass. And look, I was only trying to be supportive before. Not competitive." Beth pauses. "What about the friend, Chloe? Has she been helpful?"

"Nah, she still hates me and won't even look at me when I see her at the hospital."

"Still doesn't believe you, huh?"

"I haven't seen Ari since the first time I was at the hospital—I feel like I shouldn't be there. I mean, I hardly know her." Michael runs his fingers through his hair. "Argh, it's just…so messed up."

"Just keep going in to seeing Macy. Do the small talk with the Hennigan's when you bump into them. They can't ignore you forever."

"I guess."

Beth shakes her head. "This whole thing is still blowing my mind. I can't believe it's Ariane Hennigan, of all people. I still don't understand how you didn't recognise her at the bar."

Michael shrugs. "I was already a few drinks in. To be honest, I was impressed I even remembered her name the next day."

"Classy." Beth rolls her eyes. "Make sure you don't repeat that to the family."

"Yep. Thanks for the tip."

Silence envelops them for a moment.

"Look, Mikey. In time, Ari's parents will get to know you, and the more time they spend with you, the more they'll realise…"

"That I didn't actually abandon Ari or my child?"

Beth nods.

"I don't know about that. Why would any parent believe a stranger over their own child?"

"I get it, but they're going to have to deal with you one way or another. It'll be easier on them if they make it amicable."

"The other thing is what happens if Ari wakes up and is pissed off that I was contacted? I mean, think about it; she didn't want me to know."

"But you should be more furious than her. And remember, that was Chloe's idea, not yours. Also, I've spoken to that friend of mine who handles family law. It'll be easier for you to wait for Ari to wake up and then request a paternity test. Just to be sure."

"Yeah, okay. Thanks."

Beth's phone beeps on the bench. She looks at it, then frowns.

"Go on, get going," Michael says. "I'll be okay."

"Spoken to mum…or dad even?" Beth collects her things, already in another mad rush.

"I'll get to that."

"What about, Liam?"

Michael sighs. "No, not yet. He'll be back home soon enough, so I'll wait till then."

Beth arches her eyebrows. "He's your best friend."

"I want to tell him in person."

"And…what about, Naomi?"

Michael scowls. "What about her?"

"Are you going to tell her?"

"No. I hadn't planned on it," he grumbles.

"Don't you think you should? She's your ex-fiancé."

"I don't owe her anything. If you feel the need to tell her, then be my guest. I figured you would anyway."

Beth lets out a frustrated sigh. "Fine. Whatever. I'll see you later."

On her way out of the apartment, she almost runs into a couple huddled under an umbrella. She apologises, then gazes after them momentarily as they move on at their own leisurely space. The man has his arm wrapped around the woman's waist, pulling her close. The way she looks up at him adoringly. Beth feels a pang of jealousy. She misses those romance feels.

Chapter 3

Two weeks have passed, but nerves still plague Michael every time he crosses paths with Ari's parents; he can feel their aversion to him. And each time he sees Macy in the Paediatrics ward, he still gets confused as to how to hold her and what to do when she cries.

Today, as he arrives, the nurse from that first night greets him like a friend. "I'm surprised to see you here, Michael."

"Yeah? Why's that?"

She looks puzzled. "With Ariane's passing last night…did you leave some belongings here?"

The nurses' words are like a blow to his stomach. "What? There must be some mistake?" All of a sudden, it's hard to breathe.

"I'm sorry, love. I assumed you knew. I know it's a difficult time."

"And…Macy?" He is able to muster.

"She went home with your parents-in-law. She was given the all-clear. They didn't tell you?"

"Yes…of course. I suppose, I wasn't thinking and just ended up here."

The nurse looks at him with compassion.

Michael lowers his head and looks at the ground. Ari. She's gone. And poor, Macy. *What the fuck do I do now?*

He looks up and thanks the nurse, then pulls his phone from his satchel as he heads off down the hall.

The nurse calls after him. "Michael?"

He turns back.

"You aren't on the birth certificate. That's why Macy could leave with them. Good luck." She smiles with kindness.

Michael nods in appreciation, then calls Beth on his way out of the hospital.

"Oh, my God! That's such awful news about Ari. So sad. And they took Macy home without telling you?"

23

He sighs. "Yes…"

"What are you going to do?"

"I've just had an idea."

"No. No. No. I know what you're going to do."

"I'm not going to go and start banging on doors. I'm just going to leave a note."

Beth sighs unhappily. "How do you know where they are?"

"I'll find out."

*

After pulling some favours via the celebrity and gossip department of his workplace, The Boston Globe, Michael finds himself at the gate of a grand apartment building overlooking the Charles River. A doorman in a black suit greets him suspiciously, asking for his identity and reason for calling in. Michael explains that he just needs to make sure the Hennigan's receive his business card with a note on the back to call him. The doorman doesn't say much but asks him to wait.

Moments later, the doorman asks Michael to follow him to the lift area. Michael swallows hard, holding onto his business card and fiddling with it nervously. This may not have been the best idea or time to do this. The doorman presses the button for the top floor.

The lift opens out onto a foyer. Paintings line the wall with grandeur—numerous still-lifes and other works that look like generations of family portraits. The main picture in the middle of the hall is Ari and her parents. She looks younger compared to the woman he met in the bar. Ari is smiling and the painter has captured a sparkle in her eye—a young woman on the verge of opportunities. A wave of sadness hits Michael again.

Winnie's voice behind him makes him jump. "Ariane had just finished high school. She disliked sitting for it—had too many social events on, of course. But I thought it would be a lovely memory for her…as she got older…anyway…" Winnie seems to be collecting her thoughts. "Why are you here?"

"I…I'm so sorry about Ari."

Winnie nods a slight appreciation. "How did you know where we lived?"

"I'm a journalist, so I'm good at finding people. I was just going to leave a note and give you some time. It's just that we never exchanged numbers."

"Numbers?" Winnie looks puzzled.

"I was a bit surprised that you'd taken Macy home."

"Surprised? Why would you be surprised? This is her home, and we're her family."

"I get that, but I just thought you might contact me."

"Our daughter has just…" Winnie swallows, and when she continues, there's an edge to her voice. "You're suggesting that I'm meant to call you to pass on a running commentary about what we're doing?"

"I just want to stay in the loop. I'm her father, after all."

"That might be so. But a father that deserts his family has no business here. We indulged you while we were distracted at the hospital, but with Ariane…" She clears her throat. "Let us agree that we don't need to see each other again. You don't belong here. Do you understand?"

At that moment, Harold walks through the doorway, looking dismayed. "Michael?"

A familiar face appears behind Harold, and Michael is taken aback—this is the last place he expected to bump into an ice hockey star.

"Hi, I'm Logan Realmer." Logan seems to sense the uneasiness in the air and offers an awkward handshake.

"Nice to meet you." Michael takes his hand. "Michael Wilson," is all he manages to get out.

Harold looks Michael up and down. "I didn't know you were stopping by."

Michael cringes. Perhaps, his visit is a mistake. Perhaps, he should have dressed more formally. Even more regretful is his baseball cap choice—the Boston Bruins, a rival team of Logan's. "I didn't know I would be either."

"I thought we said no more guests today, Winnie?" Harold says.

"He's dropped in to pass on his condolences, but he has to rush off."

"I'll walk out with you," Logan offers.

Logan turns back to the Hennigans. "Again, I'm sorry to drop in, but I leave for Vancouver in an hour."

"You're always welcome here, Logan. You'll always be family to us." Harold offers his hand, and Winnie kisses Logan on both cheeks.

Michael quickly holds out his business card before he's whisked away into the lift. "This is my number and email." He leaves the card on the console.

In the lift, Michael smiles weakly at Logan.

"How long have you known the family?" Michael asks.

"Long time."

"I'm so sorry for your loss."

Logan nods. Nothing else is said for the rest of the ride. Michael can't help but feel small next to this giant, whose athletic broad shoulders seem to take up most of the space. His buzz cut makes him look fierce and slightly jarring in the glamorous lift surrounds. But the gold Rolex watch shows that he's in familiar territory.

They exit the lift together.

"Nice to meet you," Michael says.

Logan looks at him indifferently, "Yeah, see ya," and walks off to a waiting car.

Winnie was probably right, Michael thinks. I don't belong here.

*

Three long days later, the Hennigans request Michael's presence.

Winnie greets him, expressionless. "Harold is waiting for you in the guest lounge."

Michael files into line behind her quick step as she leads him through a wing of the apartment. He wonders if she always looks so formal; even in grief, she's immaculately presented. He reflects on his own outfit—he's glad to have at least put on a newish shirt, clean jeans and his Air Jordan 1 High 'Chicago' 1985 sneakers, which are in mint condition. Not that the Hennigans would appreciate that.

Winnie opens the door to the lounge room where Harold is seated. He looks up from the newspaper he is reading, before folding it and placing it down next to him.

"Michael. Welcome. Would you like a drink?" Harold asks as he stands.

Winnie asks, "Harold, it's only eleven thirty."

"It's almost lunch then. Wonderful. Michael?"

"Ah. Sure." Is there a right answer here?

"At least think about your health," Winnie protests with a loud sigh.

Harold ignores her and motions for Michael to sit, while gets up and heads to the liquor cart. The only sound is the clinking of ice cubes that fall into the glass. Michael shifts uncomfortably in his seat. It creaks slightly. Probably antique, he frets, wishing he'd picked another. As he's about to get up and move, Harold walks over and hands him his drink.

"Thank you, Mr Hennigan."

"Please, 'Harold' is fine."

Michael nods.

"Although, we aren't ready to have this whole conversation yet, I think you should know that Macy will remain here for now. This is the best place for her, given she's going through an unsettled period. As we all are," Harold says. He looks to Winnie, who nods, and an awkward silence surrounds them.

"Sure, okay. It makes sense for her to be here."

"Let's have a follow-up conversation. But now isn't the time. We're sorry that we didn't notify you that we took Macy home, but to be frank, we didn't feel we needed to."

Michael shrugs. "I can see where you're coming from. I can. But obviously, this is an unusual situation for everyone...I'd appreciate it if we could keep communication open, so I can see Macy." He takes a sip of whiskey, then places his glass on a coaster, hoping that scores him some points with Winnie. He looks over at her, but she ignores him.

"I understand," Harold says. "Given this, as you call it, is an unusual situation, it would be a proper formality for you to attend the wake we're having for Ariane."

"Harold!" Winnie looks shocked.

Harold sighs. "If he's the father of Macy, then he should be present."

Winnie shoots out of her chair and rushes from the room.

Harold's sets his glass heavily on the table next to him. "Sorry. It's an emotional time."

"Of course. I should probably get going anyway. Lots of meetings." Michael stands.

"Also, Michael, if anyone asks—you're an old acquaintance of Ariane's."

"I see." Michael rubs his jaw.

Harold adds, "We don't feel now is an appropriate time for gossip. We're a small but close family. Our daughter has never lied to us." He pauses and sighs again. "Not that we know of. I'm not a complete fool. There are some things a daughter doesn't tell her old father." Harold pushes his glasses back up the ridge of his nose. "If I were in your shoes, Michael, I'd say it's worth trying to have another conversation with Chloe."

Michael nods, thanks him for his time and leaves.

Perhaps, he's just being paranoid, but as he walks out of the apartment building and down the road, he feels he's being watched.

Chapter 4

Liam knows the family name, but he's surprised at the number of paparazzi stationed outside the Hennigan's apartment—that the wake of a wealthy Boston family's daughter could draw so much media attention. Once inside, he doesn't know anyone and wonders why Michael has asked him to be here. He glances at the expensive artwork adorning the walls. Statues of ancient Greek Gods stare back blankly, much like how he's looking at the people surrounding him.

Trying to not look like an outsider, Liam takes the offering of an appetiser from a waiter and makes small talk with people, hoping he looks sympathetic enough when they speak of Ariane. The more the conversations go on, the more his guilt builds in his stomach. He hopes Michael finds him soon to explain why he's here. This is high on the list of oddest things Michael has asked him to do, especially as he's only just moved back to Boston.

Finally, he spots Michael talking to a middle-aged woman who's nursing a baby. He catches his eye and Michael looks at him apologetically. And there's Beth, next to Michael. It's been over two years, and she looks different somehow. Different to when they first met in college, when he was a freshman paired with Michael in a dorm. Not only did he and Michael hit it off immediately, but he couldn't believe his luck that his roommate had such a smart and attractive older sister. However, she was in her junior year and not overly interested in his presence.

Beth reaches for the baby. *Hang on a minute! Is it hers? But she was never clucky.* Liam's heart skips a beat. He doesn't want to stare awkwardly, so walks out to the terrace. The city view shimmers in the summer heat. As he takes a breath, the humidity engulfs him, but he doesn't mind. He's home.

A familiar hand touches his shoulder and he turns.

Michael grins. "Hi, bud. So good to see you!"

"You too." They embrace, trying not to look too ecstatic to see each other in the presence of mourners. "Can I just say I hadn't imagined our reunion would be this?"

Michael nods. "I know. This is weird. I'm sorry."

The subdued chatter inside rises slightly, and heads turn in the direction of a somewhat familiar, tall man.

"Do you know who that is?" Michael asks.

Liam wrinkles his nose. "Doesn't he play left-wing for the Vancouver Canucks?"

"Good to know you haven't lost all your sporting knowledge from being in Beijing for so long." Michael leans in and clinks Liam's glass with his drink.

"Hey, I still remember where I come from. He's Realmer, right? Now I know why the paparazzi are out front. But more importantly, I want to know why we're here."

Michael quickly grabs two drinks from a passing waiter. "This first."

Liam nods and they clink glasses, both taking a long swig, then coughing slightly at the intensity of the whiskey.

"I really needed that," Michael says. He frowns, then looks around, obviously uncomfortable. "I need to tell you something, and I'm only telling you here and now as I wanted to tell you in person. Plus, it wasn't really my fault that your first available day back coincides with the wake. So, here we are."

"I'm going to throw out my first guess. Were you dating this woman?"

"No, I wasn't. It was just one night."

"Huh? I know you're intense sometimes, but this is next level!"

"Yeah, yeah, hold on. It's not like that."

"So, what happened between you?"

Liam listens as Michael relays his news.

"Wait, wait, wait. A daughter? That baby inside? I thought it might have been Beth's."

"Shhh. Keep it down, would you? Why would you think it's Beth's? Anyway, Chloe said she knew I wasn't interested in supporting the baby but thought it appropriate to notify me."

"Whoa, I'm sorry. I need a minute." Liam pauses. "Surely, this could be a mistake, and it's someone else's?"

"I thought that, but the maths is right. Macy is just over three months old, and I was with Ari just over a year ago."

Liam rubs the back of his neck. "And Ari never mentioned it?"

"No. We've had no contact."

"Wow, I thought this sort of stuff only happened on reality TV shows!"

Michael shrugs.

Liam whistles a mimic of a bomb exploding.

Michael nods in agreement. "Heavy right?"

"My mind is blown…I'm sorry. I don't know what else to say. Fuck! Well, I know one thing: they aren't after your money." He nods to the lavish surrounds.

"Yep, thanks. Beth also mentioned something of equal comedic value."

"Sorry, I'm looking for some relief here. It's hard trying to take this all in."

"Tell me about it. All I know is, I now have a daughter, and she no longer has a mother to look after her."

A waiter walks over to them. "Would you gentleman care for another drink?"

"Yes," they reply in unison.

"So, did you contact her the next day or anything?" Liam asks.

"When a woman flees the scene in the morning, you don't go chasing her down…I mean, if you really think they're hot, you might check them out on socials, but basically, it's just one night, right?"

"I get it. I wouldn't have been sending her messages either. Shit, Mikey. What are you going to do?"

"I don't know."

"You'll get a paternity test, right? You'll actually double check you're the father?"

"I will. I was waiting for Ari to…you know…wake up. Now, I'm just trying to find the right time to bring it up with her parents. It hasn't exactly been smooth with them."

"But the sooner, the better, right?" Liam glances around, then whispers, "What if she…you know…slept with a lot of men."

"Possible. I guess, from my end, I know it's at least plausible. But from what I understand, she didn't date much, and hook ups weren't normally her thing."

"So, what were you then?"

"A moment of weakness and poor judgement?"

Liam takes in Michael's despair. "This isn't really my field of expertise, but I'm here anytime you need me."

"Thanks, bud. I really appreciate that." He slaps him lightly on the back. "And thanks for coming. But just having you here today…I needed that."

"Of course. I'm officially back from Beijing, and I'm not going anywhere. Unless they fire me for being out of the office for too long." He looks at his watch, frowns, then finishes up his drink. "So, I'll call you afterwards, okay?"

"Yep. Bring it in." Michael pulls him in for a hug.

*

As Liam heads out of the Hennigans apartment building, he retrieves his vibrating phone from his jacket pocket, but when he sees the name flash up, lets the call go to his messages. While waiting for a taxi, he half-listens to the long message from Evelyn. She'll be leaving Beijing in a couple days and will be in New York for a week, if he wants to meet up. His jaw tightens and rubs his neck again.

"Everything okay?"

Liam spins around at the sound of the familiar voice.

"I heard you were back in town," Beth says, looking cheerful. Her long dark hair dances below her shoulders as she strides towards him. She brushes a few strands of hair away from her hazel eyes and leans in to peck his cheek. Liam has always liked how tall she is, and with heels, she reaches a little more to his height.

"Yes, it's good to be home."

"So nice to have you back. I didn't see you inside?"

"I was only there briefly. I have another work situation to deal with."

"No luck with a ride yet?" she asks.

"I have one coming. I can drop you at your office?"

"Perfect, thanks."

"Pretty intense in there, wasn't it?"

"It's so sad even when you don't know the person. She was just like us, you know? Still young," Beth says thoughtfully.

Liam tilts his head back momentarily. "Devastating. And all this stuff with Mikey being a dad!"

"Thank God, he finally told you!" Beth places a hand to her chest.

"Can't say I was ready for that one."

Liam spots his ride and whistles it over. He opens the door for Beth, who gracefully glides into the backseat, then jumps in after her before the car takes off.

"So, how's Mikey been? He doesn't look like he's getting a lot of sleep."

"I don't think he's slept at all," Beth says.

"Poor guy."

"I've been checking up on him, but I don't know what else to do really. I guess, he just needs some time. I think they all do."

"I don't want to sound completely inappropriate here—I know we just went to this woman's wake—but it seems really dishonourable that she didn't call Mikey to tell him she was having his baby."

"I know. Why keep it a secret?"

"Do you reckon it's the family? Mikey can talk to anyone, but this sort of elite crowd knows an intruder."

"It crossed my mind."

"Hmmm, tough one."

"But from the sounds of it, she seemed like a nice person. Though, I suppose, no one really bitches about you at your wake, do they?" Beth pauses for thought. "I don't think I could go through with it and not tell the father. Just think—if she had never had the accident, he wouldn't ever have known about Macy."

Liam shakes his head. "I can't even think about that."

"It was probably pretty scandalous in such an elite family. Still, you would think it would be better if she had the support of the father, regardless."

"You would think so."

They fall quiet for a moment, then Liam looks at her. "I saw you with Macy."

Beth smiles. "Yes, she's quite the cute thing."

"So, I guess that makes you an aunt now, huh?"

"Yeah, I guess that does…"

Silence again.

"So, how are you going?" Liam asks.

"Me?" She seems puzzled that he would be interested in how she is.

"Yes, you. Michael mentioned the other week that he's never seen you working so hard before."

"That's probably true. I've been busy trying to land a major client. If I can do this, it might secure my partnership."

"Ah, yes. Mikey said. But whatever happens, it sounds like you've already achieved quite a lot."

"Thanks…I'm sorry we haven't chatted much—you know, since you've been away in Beijing. We should probably have a drink and catch-up properly."

"Sure! But don't apologise. We all have our own lives now."

Beth nods. "Are you glad to be back?"

"Yeah. At the moment, I am. I've missed my old haunts. I miss the coffee, good pizza, the company of course." He winks.

"Of course!" she agrees playfully, placing a hand on her heart.

"I'm sure, I'll miss Beijing though. But I think it was time to return. Two years is enough, and I think the longer you're away, the harder it gets to come home. I was a bit worried about coming back—everything being so different."

"Don't worry. Not too much has changed. Well, up until a few weeks ago, anyway. Until then, everything was exactly the same. Oh, but Reggio's closed. I remember how much you loved their spicy salami pizza."

"You remember that?"

"Of course. You made us order it all the time. And it was pretty good, so I complied."

"But now it's closed. I can't believe it. My one reason for coming back!"

Beth laughs.

"So, what else? No children you want to let me know about?"

Beth snorts. "I haven't been dating for a while. I'm pretty much constantly surrounded by colleagues and clients. And for the record, I don't sleep with them."

"Good to know." He grins back.

"So, what about you?"

"Hmmm, I was sort of seeing someone in Beijing, but nothing was going to come of it."

"Holiday romance, hey?"

Liam shrugs with amusement. "Something like that."

"You look different to me."

"I think I've put on weight. I ate an obscene amount of rice, noodles and dumplings."

Beth giggles. "No, you haven't. Maybe it's your hair. It used to always be so long all over, but now you have a wave on top. A tailored suit. And your glasses, quite dapper. Sort of a Clark Kent vibe going on."

"Oh...thanks." He takes his glasses off. "I only really need them for reading." He slips them in his top suit pocket. "But I dare say, it's probably just being older that makes me look different, you know, working longer hours and looking tired all the time."

"We all have that problem,"

Liam rolls his eyes. "Beth, you look just the same as I remember."

"Thank you. You're sweet."

The taxi pulls over to let Beth out.

"Anyway, it was good to see you again, even though it was brief."

"You too."

"You on a new number?"

"Yes."

"Here." She motions for his phone. Liam passes it over. She adds her number. "There you go. No excuses now."

"True. Guess, I'll have to call you for that drink."

"You better!"

He leans over and kisses her cheek before she gets out of the car.

Beth smiles. "It's good to have you back."

"Thanks. I didn't know you missed me so much."

She grins now. "See you around, Liam."

Liam daydreams for the rest of his trip back to the office. Despite Michael's issues weighing heavily, he can't help but feel elated to be back in Boston.

Chapter 5

Chloe discreetly watches Michael throughout the wake, wondering why he keeps turning up. And why now?

She'd been so angry when Ari had said the man didn't want anything to do with the baby. How could someone do that to her best friend? Leave her deserted and alone. How could they not want to be a part of their own child's life? Eventually, she'd pressured Ari into giving her the father's name, and that's when she searched online, trying find out as much as she could about him—a few photos from his engagement party, posted publicly on a friend's social media profile. Michael had probably been married when he and Ari slept together. That would explain why he didn't want to have a baby with her.

Macy's squealing brings Chloe back to the present. The baby is being bounced around by various members of Ari's family. *Such a beautiful girl.* Chloe's eternally grateful to be her godmother, but it makes her distraught to think that Macy will never know her amazing and caring mother.

She looks around for Francis. He's on the other side of the room, looking like he's almost enjoying himself. He's hardly made a backwards glance at her. He'd easily believed her when she told him she was okay, leaving her to mingle alone. A doting boyfriend, he was not.

Too many emotions creep up on her at once, tears running down her face. She rushes off to the nearest bathroom to take a moment, wipe them away. In the mirror, she looks at her red blotchy and puffy face. Annoyed, she splashes water on herself. She just needs to get through one more hour, she tells herself. Just treat it like a performance. She braces, takes some deep breaths and finds her stage persona. Exiting, she immediately bumps into Michael.

"I'm so sorry. Ah. Hi, Chloe."

"Hi," is all she can muster.

"So…how are you?" he asks. "Another tough day for you, huh?"

"I'm sorry, but I don't really feel like chatting at the moment." She turns to walk away.

"Wait. I was hoping we could talk. I don't mean today. But another time."

She narrows her eyes.

"Please, give me a chance."

"I've heard this all before."

"I need to understand why, and you're the only one who can help."

"You're wasting my time." Her words come out more venomous than she anticipates, but she can't help her anger.

"You don't think I'm sticking around, do you?" Michael says.

"I…"

"It's fine. I get it. All you see is a guy who abandoned his child."

"And cheats on his wife," she adds.

"My wife?"

"I did some digging."

"Wow. Okay." He looks stunned. "Do you think I'm here for some free drinks and then I'm done? How about you get to know me before you make any more judgements about the type of person I am."

Chloe baulks at Michael's breathless, angry tone. "How dare you come here today and start criticising me."

"I'm not. I'm just extremely frustrated, and you won't even give me a chance."

"Today, isn't about you. I'm mourning the loss of my best friend!" Chloe eyes well up. "Oh God, not again." Her tears spill over, and she wishes she could run, but her legs have become heavy as cement.

Michael ushers her to a quiet corner and out holds out a napkin. "That's the best I can do."

Chloe hesitates, until Michael whispers, "There no crab cake residue on there, I promise."

"Thanks." She sniffs, accepting it with a small chuckle despite herself.

"I'm sorry. I didn't mean to upset you."

"Wasn't entirely your fault."

"I'm sorry, anyway."

"I just need to be alone, please."

"I understand…but if, on another day, you could put up with me for one coffee, I'd be grateful."

"I'll think about it."

"Thank you. I'm sorry, by the way…about Ari."

"Thanks."

As she watches him walk away, she ponders on how he'd seemed genuinely frustrated with her comments about his wife. But maybe she's just extra emotional today, and it's clouding her judgement.

Ari's mother calls out to her. "Chloe? Aunt Margaret is leaving and wants to see you."

"I'll be there in one moment." She dabs at her escaping tears, then sets off to find Aunt Margaret.

The woman is in another room, sobbing.

"Chloe. Come here, pet." She motions for her to come over.

"Aunt Margaret, please, you'll make me cry again."

"Chloe, I've always considered both you and Ariane my nieces, and I don't want that to change."

"I hope it doesn't either. You'll always be an aunt to me." Chloe hugs Margaret, who hangs onto her hand for reassurance.

"I've lost Ariane, but I can't lose you too," she says.

"You won't," Chloe affirms, her tears starting again.

She squeezes Margaret's age-weathered hands, still immaculately manicured, each of her rings bold and eye-catchingly sparkly. She'd always been amused by the thought of how much each must weigh.

"I heard you were talking to a man?" Aunt Margaret says.

Chloe reaches for some tissues and hands them to Margaret. "Do you mean Michael?"

"Yes, him." Aunt Margaret motions for her to lean in closer, then whispers. "Winnie told me he's meant to be Macy's father. We better keep an eye on him. Showing up now, probably for money," she hisses.

Chloe sighs. "I didn't think Winnie was going to mention anything yet."

"Nonsense. She tells me everything." She pauses a moment. "I just don't understand why Ariane didn't marry Logan."

"Well, for one thing, he never wanted to be married."

Aunt Margaret scoffs. "He would have sooner or later. He's here, you know."

"Yes, I've seen him." Chloe isn't interested. Logan knows how she feels about him, so he keeps his distance.

"Such a rare gem that one. Sometimes, you only get one love in this lifetime."

Chloe smiles weakly as she remembers Margaret's late husband.

"Chloe, dear, I really wish you would get married soon and settle down. Start a family." She reaches for her hand again.

"Oh, Aunt Margaret, maybe soon. Francis likes to take things slowly, and we're both really busy with the orchestra at the moment."

"Everyone is too busy these days, but don't wait too long. You'll be thirty next year. You have such a pretty face, my dear, but it won't last forever. Look at me!" She chuckles. "But you might be luckier than me, you have your mother's wonderful Caribbean complexion, hides the wrinkles for longer."

Chloe doesn't know how to respond, so she simply leans in for a quick hug. Looking over Margaret's shoulder Francis is busy having a chuckle with a couple she doesn't know. Then she feels a gaze upon her. Chloe straightens up and looks behind her. It's Michael. He nods her way and keeps walking.

*

Chloe can't sleep; the heat from the day still lingers in the night air. She takes a deep breath to relax, but the warm air feels suffocating. Or is that her grief? Maybe the air conditioner will offer solace. She drags herself out of bed and tries to turn it on with no luck. "Ah, you piece of shit!" she yells, flinging the remote across the room. It slams against the wall. "Is the world against me?" She moans, flopping onto the couch.

She stares at the ceiling, her mind drifting to Ari. *Don't go down this rabbit hole again!* She gets up and finds her phone for distraction. Another concerned message from her mother, who's wondering whether they should fly up to see her. The flowers her parents sent are looking a bit tired, the water murky. Brown-edged petals have drifted to the floor in a mess. It almost depicts a live art exhibit, emotions the inspiration.

Francis isn't here tonight. She wishes he was. He's been strangely distant lately. Sure, their work and practice schedules are hectic, but he seems to be pulling away—oddly absent since Ari's accident. Chloe can't help thinking back to Margaret's comments; she always assumed she would get married someday. She's been with Francis for almost three years now, which isn't a terribly long time, but she's growing impatient for what might happen next. If anything.

Perhaps, the daily news might be a better and more calming time waster. She's been so switched off from the outside world recently. She taps the Boston

News App and scrolls until she hits the business section. Michael's name flashes up on a byline. *Huh. There he is again!* She can't get away from him. She reflects on the couple of times they've met. He seems like a nice guy when he's not agitated, but perhaps it's all some sort of diversion from the truth. As Aunt Margaret said, he could be after money. Maybe he thinks he's entitled to some of the family's wealth.

She drops her phone on the couch, then reaches for the only thing she has left—her violin. The walls are soundproof, and the windows double-glazed, but without the air working, she leaves them wide open. As she prepares to play, she spies a couple out on a distant balcony having late-night candle-lit drinks. She imagines how happy they are, whispering to one another how they'll always be there for each other. She sighs and begins to play Tchaikovsky's *Violin Concerto in D major, Op. 35*.

Why not feel even more miserable and alone?

Chapter 6

Beth is sitting in her office, staring blankly at her desktop screen, when an Instant Messenger notification pops up, startling her. A note from Jordan.

"Warning! James is coming your way."

She types back an angry emoji symbol. In the last year, she's taken on more work than James to prove she's capable of making partner, but recently he's been pulling in more clients for the firm. They're both young and as eager as each other, and James is standing in the road of her end goal. She has to find a way to defeat him.

"I heard you had another late night?" James pretends to look saddened as he enters her office. "You know, you shouldn't work so much. A woman your age should be thinking about a family."

"Ahh, James. What a pleasant surprise. I didn't know I'd be in for such a treat today with your chauvinistic attitude. Nice bow-tie, by the way."

James sits opposite her desk and reaches for his yellow-spotted bowtie. "Inspiring, isn't it?" He grins with mischief. She must admit the colour suits his dark-brown skin and shaved black hair, making him *slightly* attractive.

Beth focuses back on her desktop. "Perhaps, if you make an appointment with Jordan, he can make sure I'm able to squeeze you in, but now isn't really a good time."

"Surely, you aren't that busy, since I have all the new clients at the moment?"

She looks at him and his smugness. "I'm not in the mood for your banter."

"I was just seeing if you could read over my speech for Neil's farewell dinner. It's such an honour being the only non-partner to be asked. But I'm sure, it doesn't mean anything, Beth. I'm sure you're still in the running for partnership. I wouldn't read too much into it."

Ignoring his dig, she forces a smile. "James, can you please go and bother someone else?"

He smiles back and gets up to leave but turns around. "Oh, one last thing. My secretary has added me to your table tonight at the restaurant. Mr Bourke insisted you take me along as I have a bit more experience with the transport sector. Jordan is probably on the phone with them now making the arrangements. I knew you wouldn't mind."

The rush of blood to her face forces her to take a breath. "I see…fine. Whatever is best for the firm." Another forced smile.

"Great. I'll leave you to it. I'll see you tonight." He tugs at his bow tie, grins and leaves her office.

Beth waits thirty seconds, then hurls a pen at the open door.

Jordan pops his head around the corner. "I hope that wasn't directed at me? I'm sorry I had to get James a seat at the table."

"I'm sorry, he's so," she lets out a deep breath "so infuriating. He makes me act like a child."

Jordan brings the pen back to Beth's desk, his smile sympathetic. "His secretary literally just called me."

"Wow. Did he, like, sprint from his office to tell me? He knew it would piss me off." Deflated, Beth sighs then focuses on Jordan. "I need to be on my A game tonight. James is going to be making a point of showing me up."

"Just be your normal charming and intelligent self."

"Thank you. You're sweet for the pep talk. But it won't be enough. I need something…I need to get the two chairpersons on my side, and I need the partners to hear about it."

Jordan's face lights up. "A challenge! I'll see what I can dig up—a soft spot or a personal interest angle." He gets out his phone and begins his hunt. "What about, Mr Williams? Does he have a partner? Wife?"

"No, he's solo. He seems too creepy to be married." Beth wrinkles her nose at the thought of their initial meeting, where all he seemed to do was stare at her chest the whole time.

"Let's avoid him as much as we can then," Jordan says with a concerned look.

He wanders off but returns ten minutes later, looking triumphant. "I think I've got something." He rushes over to her side of the desk with his phone.

"Whose Instagram are you stalking?" she asks.

"It's Mr Carindale's son, Kent. Remember how his son was in a skiing accident a couple years ago?"

"Ohhh, yeah. That was awful."

"Looks like he's back on the social scene now. I mean, he always was a bit of a ladies' man."

"How do you know this?"

"It's all on here." He motions to his phone.

"Duh, of course." Beth realises she hasn't kept up with the socialite scene as much as she once did.

"He seems to be hosting lots of charity events to raise awareness for experimental treatments into trauma cases that lead to disabilities…"

Beth jumps out of her seat. "That's it! We need to expand on the company's pro bono commitments, and we could do this with free legal advice to people with disabilities. It's perfect! I'll ask the Carindale's tonight."

Jordan nods.

"Jordan. I'm forever grateful, you're working with me and not James. Please never leave me."

"I would never leave you, Beth." He winks as he leaves her office.

Beth blushes despite herself. She makes a mental note to reconsider setting up another online dating profile.

*

A few hours later, she's dressed in a stylish black-silk jumpsuit with an embroidered evening jacket and—her ultimate weakness—René Caovilla heels. Her hair and bangs are perfectly straight, her eye makeup subdued, her red lipstick, the hero. A YSL clutch under her arm, and she's ready to head to the downtown area. She tries to ignore her inner chitchat about not taking a plus one to the dinner. Who would she have even invited? Couldn't be a date. Had to be a friend. Maybe Liam? He's back in town and they're friends. Perhaps, next time she would.

Tonight's dinner is her focus; she needs to land these clients for her career and for the firm. To do this, she needs to keep James's interaction with them to a bare minimum—an almost impossible task, given he enjoys the spotlight so much, particularly when it means taking the focus away from her. Tonight, has to be flawless.

She's the first to arrive. She's made a point of it so she can have a moment with the sommelier, the maître d' and the waiters, to hint at a very generous tip if the meal is seamless. Unfortunately for her, James is also early with a leggy blonde on his arm.

"Beth, are you struggling to control the wait staff already?"

"Just making sure tonight goes well. You know how important it is for the firm."

"Of course, the firm. Not just for you?"

"I might remind you that this is my client dinner. You're here to help me."

"I didn't think you needed my help."

"I don't. This wasn't my choice."

"Obviously, the partners feel you're lacking in this field. But don't worry, Beth. I told them I'd ensure this would be a successful evening."

Anger rises in her body. "Better be careful you don't come across as narcissistic."

"Now, now, Beth. I thought you were working on your anger issues with some yoga."

Beth scoffs. "My only 'anger issue' is with you."

"But, Beth, your life would be pretty boring without me. Aren't I the only man in your life?"

"You're not in my life, James. And don't think for one minute that I give you a second thought the minute I leave work."

"Sure, you don't, Beth." His eyes twinkle. "I've seen you checking me out."

"Don't flatter yourself." Beth hopes she looks disgusted rather than guilty.

The woman on James's arm is staring at them blankly. Beth apologises and introduces herself, betting that James has forgotten her name already.

Luckily, the maître d prevents any more sparring by informing Beth the clients have arrived. Beth and James follow to greet them in the restaurant foyer.

"Mr Carindale, so lovely that you can join us for dinner tonight. And your lovely wife. Beatrice, isn't it?"

"Good evening, Beth and James. Yes, this is my wife, Beatrice."

"Hello, lovely to meet you both," Beatrice says sweetly. "Thank you for having us tonight. We've been looking forward to it."

"The pleasure is all ours," James intervenes, smiling. "And this is the lovely, Kiki." He motions to the blonde.

"And, Mr Williams. Always a pleasure," Beth says with as much enthusiasm as possible.

"Hello again, Bethany. It's been too long," he says with a sleazy smile that makes Beth's skin crawl.

James offers Beatrice his arm and shows her to the table while Kiki and Mr Carindale follow, leaving Beth to direct Mr Williams to the table.

As Beth anticipates, Mr Williams leers at her all evening, while James talks non-stop about himself and what he can do for them at the firm. Beth waits for James to take a sip of his digestive so she can change the subject.

"As you know, Mr Carindale…"

Mr Carindale stops her politely. "Call me, Arnold, please."

Beth nods and smiles. "Arnold…we're looking at ways to show our commitment to pro bono representation. It's been a hallmark of the firm for some time, but we'd really like to expand this service. I'm hosting an event next month to showcase our charity work, and the firm would love to have you and Beatrice there…and you of course, Mr Williams."

Mr Williams makes eyes at Beth again. She shifts uncomfortably in her seat.

"Of course, Beth," he says. "That would provide great insight into your firm, and of course, anything for a good cause. What fields are you looking at this year?"

"That brings me to my next question. We'd like to focus on providing specialist legal advice for people with disabilities." Beth turns to the Carindales. "I wanted to ask you about your son, Kent. If you think he would be interested, I'd love an opportunity to speak to him about being a guest speaker at the event."

"What a splendid idea!" Arnold says.

Beatrice looks thrilled. "Certainly. He would like that wouldn't he, Arnold?"

"Yes. I'll speak with Kent first thing tomorrow, then pass on his details."

"I think it's a wonderful idea." Beatrice pats Beth's hand. "Smart, kind and pretty."

Mr Williams chimes in. "She sure is."

He trawls a look from her face down to her cleavage. Beth does her best to not let it bother her. But later, upon leaving, Mr Williams puts his arm around her waist and kisses her, too close to the lips. Beth pushes back, shocked by his forwardness. He leaves, looking smug at their encounter.

James lingers behind while Beth fixes up the restaurant bill.

"James, you're still here? I didn't notice." She yawns. "Is there something you wanted?"

"Kiki is in the ladies." He grabs a handful of mints at the counter and starts popping them into his mouth, munching on them loudly.

"You're only meant to take one mint."

James shrugs off her comment. "The clients seemed to like the idea of the charity." He almost sounds impressed. "But it's a bit obvious, don't you think? They happen to have a son with a disability, and that's what you want to support this year?"

Beth shoves her clutch under her arm and looks him in the eye. "It's a good cause. Plus, we support other community events. So, what's your problem?"

"No problem here."

"Go home, James. I had a great night tonight, despite you being here. It was a huge success and nothing you can say will change that." She turns to leave.

"I suppose if the charity night doesn't pay off, and you don't make partner, you always have Mr. Williams to fall back on."

Beth spins around to face him. "What are you talking about?"

"I saw the way you two were eyeballing each other."

"You have a very vivid imagination. Apart from being my father's age, he's a client."

"Sure." James seems unconvinced. "I'm onto you. Mind you…maybe I should be encouraging this business lead. You can marry one of the most affluent men in the city and never have to work again."

"Take your hired date home, James."

James tilts his head. "Maybe you should try it, Beth. A little action in the bedroom might actually make you a nicer person to be around."

"Arsehole."

*

After a few blocks of brisk night air, Beth calms. She passes a familiar bar she used to frequent years ago, an eternity ago—Michael, Naomi, Liam and herself—and is lured in for a night cap. She sits at the bar, and while she sips her drink, thinks about Liam again. It was good seeing him again the other day; she'd missed his company. He did seem different, though. Perhaps, he's been working out? More masculine? Or has he always looked like that?

Her thoughts are interrupted by an attractive guy with short blonde curly hair, in a grey plaid suit who offers to buy her another drink. She agrees and enjoys his company for a while. Maybe, she does need to loosen up a bit? It's been a while since she's taken someone home, but no one seems to ever measure up. To whom that person is, she doesn't even know. While he's in the bathroom, she leaves money on the bar for his next drink and heads home alone.

Chapter 7

Michael is walking in the mid-afternoon sun through Titus Sparrow Park. A southwest wind does little to relieve the humidity. Despite the heat, runners and walkers jostle for space on the pavement and kids run around the playground. He glances over at their delighted squeals. He wonders what Macy will be like when she's a toddler. Would he be kicking a ball to her or pushing her on a swing? The church bells nearby ring and he checks his phone. He's a bit early for his meeting with Chloe but pushes on anyway.

The front of the Symphony Hall, where he was asked to meet her, is deserted. The journalist in him wants to snoop. The back-entry doors are open. One of the security guards spots him and calls him over. "Are you after tickets?"

"No, I'm not. I'm just meeting someone here…"

"Hey, I know you. You're a reporter, right? My sister works at Bank of America Europe. You interviewed her a couple months ago—Mary Barnett."

"Ohhh, yes. That's right."

"She loved the piece. You can wait inside."

"That's great, but I'm not here…"

"It's so hot out. Come in." He ushers him in. "They're almost finished."

The security guard answers a call, so Michael shrugs and walks in. Stage crew and other staff are milling around, but no one pays him any attention. He finds a spot in the backstage area where he can see most of the orchestra in full swing of a rehearsal. The hall feels so different with empty seating; he's never seen it like this before.

He spots Chloe…in the orchestra. She's playing violin. A lightbulb moment. *So that's why she wanted to meet here.* He hadn't actually given much thought to what she did for a living, but here she is—hair pulled back in a neat bun, lights reflecting off the perspiration on her face, showing an ownership of power, but something else too: passion and intensity. The longer he listens, the more exquisitely the music flows through his body.

It stops abruptly, and the maestro curses, yelling something in French Michael can't understand. All the musicians start packing up, including Chloe. A few of them walk past him with suspicious looks. Michael backs away and heads out the way he came in.

"Can I help you sir?" A stagehand asks.

"I'm here to see Chloe."

"You can wait down there." The man nods down the hall.

He isn't sure if he should venture forwards, but it would look odd now if he continued out the exit door. He keeps moving, then pauses as he hears the maestro's French accent coming from a room up ahead. A female voice responds. Chloe? A few other musicians walk by, peering into the open room, then making haste past the doorway. Michael does the opposite, moving closer to hear what's being discussed.

"Miss Chloe, I never anticipated that I'd have to remind you that you're in one of the best orchestras in the world."

"Yes, Maestro, of course I know that. I'm sorry. I know I missed my cue today. It won't happen in the performance," Chloe says.

"We don't make mistakes!"

He mutters something in French, then reverts to English. "I know things are difficult right now, yes?" His voice lowers, almost with a hint of concern.

"Yes."

"You have fire at the moment, but it's not the good kind."

"It'll pass."

"This isn't just about the last month. You've been distracted this whole season. Where did your spirit go? Without your spirit, you're just playing music. That's not enough. Then we're just like every other orchestra. We're not like every orchestra are we, Miss Chloe?"

"No, Maestro."

"You're a leader here. Everyone looks up to you."

"I know."

"I will inform the directors that you're taking a leave of absence. Anna will be first chair."

"But what about the Eastern European tour? We're leaving in two weeks!"

"I know. But I need the best for this tour. At the moment, that does not include you. I'm sorry."

Michael suspects she's holding back tears, but he doesn't hear her response.

The maestro's voice grows louder as he approaches the door. "Take a break and come back to us."

As the hatchet-faced maestro exits past Michael, their eyes briefly meet. Michael looks down at his phone, pretending he hasn't heard any of the conversation. He didn't mean to eavesdrop on such an important conversation, but he couldn't help but listen.

Chloe comes rushing out of the room and startles to see him standing there. "Michael?"

"Umm, hi. Sorry. I didn't mean…I was early and heard the music. Then some guy from staging said to wait back here…"

Chloe has tears in her eyes.

"I'm sorry," he says again. "I shouldn't be here. I can wait for you outside."

"Wait there. I just need a few minutes." Chloe doesn't wait for a response.

Michael waits. Other musicians walk past him, carrying all sorts of instrument cases. They all take him in, curious to know who he is.

Chloe re-appears dressed in a peach jumpsuit, a geometric scarf tied around her neck and gold sunglasses resting on her head. She looks like a model straight out of a summer campaign strutting towards him. Her face neutral, as if the conversation he just overheard had never happened. Michael's eyes strangely full to her hips as she got closer and then he spots the violin case in her hand.

"Can I carry that for you?" Michael points towards it.

"No, thank you." She seems to grip it tighter.

"Okay." He holds the door open for her as they head outside and is almost blinded by the bright summer light.

"I see why now big sunglasses are handy."

"What was that?" Chloe says as she pops her sunglasses on.

Michael falters, careful in case she decides to cut short the coffee. "Ah, never mind…Hey, are you hungry?"

"I suppose I am…I suddenly seem to have more free time on my hands."

"Great." Michael relaxes a little and leads Chloe to a nearby seafood restaurant.

They're ushered to a booth. Chloe places her violin case and handbag on the seat next to her and Michael sits opposite. She seems to avoid looking at him, burrowing her face in a menu.

The waiter appears and she orders immediately. "I'll have the lobster roll, with beurre blanc and lobster roe, and a glass of the pinot grigio, please."

Michael tries to hide a smile.

She catches him and raises a questioning eyebrow. "What?"

"Nothing." Michael shakes his head and looks back at the waiter. "Just a regular roll with mayo, and your, on-tap house brew."

The waiter nods and scurries off.

"So, you got me here. What did you want to talk about?" She whips off her sunglasses, pulls a case from her handbag and neatly packs them away.

"I guess I was hoping for some answers."

"And you think I can help you with this?" She says bluntly.

"Look, I'm just going to cut to the chase here, which may not be the best approach, but here goes…I want to know what exactly Ari told you when she found out she was pregnant. What did she say about me?"

Chloe sighs. "Ari barely mentioned you. In all honestly, it was quite a short conversation."

"Are you sure that was it?"

"What would you expect her to say? She hardly knew you."

"I know. I get that. But I don't know why she would tell everyone about me, then keep Macy a secret from me, the actual father?"

The waiter interrupts them to deliver their drinks. Chloe reaches for her wine and takes a long sip before she speaks.

"I didn't push her for details because she didn't want to talk about it."

"And you just believed that the father wouldn't want to be involved?"

"I didn't have any reason to *not* believe her, and plus, this sort of thing happens. Just because of our upbringing, doesn't mean this sort of thing can't happen to one of us."

Michael is aghast at her remark. "Because of where you're from?"

Chloe ignores him.

"You think you're above me, don't you? That the two of you and your families, are all so elite, and I'm just white trash? I come from a pretty decent family; in case you were wondering. I have a good career. I may not have gone to an Ivy League College, but Penn State is pretty good, although none of this probably lives up to your standards."

"Pfft. This has nothing to do with money or family names. I'm not that pretentious."

Michael pretends to cough. "You're not? Perhaps, if you were more open-minded, people might surprise you."

51

"But I am open-minded."

"Really?"

"It comes down to being an individual with strong morals and values."

"Right, so now I'm not a decent person?" Michael takes a gulp of his beer stunned by her comment.

Chloe reaches for her napkin and begins to re-fold it. "Are you going to tell me about your wife?"

Michael almost spits out his beer. "Yeah, you mentioned that the other day. I'm not married. In fact, we split up, which is why I ended up here, in this situation. I never would have met Ari if I were still with my fiancé. This will be a bombshell for you—I don't cheat on women I'm dating or engaged to."

Chloe looks surprised but doesn't say anything.

Michael shrugs. "Look, I never knew about Ari being pregnant. She ran out on me before morning, and I never heard from her again."

Chloe remains silent, though her shoulders seem to slump slightly.

Michael continues. "I know you have a lifetime of history with Ari, and I'm just this random guy. But please, look at it from my point of view. I'm really pissed off about this. My life has been turned upside down. I have a child who was kept from me. Do you have any idea how insanely difficult that is to stomach?"

"You don't need to get mad at me."

"I'm not mad at you." Michael sighs with exasperation. "Hypothetically speaking, if she was going to lie to you, would there be any reason?"

Chloe shakes her head. "She would never lie to me."

She holds his gaze. Michael cocks his head. "Can you workshop an idea with me here? Maybe she didn't think I'm good enough for Macy, for her family?"

"That could be true. But she would have still told at least me. We knew everything about each other's lives, and the only time we ever fought was about her ex-boyfriend, Logan. You know the NFL player."

"I didn't know they were together."

"They haven't been for over three years. It was hard on Ari, and me, consequently. He's everything you read about. All the scandals about his party lifestyle. They're all true, plus, so many more that never got leaked. I probably shouldn't be telling you that."

"I'll consider this an off-the-record conversation. So, out of interest, if he was such a playboy, then what did she see in him?"

"He wasn't that bad when we were younger. He was always a typical jock of course, but with all the fame and money, things got worse. More lies, more cheating. Anyway, he was the only man in her life, but it ended."

Michael grunts. "So, I can't be that bad then. Surely, Harold and Winnie wouldn't have approved of him?"

"Their parents are friends. He's ingrained in their family. And I'm sure they didn't know the full story of what went on between them."

"I see. And then what happened? There was no one else after Logan?"

"No, she wasn't seeing anyone. I mean she dated on occasion, but it was just drinks or dinners. I heard about you. There was never anyone else. There was never any doubt that you were the father."

Chloe keeps her gaze on her wine glass. One strand of a curly hair is loose from her bun, but she quickly smooths it back into place.

"I see."

"I'm sorry, there's nothing else I can tell you."

"I see…thank you for listening to me."

Their lobster rolls arrive.

"Do you always order the same thing?" Chloe asks.

"How do you know I always order this?"

"A good guess."

"I think the classics can't be beaten. Know what I mean?"

"True…I guess I like traditional things, the classics. They're the foundation for everything new."

"Just like music, right?"

Chloe raises her eyebrows with interest. "That's right."

"Wow, we actually agree on something," he says, slightly amused.

Her chin lifts. She seems unimpressed by the remark. As she shifts in her seat, her scarf dips further down her neck, revealing a bruise or love bite.

"What's that on your neck…enthusiastic husband?"

Chloe quickly tightens the scarf and pushes it up higher.

"Nothing."

"I'm sorry, I didn't mean to embarrass you."

"I'm not embarrassed, I'm just…it's easier to hide the marks than to explain. It's from performing."

"Does it hurt?"

"You ask a lot of questions."

"That's my job, sorry."

"It's called Fiddler's neck."

"Does it happen often?"

"A lot more when I was young and being graded, then the audition process for the orchestra. I corrected the way I hold my violin, but now I'm just…just not focusing at the moment."

"I see. Tough profession. How old were you when you started playing?"

"I was four. My mother sang in the choir and my dad played the French horn. There was always music in the house. Whenever we went out to see an orchestra, I'd sit there and be mesmerised by the violinists, and I imagined one day I'd be just like them…so, here I am."

Her mood shifts as she gets caught up in the moment, her dark-brown eyes lighting up with the memory.

Michael can't help but smile. "You must have been driven."

"That's one word. Some people would say obsessed."

"Nah, I say passionate. It's inspiring. I interview a lot of people who just do what they do for money, power, prestige. So, it's a nice change of pace."

She smiles back, highlighting her fine features. Then she looks away almost embarrassed.

"So, do you ever get time off? I mean, your life has been kind of…you know, emotional lately," he asks.

"No, not really. We can't afford to stop practicing; we need to keep up with our fundamentals. And even on holidays, we don't stop."

"That's certainly a strong work ethic."

"Did you hear what the maestro said to me?" Chloe asks, staring down at the table.

"Ah, not really…maybe a little. And what I did hear, I won't repeat to anyone."

She nods in appreciation.

"What will you do?" he asks.

"Not sure."

"What about a holiday? Take a break from everything?"

"I don't really feel like holidaying right now. Plus, there's no way my boyfriend would go."

"Is he in the orchestra too?"

"How did you guess?"

"Wild stab." He smiles.

"You know the story—late nights, working weekends. You only seem to meet people in the same industry."

"Yeah, I bet. I should have said hello to him at practice."

"He's in New York."

Michael nods, sensing it isn't an area to press her on.

Chloe pulls out her purse. "Do you mind if we finish up? I'm kind of tired from practice."

"Sure, of course. Thanks for the chat. I've got this." He takes the bill off the table.

Chloe nods. "Thank you."

"You're welcome."

Out front of the restaurant, Michael hesitates. "Okay, so I might catch you again?"

"Maybe." She busies herself re-arranging her handbag and violin case. "Bye," she says scurrying off.

"If you think of anything, anything at all, let me know," he calls out after her. He scratches his head as he watches her walk off. One moment, he'd been frustrated and the next, he was enjoying their conversation. And now, she's shut him down again.

Chapter 8

Liam strides down the office hallway, phone to his ear. "Hit me, Mikey, I've only got a few minutes before my boss is due to see me in my office," he says hurriedly. A few colleagues look up as he passes their offices either busy on their own phones or laptop. Liam waves an acknowledgement, trying to look as if he's on a very important call.

"I won't keep you long. I just met with Chloe." Michael says.

"Who? Oh yeah, Chloe. What did she say? Did you find out anything?"

"No, but I don't think she hates me as much."

"Awesome, that's a start."

"Or it could be that she was having a bad day and didn't have the energy to hate me."

"Either way, at least you got to sit down with her."

Liam checks for his name on the door in front of him, as he has all week, to ensure he is in the right place. His new corner office with floor-to-ceiling windows has a view down to the bustling pedestrian malls below and the Old South Meeting House. The Financial District was a melting pot of old and new and he couldn't wait to get back out there and see what had changed.

Liam whips out his laptop from his satchel whilst juggling the phone. "You almost sound upbeat." He arranges his laptop on his desk and straightens it exactly square and positions his pen holder in his preferred spot to the right.

"You know I hate it when people don't like me. I thought she was, you know, a bit cold, but I think she's actually nice underneath."

"Sounds like a positive start."

"Yeah, it ended up not being as bad as I thought it would be."

Liam spots his boss heading towards him, "Mikey, I've to go, but I'll call you later."

Malcolm Joyce, Liam's immediate boss, is a short, rotund man with an angry demeanour when things don't go his way. But he's reasonable and incredibly smart, and Liam likes working for him.

"Liam, how are you enjoying the new quarters?" Malcolm bellows across the room.

"Great. I feel right at home." Liam says as he takes a seat at his desk, quickly checking his tie is in the right place.

Malcolm sits down with a heavy thud in the seat opposite. "Like home you say? Funny. That's what I want to talk to you about."

"Should I be worried?"

"No, of course not, nothing like that. Things have changed, and we need you to go back to Beijing. The cross-office project was so successful, we're thinking of making the position permanent. With your expertise in the market, we don't think anyone else would be as suited."

Malcolm sneezes. He always seemed to have hay fever and was constantly carrying a handkerchief which he struggles to always get out of his inner pocket. Liam is relieved to have a moment to absorb the change of plans. "Thank you, sir. I appreciate the acknowledgement. But I thought Max would be the obvious choice."

"To be frank, you're a better fit. Max hasn't been over there in four years. Despite him being more senior, you were my first choice. So, I take it you would be interested?" Malcolm stops walking and looks at Liam directly, waiting for the answer he's after.

"I am…but can I've some time to think about it?"

"You need time? I thought it would be an easy one for you. You know, given your lifestyle."

"My lifestyle?"

"Being a bachelor. No ties."

Liam rubs the back of his neck, "Ah, I see. I just got back and…leave it with me, sir."

"I'll send you the contract to look over. And don't forget about this dinner tonight. Some of the Shanghai office, along with your colleagues from Beijing, will be there. Perhaps, they can persuade you to go back if you need some more convincing. Everyone's bringing a partner to keep the formalities more casual. I take it you're bringing someone aren't you?"

"Of course, sir."

Malcolm nods and walks out. Liam's forgotten tonight is plus one. He wonders who he knows in town that he could ask. He hasn't been home long enough to reconnect or meet anyone new. *I wonder if Beth would do me a favour?* He sighs. *She's probably busy.* Still, he has no other option but to ask.

*

Hours later, waiting outside the latest restaurant opened in the financial district, Liam thinks about his life back in Beijing. He's fortunate he hasn't had to deal with combining his career with family yet. He needs to be right where he is on the company ladder without any permanent distractions. Not having a girlfriend had been a blessing in disguise when he was first asked to go. Partners were always welcome, but he didn't know many women who would just up and leave their lives and move countries, especially at an early stage of a relationship. Perhaps, he's destined to end up an eternal bachelor, never spending enough time in one city.

Then he sees Beth.

She's sashaying towards him, wearing a long silver-coloured dress that hugs her perfect curves, an elegant slit up one thigh. Her brunette hair is swept back off one side of her face in a clasp, highlighting her cheek bones and drawing attention to her red lips.

Holy crap. Has she always looked this good?

Liam leans in to kiss her cheek, catching the scent of jasmine. "Wow, you look stunning!"

She steps back. "Why, thank you." She raises her shoulder and tilts her head. "I must say your three-piece blue suit is quite fetching." She reaches out and glides one of her hands down the lapel.

"Thanks, it's new. And I'm so sorry to ask you last minute…and the fact that you could even come…I truly can't thank you enough."

"It worked out perfectly; my client dinner was cancelled, and I've been wanting to try this restaurant anyway."

"I owe you big time," Liam promises.

"I know you do, and don't worry, I've already put you down as coming to my fundraising event. You'll make a big donation."

Liam laughed. "Will I? Okay, done. Parties are easy, business dinners are hard work."

"I didn't say that was all." Beth grins.

"Liam?"

Liam spins around at the familiar voice. He's suddenly filled with a mixture of surprise, happiness and anxiety, all rolled into one. "Evelyn!"

"Surprise!" She throws her arms around him before he knows what's happening, then kisses him close to his mouth.

He glances over at Beth, who's trying not to gawk at the greeting, then back at Evelyn, whose eyes seem to narrow as she notices Beth.

"Beth, this is Evelyn. She works at the Beijing office, and Evelyn, this is Beth."

"Ah, so you're, Beth." Evelyn seems relieved and smiles.

"Yes, that's me, and I've heard a lot about you, Evelyn."

Liam looks at Beth with intrigue. *Why would she lie for me?*

"Ohhh, how nice," she coos, then looks at Liam.

Liam smiles weakly, looks down and shifts his feet.

"I heard you're just like a sister to him," Evelyn says to Beth.

Beth seems to hesitate. "Yes, of course. We've known each other for a while."

"That's so charming." Evelyn beams back at Liam.

Liam tries to change the topic as he ushers both of them into the restaurant. "I didn't think you had time to come to Boston, Evelyn?"

"I had a last-minute change of work plans. I was leaving New York early and thought why not surprise you here."

"Great." His mind is working overtime, trying to overcome the awkwardness of seeing Evelyn, right now, right here, in his neighbourhood. And how she looks in her figure-hugging black dress—it's revealing back, showing off so much of her body familiar to him. Liam rubs his eyebrows, trying to concentrate.

In the private room, the table is set for thirty with place cards scribed above each setting. Beth is seated at Liam's side, Evelyn opposite. *Jesus, this could get complicated.* They are all seated and Liam keeps the conversation on updates from their office and avoids any personal conversations. A while later, Beth excuses herself to go to the ladies' room, and Evelyn takes her chair.

"I heard that you're considering the job offer in Beijing?" She says.

Liam notices her doe-eyed look. "How did you know about that?"

"I have my ways."

"Of course, you did…I only just found out about it. And I haven't even seen a contract yet."

"We're all hoping you'll come back," she says. "I think it would be a good career move for you."

"Do you now? I wonder why that is?"

She smiles sweetly. "What's the hesitation? It's not like you have anything here holding you back. Plus, you know your way around Beijing…and your way around me." She discreetly places her hand on his leg under the table and gently glides it towards his crotch. Liam coughs and tries to wriggle her hand away just as Beth returns to the table. He notes Beth's disappointment and gives her a wink as she slips into Evelyn's vacated seat opposite.

"So, Evelyn, how long are you in town for?" Beth asks.

"I'm not sure. I was meant to be leaving tonight, but we'll see what happens." She pauses and looks at Liam, who reaches for a sip of his drink, trying to ignore her glance. Evelyn continues. "Regardless, I'll be back in two weeks for another meeting in Chicago, so I could drop by."

"If you're going to be in town, my firm is hosting a charity gala, you should come along. Liam can bring you. He has all the details."

"Wonderful. Consider this your RSVP," she says with delight, squeezing Liam's arm.

Liam forces a smile, needing a moment to press pause on everything.

As the evening progresses, he listens to the directors' speeches, then watches as their wives circulate to chat with his colleagues plus ones about non-work issues. As one sits next to Beth, he takes the opportunity to excuse himself. Evelyn has been noticeably absent for the last ten minutes. Liam looks for the bathroom. Turning the corner, he bumps into Evelyn. His heart races.

"She's nice," Evelyn says as she reaches to play with his tie.

"Beth? Yeah, she is."

"Pretty too," she adds, obviously pressing for a response.

"Look, Evelyn, I'm sorry I've been distant since I got back. I'm just trying to resettle my life here."

"Sure, I understand." Evelyn leans in and kisses him.

Liam kisses her back. It's hard for him to stop, but he pulls away. "Wait. I don't think this is a good idea. You knew I was always coming home. We both knew."

"But now you have an opportunity to return to Beijing, and you're hesitating. Why?"

Liam looks into her eyes. "I had my time in Beijing. Now, I'm ready to make my life back here again, settle down."

"But you can settle down with me."

"Is that really want you want? We never really talked about it."

"Of course, it is. You must have known that."

"Evelyn, I need some time to focus on my next step. Can you give me some time?"

"Okay." She sighs.

They head back to the table, Evelyn's mood a little less peppy. Liam keeps shifting in his seat, strangely uncomfortable now. He glances at Evelyn, but she won't look at him.

As the night comes to an end, colleagues stand around the table saying their farewells. Liam is glad the dinner has ended. Even though it's been good seeing some of his colleagues from the other offices, he doesn't want anyone to be clouding his judgement about the offer.

Beth is talking to one his colleagues. He smiles at her. She looks so at ease, as if she's been to a million of these dinners with him. He looks for Evelyn but she's gone.

Damn it. Did I upset her that much? I'll need to talk to her.

*

Liam and Beth are strolling down the street, away from the restaurant, when Beth's phone beeps. She pulls it out, then hastily shoves it back in her clutch.

"Everything okay?" Liam asks.

"Ah...yes, just work. Sorry. I...I dropped Michael's baby bombshell on Naomi, and she sort of hung up on me. She's not responding to any of my messages. I was hoping it might be her."

"I can imagine she is taking it hard. It's taken us a little while for the news to sink in...I'm sure she'll call you soon."

Beth looks gloomy.

"I don't suppose you want a night cap?" Liam asks.

"I do. That would be great."

"Let's see what tavern at the wharf will take us in."

They wander down to the waterfront where the city lights seem to be captured in the ripples of the ocean. A gentle sea breeze has the sailing boats in a waltz. Liam looks up at one of the grand sandstone archways. "I don't think I've ever appreciated how nice this area is. Obviously, I've been out of town too long. I've turned into a tourist!"

"I must admit I'm usually rushing around, but right now, being in the moment…it's a good change of pace. And the company helps, of course."

"It does." He looks over at her. Her head is lowered, trying to hide a smile.

Laughter and music from a nearby Irish Bar calls their attention. They look out of place in their formal dinner wear, but who cares? They walk in. Liam is confident every man is eyeing Beth. And why wouldn't they? He orders gins at the bar, then takes them over to a booth Beth has found.

"Can I ask why you covered for me earlier with Evelyn?"

"Oh, that…I know what women are like. It's nice to know if someone you're interested in is talking about you. Plus, we *are* friends, right? And we have each other's back?"

"Cheers to that," Liam clinks her glass. "How do you know she's interested?"

"I could tell by her greeting." She grins.

"Hmm, yes, it was more than a standard work greeting."

"So, was Evelyn the holiday romance or is she more a long-term thing?" Beth muses.

Liam frowns slightly. "It's been on and off the last year, but I don't know…we never really talked about how serious it was."

"Well, she seems nice. Sorry if I made things more complicated by inviting her to the gala. I opened my mouth too quickly. I should have checked with you."

"No, it's fine." Liam takes a sip of his drink.

"So…you said I was like a sister, hey?"

"Ahhh…it was kind of a diversion tactic. She was quite jealous of my life back here. Especially, when I talked about people back home."

"You talked about me?"

"Of course, I did."

Beth swirls her straw in the glass, looking pleased. "So, what do you think will happen now?"

"Let's just say that I thought I had already left the past behind."

"And are you happy with that decision?"

"We'll see. At least I don't have a child to worry about."

"When did we get so grown-up all of a sudden, talking about kids?"

"I know. It's crazy, right? So have you…thought about…"

"Kids? Never been a priority. I suppose, if I found the right person. Someone who's not the on-off type?"

Liam's taken aback for a moment, but Beth smiles cheekily.

"Yeah," he says, "that would be a good start. What about you?"

"Same as you—one day it would be great, but not right now. Obviously meeting the right person would be helpful."

"And someone that can deal with all the late meetings and work events." He winks at her.

"True. Hey, you know…I don't remember being at a work dinner with you before. I was…impressed."

"You're pretty impressive yourself." She blushes in response.

They talk late into the night, then reluctantly call a taxi to share—they both have long days at work tomorrow. As the taxi pulls up outside Beth's apartment, Liam leans over to kiss her goodnight on the cheek. Beth turns towards him at the same time, raising her hand to gently touch his face. Their lips half meet in passing. Her perfume is softer now, and Liam lingers longer than he should. He quickly shakes off his daze and pulls back as she drops her hand. She looks almost as confused as he feels.

"Th…thanks again for coming tonight," he mumbles.

"You bet. It was fun." She hastily exits the car.

Liam sits wondering what just happened. Probably, just the extra drinks.

Chapter 9

Chloe's sits at her writing desk, gazing at Ari's laptop. She'd been combing through it before the wake, looking for photos to share. Luckily for her, Ari had kept the same login since high school. She tears up now as the images come to mind, hundreds of them. Some familiar, others new—Ari with friends, with family, with Logan.

She pauses at the thought of Logan. Had her best friend lied to her? Is Michael lying now, trying to deceive them all? She doesn't think so; he seems generally interested in Macy.

Chloe reaches for the laptop, hesitates momentarily, then logs in. Ari would have done the same in this situation.

She snoops through Ari's emails, all pretty tidy. Most of the old ones seemed to have been deleted. She checks Ari's calendar, looking back a year, to before Ari found out she was pregnant. She finds plenty of flight reservations. Not unusual—Ari often had to travel to New York for head office meetings, but most of her work was in Boston.

That's weird. She takes a closer look at the destinations and dates listed. Flights to Montreal, Dallas? The trips were short enough that Chloe wouldn't have even noticed Ari's absence. But why would Ari not have told her about all these trips? Sure, she'd rescheduled their meet ups often, but Chloe hadn't thought much of it at the time. Everyone's so busy these days.

Chloe googles the dates, hoping to understand why Ari might have gone to Montreal. Nothing. She tries the next one. Reading the search results, she sits back in disbelief, her hand over her mouth. *What?* She stares at the screen a few moments as a thought threads its way into realisation. *No!* Sitting forwards again, she opens the browser history from the same time period. It's the same search over and over. *Why, Ari? Why?*

Chloe grabs her bag and flees the apartment, heading straight to a place she hasn't been to in a very long time.

The noise from the ice hockey stadium is deafening, even for a pre-season game. Chloe hasn't been here since she was a teenager. She didn't mind watching the games then. When she had time, she would occasionally go to a game with Ari. Then Logan started to get noticed by all the national team reps, and more and more women. The first time he cheated on Ari—in high school—Ari blamed herself, as she'd been away with her family in Europe on a skiing holiday. Then, she and Logan had gone to different colleges, so she blamed distance, even though they were still in the same town. Next, she was studying, so Logan felt ignored. There were countless other times. Ari eventually saw the light and broke up with him. But she never really seemed to move on. To be fair, he was in major campaigns, all over social media, or on TV. His face was everywhere.

The buzzer goes for the end of the game, and Chloe heads down to the ground level to find the player and media access areas. She waits. A few girlfriends, or young wives, who have been watching the game, stare at her. One mutters 'you wish' under her breath, then walks away with the other women, their giggles and heels echoing after them. Logan finally appears from the locker room.

"Chloe?" You're the last person I'd expect to see here. "Come to watch the game?"

"Err, no not really." She nervously looks around at the other players coming out of the change rooms. One of them raises his eyebrows suggestively when he catches her gaze.

"Look," she says, "I came to talk to you, and I was hoping to do it privately?"

"Sure, we can talk. I'm staying at The Four Seasons. I've got a car. Want to ride together?"

"Thanks."

They swap polite chat until they get to the hotel. Chloe chews her nails, wondering how she's going to ask what she came to find out. She's absorbed in her thoughts, and it seems only seconds before they get to the hotel where the lift opens to the lobby to a top-floor suite.

"Isn't it odd staying in a hotel when you grew up here?" she asks.

"Nah, not really." He shrugs. "This city hasn't been my home for a long time now."

"Don't your parents mind?"

"No. They come to see me sometimes, but they're too far out of town, and I like being in the city. And check out the view!" He opens up the bi-fold doors in the lounge, revealing a terrace with breath-taking view of the city.

"Nice," is all Chloe can muster.

"Can I get you a drink? Champagne, wine or scotch. What do you musicians drink anyway?"

"A white wine, please."

He walks over to the bar and pours them both a wine.

"Is that allowed?" she asks him.

"Not really, but it's off-season. But yo, don't tell my sponsors. I have a new vitamin company."

"Don't they test you all the time, for everything?"

"Sometimes, but you get a heads up." He grins.

Chloe shakes her head in disbelief.

"Cheers." Logan hands over the glass of wine and takes a long swig. "Didn't really see ya at the wake."

"I guess, I thought you would have stuck around for a bit longer, especially as you seemed to be spending more time together lately." Chloe takes a sip from the glass keeping her eyes on him for a reaction.

Logan's brow furrows, "What do you mean?"

"I found all her calendar appointments—flight details, everything. I know you guys were seeing each other. Quite a bit."

"Once a fan, always a fan, right?" He shrugs and finishes of his wine.

"Don't joke around with me on this. It's hard enough thinking about Ari, let alone talking, without getting emotional, and you just treat this like it all means nothing to you."

"I lost someone too, you know!"

"Really? You never seem to act like you cared about her."

"I'm capable of feelings, Chloe. Didn't you catch the sport headlines? We were halfway into a friendly game, and I shouldn't have gone back on the ice when I found out about the accident, but I didn't know what else to do. I crashed into the first opponent I saw and punched him square in his face, then kept punching until the ice was covered in blood. See all these scars?" He points to his chin. "His teammates made me pay for it later. I deserved it."

"So, what you're saying is you got into a fight to show how much you care?"

"I just know that you think I'm a dick."

"I don't just think. You *are* a dick!"

"Yeah, okay, I get it. I know you hate me, but a part of me will always love Ari."

"So, I'll ask you again then." She lowers her voice to a warning tone. "What was happening between you two?"

"There was nothing happening. Plain and simple."

"Then why was she coming to see you?"

Logan sighs loudly as he grabs the bottle of wine again and sits on the couch. "She never said anything?"

Chloe sits opposite him. "No. That's why I'm here." Chloe places her glass down on the coffee table in front.

Logan tops up his glass. "When I was back in town one night, about a year and half ago, I bumped into her after a game. I was with a couple of guys from the team, and she was with some work friends. I kept seeing her for a while after that—just hanging out as friends—but then we had a massive argument."

"What was the argument about."

"I already had a girlfriend. She wanted more. I said no."

"You know she was infatuated with you. Why did you lead her on again?"

"It wasn't like that. I swear. Nothing happened between us."

"Nothing happened?"

"Like I said, we were just friends. I was with someone, and it was pretty serious."

"Hasn't stopped you before."

Logan tsks. "You can think what you want. I don't give a shit."

"Okay, fine. Just tell me why was it a big secret?"

"She probably didn't want you getting mad at her again for trying to see me."

"And she would have been right about that."

The apartment's door reader makes a sound, and in walks a tall, thin, red-haired woman with a delicate face and pouty lips.

"Hi, babe, I didn't know you had a meeting?" The woman observes Chloe.

Chloe ignores her and focuses on Logan. "Do you hand out your hotel key-cards to every woman in the city?"

He shrugs.

"I'm Stephanie. I'm actually his girlfriend," she gloats.

Chloe rolls her eyes. "Girlfriend? Maybe in *this* city. Good luck with that." She gets up and grabs her bag from the table.

"You don't have to leave; you haven't even finished your wine!"

"I think its past its used by date."

"So? You can stay for what comes after the wine. Stephanie doesn't bite and I don't mind an audience." Logan swirls his wine glass with a sly grin.

"Screw you, Logan. I hope our paths never have to cross again." Then she's out the door and down the hallway to the lift.

She walks home, stewing, until she reaches all the bars and cafes. Now, she relaxes, her anger subsiding as she gazes at people sharing bowls of pasta and enjoying drinks with friends, laughing. They look so happy and content with their lives.

She used to relish leading a different life and even enjoyed the solitude of eating dinner at 1am after concerts. It made her feel elitist to be on a different schedule to everyone else. But now, she realises, she envies them.

*

When she arrives home, Francis is pacing the lounge room, a large glass of red wine in his hand. His dark curly hair is a little shorter than normal—a fresh haircut. He places his wine on the coffee table and greets her. She'd forgotten he was coming over. He kisses her but not as warmly as he normally would. Something isn't right.

"What's going on?" she asks.

"Come sit with me." Francis moves to the couch and pats the spot next to him.

Chloe follows his lead and sits next to him sliding her bag onto the floor next to her feet.

Francis takes her hands, "I need to tell you something important."

"You're sort of freaking me out. What is it?"

"I've been offered principal flute at the New York Symphony Orchestra."

Chloe's heart shatters.

"I know this isn't good timing," he continues, "but you know, I've been waiting for this opportunity. Everything has finally fallen into place" He quickly adds, "And New York isn't that far away."

Chloe stays silent, winded.

"Please say something." He squeezes her hands.

"You're right about the timing. So, this isn't even a discussion then?"

"I...I had to give them an answer."

Chloe pulls her hands away. "I can't believe you accepted without even talking to me!"

"They offered it on the spot. There was no way I could turn it down."

"I...I...would at least have had the decency to ask you first...and you told me it was nothing, just an ordinary meeting. You said maybe something would open up in a few years."

"The situation changed."

"You already knew that didn't you? But you didn't tell me."

"I...Chloe. I'm sorry."

"When do you leave?"

"Tomorrow." Francis lowers his head, unable to look at her.

"No, no, no!" Chloe shakes her head.

Francis kneels in front of her, reaches for her hands again and tries to look her in the eye. "Chloe, look at me please. This isn't the end for us. It's easy to commute back and forth."

Chloe's chest and throat tightens. "How?"

"We can make it work."

"I hardly see you now, mostly at the theatre."

"But this is the life we chose."

"And you're choosing your instrument over me."

Francis huffs, drops her hands. "But you would do exactly the same thing."

Chloe shakes her head in disbelief. "I don't know if I would anymore. Sometimes, I wish we could just be like everyone else, sitting down for dinner at a normal time. We'd get to see our friends and family on a weekend, go on a holiday and even have a normal relationship."

"But you've never wanted that. You love the life you have."

"Do I? What do I have? Nothing. My best friend has died, my family live in another state, and now you're leaving me too. I have my music and that's it."

"You have me!"

"Really? I've barely seen you this last month. You've been so distant."

"I know. I'm sorry about that. I just felt awful keeping this from you. Perhaps I could've handled this better."

"I needed you," she manages to say, her voice small and vulnerable.

"I know, I know. I should have...done things differently." Francis sits next to her and puts an arm around her.

"Yes, you should have. Please…just leave."

"Chloe, please think about it."

"Just go." She gets off the couch and turns away.

"Chloe?"

"Go!" She can't help it. She's so full of anger and sadness.

Francis gets up and walks out the door. She waits a moment, then grabs his wine glass, closes her eyes, and drinks the whole thing in one gulp.

Her phone beeps. Francis, she thinks, about to ignore it. But it's Michael, thanking her for meeting up with her the other day and suggesting they might see each other again soon.

She wonders if there's any man she'll ever trust again.

Chapter 10

The concierge at the Hennigan's apartment sneers at Michael's arrival. He counters with an over-the-top greeting. "Good morning, Victor! Looking sharp today." Victor looks away, unamused. Michael enters the lift and presses the button for the Hennigan's floor, feeling like a pro now. The doors spring open at the Hennigan's foyer, and Roberta, the maid, motions for Michael to follow. She mutters in Spanish, rubbing her lower back. Michael makes out something about 'pain.'

Harold and Winnie are seated in the lounge room, waiting for him. The room seems tense. Roberta scurries out.

"Michael, Winnie and I've been discussing a few things this morning, and if you're interested, there's a park around the corner. Perhaps, you would like to take Macy there for a walk today?"

"Ah…yes, of course. It would be great to spend some time with her."

Harold nods and Winnie adds, "Roberta has done her back in, so she needs to take things easy."

"That's a shame…whatever I can do to help."

"We'll see," Winnie mutters, smoothing a non-existent crease in her long skirt.

Harold gives her a displeased look, which Winnie pretends she doesn't see.

Harold continues. "You've shown us your enthusiasm thus far, and…well, you keep turning up. So, here we are."

"Thank you," Michael says, uneasy. They don't trust him. That's obvious. But Harold at least attempts a smile, and Michael nods to him.

"For the Fourth of July weekend, we're heading to the Cape. It's what we do each year as a family. We also have friends there, and it'll be good for us to see them." Harold pauses. "We thought you might like to join us, get to know each other?"

Winnie adds, "But it's late notice, and I'm sure you have other plans."

Harold cuts across her. "We don't need an answer immediately, but please let us know what you decide. Invite your family and a few friends if you like, and I'll have my secretary make the necessary arrangements for you."

Michael doesn't hesitate. He should go for Macy's sake. "Thank you for the invitation. I don't have any plans, so…I can't see why not." It's going to be awkward, but he'll persuade Beth and Liam to come with him as support.

Macy's crying carries from another room.

Michael can't believe he'd ever be thankful to hear a baby cry. "Must be my cue to take Macy out."

Roberta re-appears with Macy and motions for Michael to follow. She mutters in Spanish again, and shows him the brakes on the pram and the release device.

Winnie's voice from behind startles him. "You should be back no later than an hour. It will be her nap time."

"Of course. No problem." He forces a calm response, although inside, he's panicking. He's never walked a baby before, let alone his daughter. He fumbles with the brakes; sure they're judging him.

He relaxes a little once he's out the Hennigan's apartment, away from any more awkwardness. But now Macy looks up, her bottom lip quivering. A few unhappy sounds quickly escalate to crying. He pushes the pram faster. No improvement. He tries rocking it side to side. That doesn't work either. He stops and scoops the baby out of the pram. "I'm sorry, Macy. I have no idea what I'm doing." He bounces her, then tries to hum a tune—nothing in particular. Heck, he doesn't even know a full nursery rhyme. Macy cries more urgently and loudly. He jiggles her, then reaches for his phone in his back pocket and calls Beth.

"What do I do when they cry?" He blurts over the crying.

"I'm guessing you're referring to Macy. Is that her crying in the background?"

"The background? You meant the foreground. I can't even hear myself think."

"Are you with her by yourself?"

"Yes. They let me take her out for a walk."

"That's a promising step."

"It is, but now look at me. I'm haven't even made it to the park." He almost yells to be heard. "Why is she crying?"

"Is she hungry?" Beth asks.

"No. Apparently it's her nap time soon," he explains.

"Just push her around in the pram some more."

"I did, but then she started crying."

"Keep pushing then?"

"Are you sure?"

"No. Why would I know?"

"I don't know. I'm desperate."

"Call mum and ask her."

"I haven't told her yet."

"You haven't told her?"

"I wanted to tell her after I knew for sure. Plus, I don't think I can deal with that yet. She is probably in the middle of a cruise through Greece and can't get off the boat anyway."

Beth groans with frustration. "She'll find out."

"Not if you don't tell her, or post anything online."

"Fine!"

Macy's crying is a wail now. "Beth! The crying?"

"Just try not to panic. Keep moving about. I see mums doing that all the time on the street."

"I tried that already."

"Just keep doing it."

"Okay then…how did I get into this mess?" He places Macy back into the pram amid continued protesting.

"You went out one night and slept with a mysterious blonde woman."

"Thanks. I don't need a recap. Although, it would be nice just to go back to that time when I was happy, single, carefree, childfree."

"Were you happy?"

"Sure."

"Really?"

"Argh…I don't know. Maybe I wasn't?"

Beth sighs again. "Just keep going. You'll get the hang of it. Just remember one day at a time. You also need to get that test done ASAP."

"I know. I'm doing it."

"Why are you procrastinating? Just do the test. Then, we can know for sure. At the moment, they're calling all the shots."

"I actually don't mind that. Imagine if they said, 'here take the baby she's yours. See you at Thanksgiving.' I don't even have any nappies at home!"

"I guess that could happen, but I don't think it will. They seem pretty keen on hanging on to her."

"Okay, shhh, I have to go. I think she's starting to go to sleep," he whispers, easing her back into the pram.

He keeps walking around until his full hour is up, then returns to the apartment. Completely stressed out, but also impressed, he delivers Macy back in one piece, asleep. Roberta gently brushes her cheek.

On the way home, Michael decides to head to the shops and heads straight to the baby aisle. Every product is labelled 'must have' or 'number one choice.' There's baby care kits, nappy changing tables, nappies in different sizes, and what looks like to be a hundred different lotions.

He gets out his phone to check the notes he's been making. At least he's an expert in cross-referencing and checking credible sources. In under a few weeks, his life has gone from share prices and merger information to the best guides on single parenting and baby products. He leaves the shops with a bag of what he hopes to be the most important 'must have' baby items.

Chapter 11

Beth stands in her office lift, admiring her shorter hair in the mirrored wall. She's feeling confident—things are starting to shift in her favour at work, even if James has arranged everything for Neil's farewell dinner tonight. This is the one event James has complete control over; hers is the gala. For Neil's sake, she hopes tonight is a good evening, but the gala has to be the clear standout.

Jordan's already waiting for her to come out of the lift. "And what time do you call this? Everyone's already gone home...ohhh, I love the new hair."

"Thanks! I felt like something different. Just took a little longer than I expected, so I don't have as much time to change."

"We can walk and talk. So...guess what? Remember, when I said my friend designs bespoke couture dresses?"

"Yes, I remember. I followed his account after you showed me."

"Well, I have a dress on loan."

"A dress?" she says. "I already have a dress in my office."

"Beth, you can't say no to *this* dress. It's a work of art!"

"I don't know. I'm trying to make partner, not win a beauty pageant."

"I know, but it's the right amount of sophistication and a l-i-i-i-t-l-e bit sexy."

"Sexy? For work?" She raises an eyebrow.

He gives her a sly look. "This was made for you."

"Since when did you become my wardrobe assistant?"

Jordan shrugs and tsks.

"I guess I can have a look at it."

"Great!" He drags her to his office, shuts the door behind them, then opens the dress bag hanging on the back of the door.

Beth gasps. "It's...so beautiful. Look at that back...the train. Oh my, it's just so fabulous!"

"See? I told you."

"I couldn't possibly wear that. It looks so expensive and glamorous. What if I spill wine all over it?"

"Umm…we can expense it?" He winks shamelessly. "Just try it on."

Beth agrees and runs off to the office bathroom, Jordan in tow.

"I'll be waiting here at the door. If you feel the need to come out and show me…" he calls out to her.

After a few minutes, Beth opens the bathroom door and grins as Jordan covers his mouth. "Wow."

She walks down the hallway, looking in the floor-to-ceiling mirrors. The cobalt blue dress is shaped to her body perfectly. Crystals sparkle across the front in an elegant pattern which trail around to the plunging low back. Eyes wide at the amount of skin it reveals. Is it too much? Does she care?

"See! Modest in the front, but a whole lot of fun at the back!" Jordan grins, pleased with himself.

Beth laughs, still admiring the dress. "I don't think I ever want to take this off."

Jordan clears his throat. "If it wasn't inappropriate to wolf whistle at my boss, I would."

Beth turns to get more angles of her in the dress. "Thanks, Jordan. You really go above and beyond."

"You're more than welcome, plus my flatmate will be happy with any social mentions of course." He glances at his watch. "Please get going before you're late."

*

Beth enters the lobby of the Mandarin Oriental Hotel and heads straight for the lift. Men pause their conversation to look at her. Normally, she would appreciate the attention, but tonight is work, and she's too focused on her internal pep talk.

"Madam, your floor," the lift operator announces.

Beth nods and thanks the man before heading across the lush carpet for the ballroom doors where she's greeted by staff. The room looks stunning—softly lit, filled with black and white balloons and elaborate flower displays. What seems to be hundreds of staff are drifting among the guests, offering cocktails and appetisers. Beth drifts across the room, nodding hellos to people in mid-conversation.

Neil walks over to her. "Why, Beth, quite an entrance tonight, and what a remarkable dress."

"Thank you, Neil. That's very kind of you."

Neil nods. "I must say, your efforts the last year and, in particular, the last few months haven't gone unnoticed."

"Thank you, so much. I appreciate that. And you know that I'd be more than ready to move into the next phase of Clifford and Marks."

"I'd like to discuss this in more detail. It's a shame you don't seem to be seated at our table tonight."

"Oh, I'm not?"

"I'm sure we'll find the time later for another chat—sorry, please excuse me. I must rescue my wife from that awfully annoying woman, Sue-Ellen, or I'll hear about it for the rest of my retirement."

Beth forces out a smile, then hurries to check where she's seated. Damn, James! Her seat is nowhere near the partners or her clients. She takes the nearest champagne on offer and makes a beeline for her rival.

"Why, Beth, didn't know you could pull off a dress like that."

"You're really bad at compliments," she says flatly.

"I feel you misunderstand me."

"Really? See, I'm pretty sure I do understand you. Particularly, when you seat me at the back of the room. I'm practically in the kitchen. You might as well get me a dishcloth so I can help clean up."

"Come on, Beth. You know I didn't handle the seating arrangements."

She grits her teeth. "No, I'm sure you didn't, but I'm guessing you instructed them."

"The MC is starting, so you better run off to your seat. And don't worry, I'm sure you won't miss out on much."

Beth turns on her heel, biting her tongue. She can't afford to make a scene.

*

The evening has been running smoothly, and now, James's speech is a standout. Why does he have to be so bloody good at everything! Beth twists her napkin with annoyance. Sensing someone looking at her, she gazes across the room and locks eyes with Mr Williams, who raises his glass. She nods with a forced smile and tries to engage with the nice older couple sitting next to her. When they query where her husband is, Beth excuses herself to the bathroom. As she pushes a cubicle open, a hand grabs her behind. She whips around in surprise.

"Ah, Mr Williams, this is the women's. If you're looking for the men's bathrooms, they're next door."

"I wasn't looking for them. I was looking for you," he says, drunken and suggestive, leering at her. He breathes alcohol over her face.

Beth backs into the cubicle. "Well…if you want to discuss strategies for your company, how about I meet you outside in five minutes?" She says firmly.

He takes a step towards her. "I think here is as good a place as any other."

There's nowhere to escape. Mr Williams brushes a hand down her arm.

She shivers at his touch and pulls away. "Mr Williams, I don't think this is appropriate."

"Nonsense."

"Please! I really think people will be noticing our absence, and we should go back outside."

"Why waste an opportunity like this when we can be alone momentarily?" He leans in and tries to kiss her. Beth squirms away, but he pushes her back against the side of the tiled cubicle wall.

"Mr Williams, please, you're hurting me!"

"Beth, I can give you everything you want." His hands move up to her shoulders, and he presses her against the cold tiles. Every fibre of Beth's body is screaming at her to get out of there, but his grip is unyielding.

Perhaps, she can negotiate with him. "Please let me go. I'd like for you to be my client, but that's all."

"Why do you think we're still considering your law firm? I don't care which one we go with, but I know I want you."

"Mr Williams, please let me go." She writhes, but his grip tightens. "You're hurting me. Let me go!"

"Don't act shy with me," he slurs in her face. "I know you're into me too."

Her voices trembles. "No…you've…got it all wrong."

She tries again to push him off, but he seems increasingly agitated with her attempt to move away and pushes her harder against the wall. The back of her head hits the wall.

"Don't ruin this, Beth," he spits with annoyance.

His rough hand grabs at her breast. She's so panicked; she can't find the air to scream out. At that moment, James walks into the bathroom. Mr Williams's whips his head around, then backs away from Beth. "If you ever approach me again for favours, I'll have you fired. You undermine the integrity of this company." He storms out, straightening his bow tie.

James stares at her in disbelief. "Wow! Lucky, I walked into the wrong bathroom when I did. I knew you were competitive, but…this is taking it too far. I…really respected you. I can't believe you would do this." He sounds genuinely disappointed.

In the trauma of the moment, Beth can't manage to speak. James walks off, shaking his head. Beth presses a hand to her heart. She can't breathe properly. The only thing she thinks is *run*. Run far away from here.

She takes the nearest stairwell and races down to ground level, her heels echoing on the dusty cement steps. She exits onto the service entry of the hotel. Staff watch her silently as they finish their cigarettes. She scrambles for her phone and drops it. She fumbles a few times before she's able to hold onto it and call Michael. He doesn't pick up. She tries again. No luck. Her breathing won't slow. She tries Naomi, but she doesn't pick up either. Her next bet is Liam.

"Hey, Beth. What's up?"

Beth loses herself at hearing his voice, breaking into sobs.

"Beth? Where are you? I'll come to you…Beth, tell me where you are."

"No, I…will…get a taxi," she says, gulping through tears.

"Okay. I'll wait out the front of my apartment. Stay on the phone with me. Okay?"

Beth nods, then realises he can't see her. "Okay."

She gets in the first taxi she sees at the front of the hotel and hands her phone to the taxi driver. He looks startled but talks to Liam and quickly drives off. He keeps checking on her in the rear-view mirror, looking worried, then tosses some tissues back to her.

"You okay, miss?"

Beth nods as tears keep rolling down her face, her breathing still rapid.

"You're sure?"

Beth sobs a breath and nods again.

As promised, Liam is out the front of his apartment. He throws extra notes to the driver before helping Beth out of the taxi and taking her upstairs.

"I'm sorry. I tried calling Mikey…and Naomi…and…and then I tried you," she stutters between sobs.

Liam seats her on the lounge next to him, then pulls her into a hug. "Hey, now, you need to take some deep breaths if you can."

His warmth around her helps her calm a little.

"Take a deep breath…in and out. That's it, keep going."

After a few minutes, he brings her some water. She takes a sip and sits back. "Thanks."

Liam faces her. "Beth, tell me what I should do. Did someone hurt you?"

Beth shakes her head. "Sort of. It's a work thing," she adds.

"I've never seen you like this before. Did…did they make that other guy partner?"

"No, but they probably will now."

"How come?"

Beth doesn't know whether to say. She thinks about it for a moment. "I had a run in with a client."

"What kind of run in?" He frowns.

She looks at the floor, avoiding his gaze.

"Please, tell me."

"I was cornered in the bathroom. One of my clients—or someone I was hoping to make a client—made a pass at me." Beth pauses, and Liam waits for more information. "He was quite forceful about it. I said no." She sobs again.

"Beth!" Liam jumps off the lounge, ready for action, but Beth looks up, reaches for his hand and pulls him back down. "Please, just sit with me."

"Tell me who did this?"

Beth tries to answer, but her tears keep coming. Liam pulls her in close again, and she leans into him. She tries to continue her story. "It gets worse. James came in and…he saw. But he got the wrong impression. Either the client will mention it to the partners or James will—he heard the client accuse me of making a move on him."

"Oh, Beth."

"There's no way I'll make partner now, and I'll probably be fired."

"That's crazy," Liam says. "How could you possibly get fired for not doing anything wrong?" He looks aghast. "This can't happen. I won't let it happen. I'll go in there myself."

Beth shakes her head. "No, it won't matter. They'll have to side with the client. It's worth too much to the firm." More tears. "I…should feel lucky. If James hadn't walked in…"

"Don't think about that. You're safe now."

Liam wraps his arm around her again, but as he rubs the top of her arm, she jerks back.

"Ow!"

"I'm sorry. Did I hurt you?"

Beth pulls her dress fabric aside and looks at her arm.

"Holy shit! No one is allowed to do that to you. To anyone. That bastard! I swear, I'll hunt him down and make him pay." Liam's face is full of rage and anguish.

"Did those words just come out of your mouth?"

"I've never seen you like this before. Damn it, Beth. I can't believe this happened to you. You have to report him."

"It'll be too much negative publicity for the firm. The partners will hate it."

"Fuck the firm. This is your life. This is a crime," Liam argues.

"Liam, please."

He seems to become aware his rage isn't helping. "Sorry. I'm just…do you want something for your arm?"

"No, thank you." She looks at her arm and wipes away the last of her tears. "It's more the thought of him near me." She shakes her head, trying to erase the memory of him looming over her, and how small she felt, how helpless. "He's repulsive."

She rubs under her eyes, mascara coming away on her fingers. She must look a mess.

"Please tell me what I can do to help." Liam gently reaches for her hands, looking into her eyes for guidance.

She sniffs. "Do you mind if I stay the night? I don't really want to go back out again."

"Of course not. The spare room is already made up. I'll get you something to sleep in. As beautiful as you look in that dress, I'm pretty sure it's not going to be comfortable." He gets up and heads off to fetch things. "There's food in the fridge if you want, or I can make you a drink?" He yells in between the noise of draws opening and closing.

"I don't need anything, thank you."

Liam walks back in with some basketball shorts and a T-shirt—all oversized for her frame. He hands them to her. "Sorry, I don't have much to offer."

"They look comfy. Thanks."

"Look, I can call the cops if you want. Let me talk to them," he offers.

"No, I don't want to do that. I just want to go to bed and forget this day ever happened."

"Okay. Bathroom's through there," he points.

Beth heads off to change.

She hangs the dress up on the back of the door and wistfully straightens the fabric. It deserved a better night out. She looks again at the tinges of red starting to bruise on her arm. She leaves the bathroom before she gets upset again.

On the way out, she finds Liam waiting for her in the hallway, to see if she's okay. She embraces him, placing her head on his chest for a few moments. He wraps his muscular arms around her, and she feels safe again.

"Promise me, you'll let me know if you want anything during the night?" he murmurs.

Beth nods and leaves the comfort of his chest.

"I will."

"I'll show you your room." Beth follows him down the hall. "I'm here," he pushes the door ajar and keeps walking, "And you're here. I've already put your things in here. Now, are you sure you're okay?"

"I'm okay. Thanks again." She tries to offer him a smile to show it's okay to leave her alone.

He seems to accept this. "Alright. Goodnight." He heads for his room.

In the spare room, Beth finds that Liam has plugged her phone in next to the bed and placed aspirin and water on the nightstand. Everything so orderly, much like his whole apartment. She manages a smile, thinking about his kindness, and slips into bed. It's somewhat comforting, even though it's not her bed, and she tries to stay calm, but it doesn't take long for her to grow anxious and restless. In defeat, she gets up and paces to the bathroom, just for something to do. Liam's bedroom door is still open. He's propped up on his pillows, glasses on, reading his kindle. She pauses, then keeps walking.

"Beth?"

"I'm so sorry. I didn't mean to disturb you," she whispers.

"You don't need to whisper. I can't sleep either."

She enters his room, and he puts his kindle down. Beth doesn't say anything. She walks over, lifts up the corner of the sheet, climbs in next to him. Liam takes of his glasses and places them on his bedside table. He switches the light off and lies on his back next to her. Beth wriggles closer, then rolls over so that her back is greeted by the warmth of his body. She senses Liam hesitate for a second before reaching his arm around her waist and pulling her close.

Chapter 12

Just at dawn, Beth's breath is warm on the back of his neck. Sometime during the night, they must have switched positions. One of Beth's arms is now around his waist, and she's nuzzled into the back of his body. He's still livid about the man who assaulted her. It shouldn't have happened, and it's breaking his heart. He wants to jump out of bed and smash the guy's face in. But Beth is lying here so peacefully, and if he's honest, he does like the feel of her wrapped around his body—even if it's an inappropriate time to be thinking of her in that way. And where to begin on the fact that they're friends, and she's Mikey's sister.

Beth stirs and he almost forgets to breathe. What if she's still upset about last night? What if she's had second thoughts about climbing into his bed during a moment of vulnerability?

"Liam? Are you awake?"

"Yeah…Can I get you anything?" He doesn't move.

"No." Her breath tickles his neck.

"How are you feeling?"

"I'm okay," she says softly.

He tries to stay focused…but she's nestled so close his body…

He gently lifts her hand and removes it as he turns to look at her. Her shoulder is peeking out of his oversized shirt, showing a slight bruise. He frowns.

"Is it bad?" she asks.

Liam lifts his hand and brushes it slightly. "There's a bit of a mark there. Does it still hurt?"

"Not unless I roll on it."

Liam looks from her arm to those hazel eyes. "I'm so sorry this happened to you," he says.

She stares back, smiling weakly. "I know…"

"I really want to help you with this. I couldn't sleep last night."

She frowns. "Sorry about that."

"Don't be ridiculous. I want to help you."

"You have already helped me."

"I've hardy done anything, Beth."

"You have—you made me feel safe. I'm just sorry I ruined your night."

Liam makes a quizzical face. "What could I have possibly been doing that was so riveting last night?"

"I don't know…watching a Netflix series? Working? Fantasy baseball league? Anything would be better than looking after a damsel in distress."

"I'm just glad I was here."

"So…you thought I looked beautiful last night, huh?"

"Heard that, did you? I thought you might have been distracted."

"Not for compliments like those." She smiles.

"Well, I meant it, even if it was inappropriately timed." He lowers his gaze, momentarily embarrassed.

"It was nice to hear."

"Good." He looks up at her again.

"Your hair…" He reaches up and twirls a lock between two fingers before gently settling it down. "New haircut since I saw you?"

"Yep."

"I always liked it long, but this is also good."

"Thanks…and again for last night. I really mean it. I felt better being here with you."

"I know we haven't been that close the last couple years, but I hope you know you can always come here whenever you need, whatever time it may be."

"I know…do you remember one night when we were in college, and I got locked out of my dorm? Mikey was passed-out naked in bed, and you had to share your bed with me."

"Yeah…I didn't think you would remember that."

"Of course, I do. It was really nice of you to let me in, then give up half your bed to me."

"Ha, I really went above and beyond to let someone like you get in bed with me."

"Someone like me?" She blinks at him.

"You know I'm teasing."

"You never made a move on me."

"And should I have?"

"I guess I thought most guys would normally try something on, given the circumstances."

"Maybe I'm not like most guys you know."

"Or maybe you found me repulsive."

"I don't think that was it." He smirks.

"Are you sure?"

"Yeah. I'm quite sure."

She laughs, and though her eyes are so familiar, there's something new there.

His phone rings on the bedside table, startling them. They withdraw from each other, and Liam rolls over to check the phone. "Err, it's, Mikey. I'll call him back."

Five seconds later, Beth's phone rings in the other room. She's fallen quiet, and he wonders if she's feeling awkward, being in bed right now with him. Or whether she's thinking about last night again. "How about I get us some coffee and maybe a bite to eat? I normally have breakfast at the office, so I don't have much here."

"Sure, sounds good."

"If you want to take a shower, there's fresh towels in the cupboard."

"Okay, thanks." She pulls the sheets up further around her shoulder. "I don't think I can put that dress back on," she says glumly.

"Just keep my T-shirt for now. I see the shorts must have been too big for you." He picks them up from the floor.

Beth blushes. "Must have fallen off when I got into bed with you last night," she says sheepishly.

He can't help but grin.

*

Liam welcomes the stroll down to the corner to get coffee and bagels—time to gather his thoughts. As awful as it was to see Beth hurt and distraught, he liked that she came to him—even if he'd been her third option. But then she'd snuggled into him all night. Admittedly, she'd been vulnerable, but she seemed okay about being in his bed this morning. It felt so natural, but also exciting. Her body in his bed. *Stop thinking about her in her underwear!* He takes a long drink of coffee and heads back up to his apartment.

He finds Beth in his kitchen getting a drink of water. Her hair is wet, and she's wearing his shorts and shirt again—the latter tied into a knot on the side. When she moves, a hint of midriff skin peeks through. He looks away. *This is not helping.* But his mind instantly goes back to how her soft bare legs felt against his skin last night.

"For me?" Beth asks.

"Ah, yes. Coffee." He hands it to her.

"Thanks."

"I think you should take today off work," he says.

"Yep. No arguments from me on that one."

"I can take the day off with you. We can go anywhere you like—a nice brunch and then the park…maybe file a police report somewhere in the middle of that?"

She doesn't say anything for a moment. "I don't think I can," she murmurs.

"Which part?"

Beth pauses, then says hesitantly, "Mainly the police report. I told you last night, it's a future client."

"That's irrelevant. You have to say something to the partners and to the cops."

"I know. I want to say something. I just need to think about how I should go about it. I'm meant to be closing the deal next week. It'll be one of the biggest clients we've landed in years. Do you know how important it is for us right now?"

"But you're more important than any of that."

"You don't get it. Everything I've been working for, everything I've given up to get to this point. I can't just let it go."

"I do get it. But it's not right. Anyway, wouldn't it mean you have to keep working with him? You can't do that."

Beth sighs. "I know, but maybe I can transfer them over to another lawyer." She heads towards the spare room.

"Are you okay?"

"I should probably get going."

"Beth, I don't want to push. I'm just worried for you."

"I know. Thank you. But it's something I need to figure out for myself."

She wanders off, then re-enters a few minutes later with her dress and phone.

"Can you call Mikey at least. I understand if you don't want me to help you, but talk to him."

"I can't."

"What? You *have* to tell him."

"He has enough to worry about. I don't want to add to his mounting issues right now."

"Beth...I..."

"Liam, just stop. Okay? You can't fix this."

He trails her as she walks to the door. "But you don't need to be alone in this..."

She swings back around to face him. "I've been doing okay on my own for some time now."

"I know how capable and independent you are, but this is different."

"You don't need to do anything for me," she snaps. "You're not my brother, and you're not my boyfriend."

Stunned, Liam lifts his hands in surrender as she turns and walks out the door.

"Yeah, I'm well aware of that," he says to the empty space in front of him.

Chapter 13

Michael rushes into his office and waves to a few co-workers he hasn't seen in a while. He knocks on his editor's door—the ageing nameplate there, 'Brian McMillian—Editor' is just as intimidating as it was on his first day as a cadet. McMillan calls out. Michael pushes open the door and wave of cigarette stench hits him.

"Michael. Sit." McMillan says.

"Still smoking, hey? Patches didn't work?"

McMillan grunts at him, "Pieces of shit those things."

"Have you tried vaping?"

"What do I look like to you? Some fuckin' hipster teenager?"

"No, sir. Just making a suggestion. Some people find it easier to move off with vapes."

"How about you stop talking and work out how to use a keyboard again?"

"Sorry, I know I haven't been in the office much lately."

"Much? I'm shocked you still remember where my office is."

Michael bites his tongue; smartarse comments won't save him today.

"To be honest, I don't fucking care if you're here in the office or sitting at Base Camp in Kathmandu. All I need you to do is file work! I'm relying on you to fill spaces, but all I seem to be doing is giving out free ad space. I hired you because you deliver hard hitting and investigative reporting—stuff people actually want to read. It gets us traction, we keep our readers, we get advertisers, and we all get to keep our jobs. I don't know why I need to remind you about how this process works. Do I need to go over this again?"

"No, Boss."

"So, tell me why I've barely seen anything from you, and when I do, it's this shit." He stabs at his computer screen. "If I wanted this standard of copy, I would've hired that college student who walked into my office last week and spilled coffee all over my desk. If you have nothing, don't waste my time!"

"I'm sorry. I've just had a lot of things going on at home."

"Who doesn't!"

"Maybe I could take some time off?"

"I'd have no staff left in here if everyone took time off for family issues."

"I know, I can't expect special privileges."

"That's right. You can't. I need work from you, or I'll get it from someone else." McMillan pauses. "I've given you more time than I would've given anyone else. You're one of my best writers. Stan brought me the Cuba story, which should have been your pitch. Find me something to publish!"

"I'll get onto it."

"I see you still have time to do your podcast, so I'm assuming your family issues aren't interfering with that?"

"Huh, I didn't know you subscribed."

He ignores the comment. "We have deadlines for a reason. Miss one again, and you'll have to find yourself another job."

Michael sighs heavily as he leaves McMillan's office. His phone beeps—a voice message from Harold asking that if he hasn't yet left to join them for the weekend away, can he collect Chloe whose car won't start. He hesitates but sends both of them a text confirming he can. At least it'll take his mind off his boss's rant for a while.

*

He leans out his car window as he pulls up to where Chloe is waiting at the curb. "Did you bust your car just so you can ride with me?"

Chloe looks frustrated. "Yes, that was my first choice," she mutters.

"I can leave without you if you want?"

"I'm sorry."

"Sorry for the attitude or sorry that you have to ride with me?" He smirks as he gets out to open the boot.

"Perhaps both." Her smile is sly.

"That's fair."

To make the journey bearable, he plays the nice guy card and opens the passenger door. "Here. Jump in and I put your bags in the trunk."

Taken aback, she offers him a weak thank you and climbs in.

A few moments later, Michael pulls out into the traffic and settles into its crawl. Uncomfortable with the silence between them, he says, "So…anything exciting happen this week?"

"Not really. You?"

"No, not really." He sighs. It's going to be a long car trip. He tries again. "So, how are you really doing, since you're not working?'"

"Keeping busy."

It's obvious she's trying to sound casual, but isn't quite pulling it off.

He glances at her. "Your neck looks a little better."

She reaches up and touches where the bruise was.

"It's good that you didn't cover it up today," he says. "It's a badge of honour."

"Yes and no. It means my style is off."

"If it makes you feel better, I'm probably going to get early arthritis with all the note taking, typing and—you know—lots of swiping." He waits to see if she bites.

Chloe almost snorts. "Too much time on Tinder?"

"Please, Bumble. I like all the women coming to me. Genius concept."

"You're so full of yourself, aren't you?"

Michael shrugs. "I bet you don't like making the first move. You want a man to fall at your feet, shower you with gifts, rose petals and all that."

"I'm not like that."

"So, then tell me. What are you like?"

As the cars on the toll road come to a stand-still, she looks over at him. "It's none of your business."

"Fair enough…but it would be weird right, for a guy to serenade you with a violin? That wouldn't work. Has that ever happened?"

"No, that's never happened. That's ridiculous."

Michael chuckles to himself.

"You should take fish oil," she says.

"For what? Dating? Not sure, chicks will dig that. Unless this is a new kinky thing I don't know about? Where does it go?"

"No! That's disgusting. I meant for arthritis. Start taking it before you get older. I heard it helps, but who knows."

"Okay, that makes more sense. Thanks. I'll try it…So, tell me something else about yourself. Musician, neck thing…any other injuries?"

91

"Hmmm, mainly just from when I was younger. Non-music related. I broke my leg while horse riding on a school camp. I was never allowed on one after that in case I fell off again and broke my arm. That suited me though, as I'm petrified of them. And my hands—let's say, I wouldn't be a hand model. They aren't very straight, and I have scars. They used to bleed from playing too much."

"I've heard about that. That's just crazy."

"I guess so. Seemed normal at the time."

"Did you stop playing for a while after it happened?"

"No. When you're young and trying to make it, you'll do anything."

"Yeah, right. I guess, I never really expected playing an instrument to be so extreme."

"Yes. It's highly competitive as you can imagine. We all have the same dream and there isn't enough chairs for everyone."

Michael scratches his neck. "So, your boyfriend, Francis. Isn't he coming up for the weekend? Not saying that I don't like the company."

"No, not this time." She looks out the window, saying nothing for a while.

Maybe he shouldn't have brought up Francis. "Do you want to hear my list of injuries?"

"Yes, please." She pulls a lip gloss from her bag and dabs her lips.

"Well, since you asked…skiing accident, full ACL rupture. I like to blame that one on halting my football career from taking off. I could've probably made it to professional level otherwise."

"Is that what you tell all your dates?"

Michael laughs. "That's right. I also had a lot of shoulder dislocations and torn hamstrings from playing. The worst injury though was to my ego—bruised because I wasn't good enough to make it professionally."

"I can imagine…I'd be devasted if someone told me to stop playing violin, especially at that age. What position did you play?"

"You know about football?"

"Enough. Plus, other sports. I'm not just a music geek."

"Hmm, didn't pick that," Michael nods impressed, "I was running back."

"I suppose at least your parents could stop worrying about you getting injured all the time?"

"My mum was probably fifty-fifty. She wanted what I wanted. But dad hated football and always wanted me to go into finance. He saw job security and didn't really listen to what my interests were."

"That's tricky. So, then what happened?"

"I started interviewing my friends after the games for the school paper, then got into writing. I negotiated with dad and did communications and finance."

"So, he must be proud then?"

Michael bites the inside of his cheek. "He never said as much. After our parents divorced, he spent less and less time with us. I thought if I kept going on that trajectory, he would all of a sudden become more interested in what I was doing. But he never did. Anyway, sorry, that got deep quickly." He feels Chloe look at him.

"Sounds like a complicated relationship," she says.

"It is."

"So, do you *actually* enjoy what you do for work?"

"Most of the time, I guess."

Chloe sighs. "That's something. And you would have turned into a real jerk if you were an athlete."

Michael raises his eyebrows and glances at her. "I thought you already thought I was a jerk?"

She folds her arms but smiles.

As they continue in silence, the traffic thins out. He glances over at Chloe, about to remark on it being a faster-paced drive, but she's drifted off to sleep. She looks so peaceful, her head resting against the car window. Even on a road trip, she looks elegant. Her strawberry-coloured lips gloss. Her crisp yellow blouse suits her dark skin tone. Around her wrist, she has a Swiss IWC watch adorned with diamonds. A bracelet with a few charms dangles in her lap. Her summery white skirt has shifted higher up her thigh, revealing more of her slender legs. *Slender but curves in all the right places.* He tears his eyes away, shaking his head in wonderment.

"Eyes on the road, Mikey. Eyes on the road."

Chapter 14

Beth glances at her phone again. Still nothing from Naomi. She gets up from her home desk and walks around the apartment. The foot traffic noise from the city is escalating through the open window. She sticks her head out and looks down the street. Restaurants have put their tables out on the sidewalks and bars are flicking on their lights. Everyone is getting ready for a weekend of Fourth of July celebrations. A couple of women walk arm in arm down the street, giggling over something they've shared.

Beth sighs. *I could really do with my best friend.* She walks back over to her phone and decides to send another message. Her phone rings immediately.

"Naomi?"

"Umm, hi. I wasn't sure if you would be mad at me."

Beth pauses. "Why would I be mad?"

"So, so, sorry I've been dodging your calls and messages. I might have overreacted. I've had some time to let it sink in—I mean, my ex with a baby?"

"I get it. It wouldn't have been easy to hear."

"Can we meet up?" Naomi asks.

"Yes, of course. Do you want to come around?"

"I'm already here."

Beth laughs and hangs up to find Naomi at her front door with a bottle of wine. They have a long hug. She steps back and takes the bottle of wine from Naomi's hand. "Can we open this immediately? I could do with a drink."

"You bet," Naomi says. "I need a break from thinking about work and this gala event of yours. Although I'm still so excited that you picked us to be the event organisers."

"Of course!" Beth leads Naomi to the lounge room. "Who else would I get to do it? Your agency is all anyone is talking about. Plus, I know you'll make this night the most talked about event of the year!"

"It's going to be Ah-mazing. I'm so excited. Have you got a dress picked out yet?"

"Hmmm, not yet."

Naomi jumps up and leaves the room. Beth hears her rummaging through her wardrobe with muffled muttering.

"What?" Beth yells as she pours the wine.

"Don't worry. I found the dress I was after!" Naomi returns triumphantly holding a short red dress with a daring neckline.

"Wow. I haven't worn that dress in years."

"It gets my vote!"

Beth laughs while Naomi goes back to look for a pair of shoes. She returns, holding them up triumphantly. "With these sexy numbers."

"You know, this is a work event, right? Not a club opening. Now, I'm worried about the brief I gave you."

Naomi waves her off with a laugh. "I've got this. Don't worry." She returns the shoes and dress to Beth's bedroom, then comes back to the lounge. "So, before we get into talking about the gala, I should say thanks." She grabs her glass of wine and has a quick sip before looking back at Beth with a little hesitation. "Thanks for telling me about Michael. He didn't want to tell me?"

"No. I think he's still finding it tough."

"It's not like it took him long to move on." She swishes her blonde hair off her shoulders.

"I don't think it was a matter of moving on—more a drowning of his sorrows and getting drunk. Anyway, now you've both moved on, and it's for the best."

"Probably. It was crazy to think he would forgive me and come back. Dumb."

"That sounds very mature of you."

Beth's phone buzzes—Liam confirming he's picking her up early in the morning to take her to the Cape. She lets out a long sigh. *Can't avoid him forever.*

"What's wrong?" Naomi asks.

"Nothing, just…don't worry, it's a long story."

"Who was that text from?"

"Ah…no one."

"Is it a new man? I hope he didn't cancel a date on you?"

"It's not as exciting as you're hoping for." Beth pours more wine for them and puts her feet up on the coffee table, relaxing into the couch.

Naomi looks at her with keen interest. "Cough it up. Did you have some hot sex last night and now he wants another round?"

Beth laughs. "No, not at all. Who has the time?"

"Plenty of people!" Naomi giggles.

"I wish I were like them."

"What? For the sex or for more time?"

"I'll take either. But preferably both!"

They laugh.

"I'm still picking up vibes that there's a man on the horizon?" Naomi persists.

"No. Like I said, I have no time to meet anyone."

"OMG! It's Jordan, isn't it! He's such a snack! I can't believe you're sleeping with your secretary. That's so Mad Men of you. I love it!"

"No, Naomi. He's hot, but I'm not sleeping with him. He works for me, and even if he didn't, he's too young for me."

Naomi looks disappointed. "Too young? Who cares?"

"I also can't work out if he's gay, bi or pan."

"Ohhh, a mystery. I love this game!"

"But I don't need to solve it. So, let's move on."

"I can imagine a six pack under that shirt and tie."

"Naomi!" Beth playfully smacks her leg. "I can't think about his body. I need to be professional."

"If he worked for me, we'd have done it several times on my desk already."

"You have no shame." Beth laughs. "Anyway, it doesn't matter, he's the best secretary I've ever had. End of story."

"Okay, fine. Do I have to keep guessing? Talk! I know when you're hiding something. Plus, it must be killing you not to tell me."

Beth sighs overdramatically for effect. "Okay. But I just want to remind you nothing has happened. And I'm pretty sure I've already quashed this."

Naomi curls her legs underneath herself on the lounge and faces Beth with interest. "Keep going."

"I don't know how to explain this…"

"Come on, out with it, or I'll start to send your sexy secretary love messages from your phone."

Beth moves her phone away from Naomi. "I stayed over at Liam's the other night."

"What?" She squeals. "Liam, as in *Liam* Liam? Not a new Liam, but the old Liam?"

"Yes, the old Liam."

Naomi looks stunned. "I don't know what to say."

"Is it that much of a bad idea that something could have happened?" Beth says.

"No, just shocked, I guess. Did something happen between you guys in college, and you never told me?"

"No, nothing happened."

"Did you have a crush on him?"

"Hmmm…I kind of liked him, and he was always sort of cute. But he was part of the younger brat pack hanging out with Mikey. And I was always dating or chasing some older guy on campus."

"Ohhh, so you *did* think he was hot and sexy?" She teases.

"I wish I'd never said anything." Beth grabs a cushion and hides her face.

"Shut up. Of course, you wanted to tell me. I just need a minute to take in all this exciting information. Wow, the re-emerged Liam with Beijing twist." She grabs the pillow and pulls it away from Beth's face. "What happened? What changed? Tell me everything. This is so exciting." She claps with enthusiasm.

"I don't know. I guess that's why I'm a bit unsure. Since he got back…he looks different…but familiar. I think we had a moment when I was at his work dinner, well it was after, anyway. Then the other night I was having a rough time, and I stayed at his place. We ended up cuddling in his bed, and it was *nice*. You know?"

"That's it? I mean, I'm excited, but also disappointed."

Beth rolls her eyes, "Sorry it's not X-rated enough for you."

"So, he's either a very rare gentleman or not interested."

"It's more complicated than that."

"Hmm. So, maybe just ask him straight out what he's thinking."

"No way! It's hard enough telling you this."

"But I feel like you've had a big revelation. You need to find out where his head is at."

"It's not a revelation. It was…cosy. I woke up in his bed, and we were…"

"What?" Naomi bounces on the couch, trying not to spill her wine.

"It was just spooning."

Naomi covers her mouth, laughing. "Spooning? That was it?"

Beth grimaces. "I'm not talking to you about this anymore." She tosses the cushion at Naomi's head.

"Hey! Watch my wine," Naomi squeals.

"Anyway, I'm sure nothing is going to happen."

"No one spoons unless they want action."

"Are you sure?"

"Have you ever known a guy to just cuddle and leave it at that?"

"I guess, I normally spoon after sex, not before."

"Hmmm. So, how did it go from catching up to bed sharing?"

"Ahh, it was a work situation. I tried calling Mikey...and you. Liam answered."

"Beth, I'm so sorry I've been shutting you out. I hate that I wasn't there for you. I'd normally drop everything for you."

"I know, but it was okay in the end. Liam was there."

"So, he became your knight in shining armour? Maybe I did you a favour." Naomi winks. "What now?"

"Well, he's still Mikey's best friend and my friend. So, I can't take it any further."

"Why not?"

"What if it all goes wrong?"

"What if it doesn't?"

"This could all be in my head too by the way."

"I doubt it. I always thought he had a thing for you."

"Really?"

Naomi raises an eyebrow at her with disbelief. "I'm more than one hundred per cent positive. Tell me what happened with the work thing."

Beth sighs. "Just one of my potential clients was a bit sleazy."

Naomi gasps. "What a scumbag! What happened?"

Beth tells Naomi her story.

"Beth! Holy crap." Naomi springs over and wraps her arms around her.

"I'm okay...I'm just still a bit rattled by it all."

"Of course, you are." Naomi keeps holding her. "That must have been so awful for you. I wish I'd known sooner." She pulls back to look at Beth. "You must have been terrified. Are you okay, or are you okay now?"

"I'm okay, sort of. Just still shaken up." Beth sniffs and wipes away a loose tear.

"Is he getting fired?"

"He owns half the company."

"Shit."

"I haven't mentioned it to anyone else aside from Liam."

"You haven't told anyone else?" Naomi is shocked. "You have to say something to your boss. Plus, you should file a police report. And, Mikey, will be so upset if he doesn't know about this."

"I'll tell Mikey later. He'll go nuts. I'd like to have it resolved before I mention it to him."

"And what have you told work?"

"Ah, I haven't. I've…just been hiding out."

"Doesn't sound like a good long-term plan. What about this sleazy dirtbag?"

"It's complicated. Our firm really needs his company. Our competitor has just gone bankrupt, and our partners are panicking that something similar could happen to us if we don't stay competitive in the market."

"That's shit though. How is this fair?" Naomi reaches for the wine and tops up their glasses.

"It's not. This is the fucked-up position I'm in. I make a complaint: I lose my job, I lose my dream, the company could fall apart."

"Shit, Beth."

"I know." She sniffs again.

"I don't want to pressure you. I can't imagine how traumatic it's been for you, but you really should report him."

"I'll think about it."

"He's probably done it to other women too."

"You're probably right," she says glumly. "I just need to get through this gala dinner next week. But I don't know what James is going to do. He might humiliate me in front of everybody."

"What does James have to do with this?" Naomi's eyes narrowed.

"He was the one who interrupted us. But he doesn't know what he saw. He thinks I was propositioning the client."

"Fuck. This is why you have to say something."

Beth sighs. "I'm just not ready yet. Do you think we can stop taking about it?"

"Okay." Naomi squeezes her hands. "I suppose talking about how sexy Liam is, is a way better conversation."

Beth squirms. "It's also a pointless conversation anyway. I forgot to mention he has a girlfriend, or ex-girlfriend, or whatever she is. And she's in town."

"Oh, really?"

"Her name's Evelyn. They had a thing together when he was working in Beijing."

"That won't last," Naomi says.

"How do you know?"

"For one thing, you're amazing. And I guarantee she's no match for you."

Beth manages a smile.

"So, what does this Evelyn look like?"

Beth picks up her phone, finds Evelyn's Instagram and holds it up for Naomi. Naomi pulls a face. "Sheesh."

"Exactly."

"I do like that you have been quick to stalk the competition."

"Anyway, like I said before, it's too risky even if I did like him." She sighs.

"So what? You're going to do nothing?"

"Yes."

"Boring!" Naomi pouts then grins, giving Beth another hug.

Chapter 15

Chloe awakes disorientated, her neck stiff from sleeping against Michael's car window. She blinks a few times. They've stopped at a petrol station. She spots Michael inside, waiting at the checkout queue. He's pulling funny faces at a child in front of him who's laughing back at him. As he returns to the car, triumphantly holding up a selection of items like a trophy, his shirt lifts up with the wind, displaying his lower abdomen and a long graphic tattoo that seems to run below his waistline. Chloe wonders where it leads to. Flustered all of a sudden, she tries to look indifferent as he jumps back into the car.

"Hey there, sleepy head—I picked you purely for company on the drive, and look what happens," he jokes.

"Sorry, I was just so tired." She straightens in her seat, then notices her skirt has ridden high on her leg. She quickly pulls it down. Michael doesn't seem to notice.

"Don't be sorry. You must have needed some rest…I remembered you drank coffee." He hands her a cup. His fingers graze hers and something inside of her flutters. *What was that?*

"Umm perfect. Thank you so much. Would you like me to drive?" she offers, sipping and swallowing coffee with haste.

"I would, but I don't see how you're going to let go of that coffee."

She manages a small laugh.

Michael starts the engine and looks for some music on his phone. Chloe has a moment of amusement when Beethoven plays over the car speakers. And they're back on the road again. Chloe makes small talk for a while but soon becomes distracted by the dread of being back at the Cape for the first time without Ari.

After a while, they pass through a gate to the Hennigans' Cape Cod property. Michael whistles. "Wow, this driveway goes for miles."

"It's a nine-acre estate. They ended up building two family compounds here," Chloe says.

"Yeah. It's slightly smaller than my holiday house, but don't go saying anything and making it weird for Harold and Winnie. Okay?"

She smirks. "Does your estate also come with some of the best views on the Cape?"

"Yes. In fact, it does!" he says.

Unfortunately, Michael's comedic banter only distracts her until the house comes into view. Chloe swallows a sudden lump in her throat. She's normally excited by coming up the driveway; it's a special place. But tonight, the house seems to loom over her, its dark windows soulless. Cold and empty.

"Chloe?...Chloe?" Michael asks.

"Oh, sorry. I tuned out."

He stops the car out the front. "You okay?"

"Yes. Of course."

"If you need a moment?"

"No...I'm okay."

Just as she responds, lights flicker on and Harold and Winnie appear on the porch. Chloe takes a long breath and opens the car door to greet them.

"Sorry. We were all in the west wing of the house. We should have left more lights on for you," Harold says.

"So glad you made it, Chloe," Winnie gushes, racing over to give her a warm embrace.

Harold offers Michael his hand, then Winnie greets Michael with a polite handshake too.

"Sorry it's so late—traffic," Chloe explains.

"Nonsense. We're happy to have you arrive anytime," Harold says.

Inside, Winnie takes Michael's arm. "Let me show you to your room and where Macy is sleeping." An unfamiliar maid scurries after them, waiting for instructions from Winnie.

Chloe pauses in the entrance.

Harold notices her hesitation. "After a day or two, it gets a bit easier." He pats her on the shoulder. "I'll let you get settled in. We allocated your usual room, but you can pick another if you wish."

"The same room will be fine," she tells Harold and herself.

"I may not be awake after you unpack, so I'll see you in the morning."

"Goodnight, Harold."

Upstairs. Chloe enters the room she'd shared with Ari ever since they were kids. Two single beds on opposite sides of the room, which they always pushed together as soon as they arrived. Chloe pushes them together once again. She unpacks quickly, but the old photos on the wall draw in her attention. Reminders about firework nights, and circus events, bands they saw over summer holidays. She feels someone in the doorway and looks around. It's Michael.

"Sorry to interrupt. Winnie mentioned they left us some food downstairs, if you're interested."

"Sure."

In the kitchen, they sit at the long marble bench with an array of late-night snacks and a couple of ciders.

"Sort of a tough one for both of us…being here. I know it won't be easy for you this weekend," Michael says.

"No. But I have to be here. It's hard, but what are my options? If I don't come back, this whole part of my life doesn't exist anymore."

"I agree. I think it's the right thing to do. You'll be better for it in the long run."

"So, what about you? Nervous?"

"Yeah. I'm glad I'm here…but kind of freaking out too."

"Nervous about all of us?"

"That and spending more time with Macy. But I need to make up for lost time."

Chloe studies his face, sees sincerity.

Michael continues. "I feel guilty. Even though I know I didn't do anything wrong. I wasn't there when Macy was born, and part of me also feels guilty for not helping Ari through this when she was alone…although, I'm still frustrated about what she did."

Chloe thinks back to her conversation with Logan. Ari had lied to her about seeing Logan. Had she lied to her about Michael too? "Can I ask you something?"

"Shoot."

Chloe fidgets with the label on her cider bottle. "After that night with Ari, did something happen? Was there anything that would have made her not want to reach out to you?"

"I wish there were an explanation. If there is one, I'm not the one who has it. I wasn't even sure if she gave me her real name. She must have remembered mine though, else we wouldn't be sitting here right now, having this conversation," he takes a sip of cider, then looks at her. "Are you ever going to believe me?"

She looks down at her cider, unable to meet his eyes. "I...I don't know what to believe anymore."

"You still don't trust me?"

"It's not that I don't trust you. Can't you see it from where I'm standing? You're this stranger who comes storming into our lives..."

Michael's nostrils flare. "Just a second...you contacted me. Remember?"

"Wait, I hadn't finished. I want to believe you, but I know Ari...I *knew* Ari. I just don't know why she would keep secrets from me—for what purpose. I've been listening to your side of things, and they all seem genuine. Okay?" Chloe turns and looks directly at him. "Why is it so important for you that I believe you?"

"I don't know. It just is." Michael locks eyes with her, and his face softens. He shifts in his seat. "But I'm glad you said that I seem genuine. I'm sorry if I raised my voice at you. I can appreciate you're in a difficult position too...I'm scared shitless about having a child, but I'm here and I'm trying to work out what happens next."

"You know, I think I'm beginning to understand you more."

"How so?"

"What you said in the car earlier about trying to please your dad and him not being around. That stuff plays on your mind. Makes you think about the other relationships you have, like say...one you would have with your child?"

Michael takes a long swig from the bottle and looks straight ahead. "Regardless of what happened with my dad, I want to do the right thing. But yeah, maybe it makes me more determined. What I do know is that having an absent parent, or let me re-phrase, uninterested parent, is pretty shit."

"Do you see him ever, or speak to him now?"

"Haven't seen him for three years. Last phone call was about a year ago. I used to call and leave messages, but then I heard nothing. So, it's easier on me that I don't ring at all."

Chloe looks down at the counter, feeling a little guilty for bringing up the subject. "That's tough. Sorry."

"Yeah, what can you do?"

"And what you said before. You don't seem scared at all about being a father...you seem pretty confident and determined to me."

"I'm glad that's what it looks like, as it certainly doesn't feel that way."

"Harold and Winnie must see it too. They invited you here regardless of the 'how this happened' story. I know they can be difficult to deal with sometimes, but they're good people, and they're handling it all pretty well, given the circumstances."

They quieten for a moment. Chloe looks over at him again—his loose jeans with a tear, a baseball cap backwards and his slouch on the bar stool are all totally out of place here in this large designer kitchen, which has appeared in interior magazines across the state. It makes her smile for some reason. "You know...you aren't really Ari's type."

"What's that meant to mean?" He sounds upset until he realises that she's teasing.

"She did date an athlete, remember? Big strong muscled bodies, chiselled jaw-lines, ripped abs." She sighs for dramatic effect.

"What? And I'm not that?" He pretends to be extremely offended.

Chloe laughs, shaking her head. "No."

"Gee, thanks. But hang on, I'm sporty though. Is that not enough?"

"Hmmm, maybe you need more protein in your diet, and a few more weight sessions."

"Ouch. Anything else?"

"Maybe less sneakers, more loafers. More dress shirts, less T-shirts and no baseball caps."

"Wait, wait, wait. All of a sudden, this seems to have turned into your personal list."

"It is not."

"Sure." He grins.

"Some women might like your type." Chloe squirms in her seat.

"That's nice to know." Michael tilts his head. "But not your type?" He chuckles.

"Definitely not." *Is it warm in here suddenly?* Chloe rubs her neck.

"A lot of women don't mind the rough around the edges vibe—messy hair, tatts, unshaven."

"I suppose. And I should add, being a gentleman is important too—being one of the good guys, someone who cares about other people, not just themselves."

"So…what about me, then. Do I qualify? Am I a good guy?"

"Maybe you are, after all."

"Wow. That's the nicest thing you've said to me so far."

Michael smiles and reaches for his cider. The condensation on the bottle makes his hand slip, and the bottle thuds back on the table with a splash escaping onto Chloe's arm. Michael quickly reaches for a napkin at the same time as Chloe. His hand touching hers momentarily, sending a quick release of adrenalin through her body. That feeling again but even more intense. She looks away. Feeling her cheeks are pink with the encounter.

"You probably need this," he murmurs and offers Chloe the napkin.

Chloe wonders if he'd felt it too. Or was it just in her head? She takes the napkin and dabs at her skin. "Thanks."

Michael seems to finish the rest of his drink quickly. "Ah, shall we call it a night?"

"Sure."

"I'd be a gentleman and escort you to your room, but I can't remember how we got here, so I'll just have to follow you."

Chloe smiles, leading the way back upstairs. And as Michael disappears into his room, she feels even more confused about him than before.

Chapter 16

Michael has volunteered to look after Macy this morning, and just his luck, she's awake and a bit grizzly before dawn. He potters around the house, carrying her against his chest to see if she might resettle. Instead, she grows more restless. He frantically searches for a carry pouch, then flees out the back door, not wanting to look as if he can't handle his first shift. If he was being honest with himself, he needed a moment from the house too. He awoke this morning strangely thinking about Chloe. The honestly of their conversation and the way she playfully teased him which he felt was almost like…flirting? Surely not. But then the unexpected excitement of when they touched. It couldn't mean anything. It was nothing…it had to be nothing.

Heading over the manicured lawn, he walks past a grass tennis court, then down a track opening up onto the beach, which seems endless in both directions. Pushing any last thoughts of Chloe out his mind he concentrates on the matter at hand. Being here, being present for Macy. Becoming a father. As the sun creeps over the horizon, Macy's breaths become longer, and her body relaxes. Michael is surprised how much he's enjoying the moment. He never expected to feel happy doing this. It makes him think. Could he look after a child on his own? After some contemplation and a long stroll, he heads back to the house.

He treads lightly down the hallway but gets distracted by happy snaps covering the walls.

"Great summer that one."

Michael startles, not having heard Harold walk up behind him. "I didn't realise anyone was up yet. I was just looking. Hope, you don't mind."

"No. They're on display."

"Everyone looks happy."

"Yes…we were. What about your family?" Harold asks. "Did you have a place you went to as kids, or now perhaps?"

"Not so much. My parents split up when I was young, so after that, things weren't really the same."

"A shame. Happens so often these days. People are in such a hurry to get married, start a family, and then they're in such a rush to leave."

Michael isn't sure if this last remark is directed at him. "You have a fantastic home here. I hope it's not too much with all of us being here?"

Harold shakes his head with a tsk. "Of course, not. It's a big place. Plus, I'm glad you're here. It was my intention that we could talk about a few things man to man."

"Sure," Michael says. Trying not to sound nervous.

Harold motions for him to follow. "Let's go to the study."

Michael spots Roberta down the hall and says a morning greeting to her. She comes rushing over to retrieve a sleeping Macy and motions that she'll put her back to bed.

Michael follows Harold further into the house, to a room with a grand walnut-coloured desk and a magnificently large window overlooking the grounds. Gardeners are sweeping up a few minor leaves that must have only just fallen. The room is as orderly as the rest of the house is—impeccable. Harold walks over to a cabinet door and opens it, displaying an array of decanters filled with cognacs and ports.

"Can I get you a drink?" he asks.

"I'm fine, thank you. Not this time of the morning."

Harold chuckles and pulls out a bottle of Pappy Van Winkle's. Michael can only guess what reserve it might be and how much it cost.

"It's the holidays after all. It's terrific with pancakes." Harold passes a glass to Michael and raises a silent toast.

Michael shrugs and holds up his glass.

"Michael, I feel that we've both spent some time getting to know each other in the last month. Obviously, not in the best circumstances, but nonetheless. I hope we can both be frank with each other."

Michael nods. "I agree, Harold. I want that too."

"Good. That's what I want to hear." Harold coughs. "I loved my daughter, of course, and naturally, I don't want to believe there was any wrongdoing on her behalf."

"Harold…"

"Let me finish." He raises his hand.

"I'm not blind to the fact that there's a strong possibly that Ariane could have made a mistake along the way."

"Regardless, I'm here now."

"Indeed, you are. Which is why I'd like to talk about the future. Family is very important in this house. I'm sure you've seen that."

"Yes. Of course. And I feel the same way."

Harold rubs his chin. "Very good. So, I was hoping you might be able to tell us if you have any long-term plans of being involved in Macy's life? It's a tough job being a parent, and it doesn't suit everyone. Being a father comes with a lot of responsibilities. I'm sure you're already starting to understand."

"Yes. Couldn't agree more. Also, I need to tell you…I'm having a paternity test. I just need to put my mind at ease, and yours too, I would say. I was waiting for Ari…umm…well, I just want to be one hundred per cent sure."

"I understand. A wise move, given the murky circumstances surrounding all of this. I don't know how long these things take, but you should know that there's another motive in why I'm asking you this." He pauses. "I've had a bit of bad luck it seems, of late. You see, I have a heart condition. I need to have surgery next month for a triple bypass."

Michael is taken aback. "I'm so sorry to hear that, Harold. I had no idea."

"Truthfully, I'm probably lucky to have made it this far." He takes another sip, then holds up the glass. "No doubt, this doesn't help, but it's too late to change course now. Anyway, back to what I was saying—the doctor tells me he can do this operation in his sleep. There shouldn't be any issues, but you never know what this old ticker could get up to once it's in the operating room."

"I'm sure the doctor will have this all under control."

"Regardless of the operation, Winnie and I are both getting older, and we can't be there full-time for Macy. And really, Roberta is our housemaid, not a nanny. We need a few more youthful options here. We have aunts, uncles, cousins, but everyone has their own life. Winnie wants to organise a live-in nanny, but maybe that's not really our decision to make." Harold stops to clear his throat. "Under the assumption that Macy is yours—and I think we're all in agreement that she is?" He looks at Michael to confirm.

"Yeah…yes, I believe she is."

"Just take some time to think about what role you would like to play in Macy's life. All new things are exciting for a while, but often lose their lustre over time. Our main aim is to give her a stable life."

Michael isn't sure what to say. "I understand."

"Let me know what you decide."

"I will."

Michael is happy to hear the doorbell ring. "Must be Beth and Liam. They were arriving early." He rushes out to the front of the steps to greet them.

"Thank goodness, you made it!" Michael hugs them both longer than usual.

"Have you been drinking?" Beth asks. "You smell like alcohol."

"Ah, not intentionally."

They look at him oddly, which he ignores. He quickly moves into hosting mode, leading them inside and giving them a brief run-down of all the rooms in the house.

"So, what's been happening since you got here?" Beth asks.

"I'll fill you in soon. Come on, I'll show you around. As best I can anyway. At least I know where your rooms are."

Michael opens a bedroom door. "I assume all the rooms are the same."

"I'll take this one." Beth says quickly.

"Okay. Don't forget about the welcome party out on the lawn at noon."

"I'll be there. I just need to do some work before then. So, I'll see you guys later?"

"Okay, sure." Michael looks to Liam, who shrugs as Beth shuts the door on them.

They walk down the hall to another room. "What's wrong with Beth?" Michael asks.

"Don't ask. It was a fun ride up."

Michael shakes his head. "Great. As if this weekend needs anymore drama."

Chapter 17

Chloe's phone rings for the third time, and she finally gives in.

"Chloe!" Francis says. "Why haven't you been taking my calls?"

"You know why."

"I really want this to work, but I don't even know where you are."

"I'm at the Cape."

"I see. Well, I guess I wasn't invited."

"No, you weren't invited. You left me!" Chloe says.

"Chloe, please. I miss you."

"You had a choice."

"I told you I wanted us to stay together."

"You knew it would never work, but you left anyway, so please spare me."

"That's not fair. I still hope every day there's a chance for us."

"You're such a liar. You could never commit properly, and now you're in another city, trying to convince me you want this to work? I can't believe I wasted all this time on you."

"Please don't say that."

Chloe hangs up.

Francis sends through a message: "I'm sorry."

But not sorry enough to stay.

*

Chloe isn't feeling in a festive mood, but the lawn party is already in full swing when she comes downstairs. Waiters are whipping in and out of the house with trays of cured seabass on blini with caviar and glasses of Dom Pérignon. A pop-up bar sits on a corner of the lawn, and a couple of young men are making cocktails while flirting with some of the female guests. The setting is tastefully patriotic with blue, white and red table decorations, and garlands hanging from the trees. Children are running around giggling and taking multiples of the more exciting kid-friendly food.

She spots Michael in the crowd. He actually looks quite decent in a crisp beige suit, white linen shirt and boat shoes. He's clean shaven, and instead of his sandy hair being a bit wild or in a baseball cap, it's neatly combed off his face, showing off his chiselled jawline. She enjoyed teasing him last night—he's in no way as broad as Logan, but that sort of oversized athletic body isn't for her anyway. And...if she's honest, Michael probably has the type of physique she likes—strong enough to effortlessly sweep her into his arms.

Michael catches her looking at him, and his deep blue eyes seem to dance with mischief. Embarrassed at being caught out, Chloe looks away. *Why am I even thinking about him like that?*

"I feel like the view gets better and better." Harold's voice from behind startles her.

"Sorry?"

"The ocean. Isn't it glorious?" He muses.

"It is." She breathes a quiet sigh of relief.

"I know it's hard for you being here, as much as it is for us. I assume that's why Winnie wanted to keep the tradition of the lawn party. Distraction more than anything, and to fill the emptiness of the house."

Chloe nods. "It's certainly different being here without her."

Harold pauses. "You'll keep coming back, won't you?" He reaches for her hand and gives it a gentle squeeze.

"I'm sure, I will." She looks at him almost tearfully and smiles.

"Winnie and I would find it even harder if you stopped coming. You are family to us, you know that?"

Chloe nods again, avoiding saying anything more sentimental. She remembers how scared she used to be of Harold when she was growing up. He always had yes-men scurrying around him with paperwork, and he always seemed to be barking orders at them or down the phone line. His snowy hair, distinguished and brushed back, would become unkempt when he lost his temper. In the last few years, that behaviour had lessened, and in its place emerged a calmer personality that made him quite charming.

Harold ushers over a waiter and takes two champagne flutes, passing one to Chloe. "Let's try and make the most of the next chapter, as difficult as that might be." They clink glasses and sip the champagne.

Harold nods towards Michael joking around with his friend Liam. "So, how was the car ride up with Michael?" he asks.

"Quite pleasant actually. We had good conversations about a lot of things, mainly about Ari and about Macy, of course."

"I'm impressed he came."

"Me too."

"And what do you make of this situation?"

Chloe bites her lip. "Hmmm, I'm not sure yet…but I think maybe I had the wrong idea about him."

"I had him looked at. Just so you know, they didn't find anything—divorced parents, some assets, nothing criminal."

Chloe nods. "That's a good result then. Still doesn't make any sense though."

"Maybe, the truth will remain with Ariane."

"Maybe."

"Time for a toast, I think." Harold clinks his glass for attention, and party goers pause their conversations to face him. His loud booming voice carries over the crowd. "It's wonderful to see you all here. It's been a difficult time for us recently, as you all know. We thank all our dear family and friends, and also our new friends." Harold motions to where Michael is standing. "Let's enjoy the time we have together. Happy Fourth of July weekend!" Harold raises his flute, and everyone cheers.

As the afternoon fades into night, more champagne bottles are poured and drunk, and by late evening, the remaining crowd moves indoors to the piano room. Ray, one of the locals, is playing 'America the Beautiful' on the piano, and many are singing along, while others chat loudly to each other. Chloe stands, taking it all in, but soon becomes cornered by Winnie and her neighbour Bernadette.

"Do tell us, Chloe, why won't you be going to Europe," Winnie says.

Chloe internally curses her mother—she must have spoken to Winnie about the news. "I've been given some time off. But it will give me a good chance to practice."

"You don't need any practice, my dear." Winnie looks baffled.

"Please, we'd love to hear you play something," Bernadette says.

Chloe sees the hopeful joy on their faces but doesn't want to fail here too, not in front of everyone she knows. "I don't think tonight would be appropriate."

"Nonsense, my dear. Every night is a perfect night to hear you play. Plus, we always keep your spare violin here, although it may not be up to standard at the moment." Winnie reaches up above the bookshelf and brings down a violin case. With a hopeful smile, she hands it to Chloe.

Cooper, one of the older neighbours, overhears the conversation and chimes in with gusto. "Chloe, how about one of our old favourites?" He goes to the corner of the room to pick up his guitar.

Michael looks over at her and offers a smile of encouragement. She nods. "Argh, okay. Why not?" She takes out the violin and tightens a few strings. Chloe checks her finger grip, places the violin into position under her chin, then closes her eyes. She breathes one deep breath, pushes all her thoughts aside and focuses.

Cooper counts her in. He always loves playing Bob Dylan's 'Hurricane.' Ray and Cooper start singing, and to Chloe's surprise, so does Michael. Everyone else claps along. But then it happens again—halfway through the song, she loses her place and stops playing for a few seconds before picking up the song again. When the song finishes, there's an eruption of applause and cheering. She smiles, glad to see everyone enjoying themselves, but her joy is overshadowed by an annoyance at her mistake. She excuses herself before she can be roped into another song and is relieved to hear Ray playing the piano again as she slips outside to the deck.

It's dark except for the stars, and a few tanker lights out at sea, sparkling between the beach heather on the sand dunes. On the balcony, she finds a bench, beautifully styled with cushions and light throw rugs. A slight breeze has picked up, and she brings the rug up around her shoulders then turns at the sound of the door opening.

"If you want to be left alone, just give me the word," Michael says.

"It's fine...please." She motions for him to sit next to her, which he does—noticeably close. His presence makes her a little nervous.

"You seem a little upset. And don't take this the wrong way, but I'm quite familiar with this side of your personality."

Chloe looks at him curiously. "Is that right?"

"You get this little frown. It's kinda cute when it's not directed at me."

"I have a cute frown?"

"Ah...ahem...you're still quite intimidating when you're mad."

"Hmmm."

"Want to tell me about what happened in there? You seemed annoyed near the end of the song."

Chloe shakes her head, looks up to the sky and sighs loudly. "Argh, just another mistake. My mind drifts for a second. I don't know…I feel like I've lost my touch."

"Look, I'm no expert, but what I saw in there…it was a pretty incredible performance. Watching you play, I couldn't take my eyes of you. Uh, sorry…that sounded creepy."

Chloe manages a small laugh. "Thanks, I think." She looks at him.

"Look, no one else noticed. I promise." He smiles.

Chloe changes the subject. "And who knew? You have a pretty good singing voice."

Michael leans back in the chair and laughs. "Really? I try. Mind you, I just realised, I probably shouldn't have sung in front of a music professional."

Chloe holds up a hand. "Please. I would never judge people singing and enjoying music. That's how it should be. Whether you sing off key or not."

"I must admit, I was also worried you might criticise some of my music choices in the car."

"I thought it was pretty amusing you assumed I only like one genre of music."

"Well…it was too risky. So, what should I have selected?"

"I like pretty much all music."

"Really?"

"Of course."

"Don't you?"

"Yes, except traditional folk music. That's not really my jam."

Chloe smiles, "I'll try and remember that."

Michael continues. "I could pretty much sing along to anything. But I like it loud, and it gets louder after more drinks."

"Sounds like fun. I miss that. Enjoying music for the sake of it."

"You don't normally get to play Bob Dylan?"

"Ha, not at all! It's nice to play a different style. Usually, a lot of the music I play has a sonata form."

"I'm nodding my head, pretending I know what the means, but can you help me out?"

"You know how pop songs have a contrasting verse to the chorus and then repeat? In a sonata form, there are two contrasting keys over three sections. The keys are like yin and yang, a feminine and masculine melody. They each have their own sound, then intertwine, then pull away from each another again. It's like watching a dance."

"Sounds like a relationship."

Chloe looks over to check if he's still interested in their conversation. To her surprise, he is leaning in focused on her. "Exactly. It's two different voices, and you need both for the song to work. It's also—in my opinion, often more dramatic when there are no rules at all, and the music takes you on a journey. Without the predictability and no pattern…it leaves the listener wanting more."

Michael swallows. "I bet."

"Anyway, I should have just been enjoying the moment more. It's hard to self-critique. You would understand—you're a writer—you want things to be perfect. You must re-edit your work so many times."

"I'm not in the same league as you, whatsoever."

"It *is* the same. You get paid to do it, just like I do. I know journalism is a competitive industry, so you must be pretty good at it. In fact, didn't I see that you had won some Press Association Award?"

"Your research skills seem to be better than most reporters I know."

Chloe grins.

"Anyway," he says, "yes, I did. I mean it's great to be recognised. But I guess, I'm just not feeling inspired at the moment. Maybe I need to find a new song as well."

"What do you normally do when you get writers block?"

"That's the thing. I don't think it's that. This is different. I'm just feeling…like I've lost my mojo. I've been doing more of my sports podcast that I usually do. I'm getting really into it. And I'm sure my five loyal listeners are enjoying it too."

"Really, only five?"

"Okay, there might be more than that, but it's still early days, and it doesn't pay the bills. So, we'll see. Maybe this weekend will help clear some things up in my head. All this sea air."

"This place can be pretty magical sometimes." She glances at him with a smile.

The rug slips off her shoulder, and she feels the warmth of Michael's hand on her skin as he reaches for it and gently replaces it.

"Th…thanks."

As he returns her gaze, her heart skips, and she quickly looks back out to the ocean.

"Are you ready to go back inside? I think Margaret is starting to warm up to me, and she might get jealous that I'm out here talking with you and not her."

"I'm sure, she will." Chloe's expression is playful. "Oh, and nice suit by the way."

"See? I clean up okay, don't I?"

More than okay, she thinks.

"Not bad."

Chapter 18

After a relaxing day on the beach the dusk is settling, and Liam is answering the call from neighbours to collect wood for the bonfire and barbeque to be held on the shared beachfront tonight. He thinks about the awkward drive up yesterday. He's been giving Beth space, but the silence and one-lined conversations have gone on for too long, so he decides to brave it and see if she'll join him collecting wood.

She's down on the shoreline. He passes by a few people collecting clams and manages to dodge squealing children running with flags and sparklers. Beth is kicking her feet around in the small waves crashing on the shoreline.

"Looking forward to the BBQ tonight?" he asks.

"Sure am." She looks at him briefly, then back at the waves.

Silence again.

"So, are we ever going to talk about the other night?"

"Which part?"

"Err…well, all of it?" He looks at her eagerly, but Beth averts her gaze.

She breathes out heavily. "I was hoping we could just avoid any complicated conversations this weekend. I just want to forget about everything and simply have a good time. Can I have that?" She looks at him now, almost pleading.

"I get it. But if you don't talk to me about it, please talk to someone else."

"I know you are worried, but please stop. And there's no point in telling Mikey, he doesn't need to know about this at the moment. Okay?" She gazes back out to the ocean as a gentle breeze blows her hair across her face. She doesn't bother removing it.

Liam nods and sighs, then walks off, leaving her to it. He knows when he's beaten.

More people come down to the beach, carrying rugs, coolers and beach chairs. The distant night sky is soon lit up with a few early fireworks for the celebrations. As they explode, a few people ooh and ah at the colours. Spirits rise as the night goes on. Liam is introduced to more of the Hennigan relatives and friendly neighbours, and they all pitch in with preparing the bonfire and cooking the clams and lobsters.

Liam offers to help with a stage being set up in front of the dunes for the musicians. Soon, the band is playing, and people are dancing. Chloe is enticed by a couple of young men to come up and play her violin. A few enthusiastic viewers clap wildly, and she gives in. Suddenly, the sound of the strings draws everyone's attention. She plays solo for a moment, then one of the men on the decks drops a beat under Chloe's notes. Then the keyboardist joins in.

Although the music is entertaining, Liam can't help but watch Beth. He gravitates to her, not really knowing what he might say this time. Something had changed between them. That night after the work dinner. It was as if she had unlocked something inside of him. He reaches out a hand towards her. "Dance with me?"

Beth slowly accepts.

He playfully whisks her into his arms. "Everyone in the town must be down here," he says, close to her ear.

"I know. It's a great atmosphere." She smiles up at him.

He spins her around a few times, and she giggles. The music changes to a gentler beat, and he pulls her close to him—the nape of her neck so near to his mouth. He tries to ignore the intimacy. His heart beating fast from the dancing.

"I don't want things to be weird between us, Beth."

"Me neither."

"I'm sorry if what happened the other night with us wasn't right. I know you were in a vulnerable position. I get that. So, please don't worry about it. We can move on. And with the other thing…I just want to protect you, but I know it's not my position to do that, so I'll back off. Okay?"

"I…I don't want you to be sorry. I like the fact that you care about me. I'm just worried about everything. About being made partner. I don't want it all to go wrong now because of this one guy." She pauses. "I deal with jackasses all the time, but this one…I think I'm scared of him, and I hate that the most. That someone makes me feel like this, you know? I feel powerless."

"You're such a strong person, Beth, but everyone needs help from time to time. You're not alone." He releases her body from his and reaches for both of her hands, squeezing them. "I'm here for you, if you want me to be."

She tilts her head slightly. "Thank you. And about us…you're right—I was feeling pretty helpless, but…it doesn't matter. It wasn't like anything happened anyway, right?"

"Sure, right. It was nothing. Good, so we're okay then." Liam can't help but feel a little disappointed as he lets her hands free. Beth seems to frown a little.

The music becomes livelier again as Michael comes up and wraps his arms around both their necks in semi headlocks. "Have you guys tried the lobster? It's out of this world."

"Sure did," Liam says, trying to sound enthusiastic.

"It's quite the party down here."

"Incredible!"

"See? I didn't drag you to such a terrible weekend away, did I?" Michael's voice trails off as he turns to watch Chloe walk by.

Liam notices her return a glance in Michael's direction and elbows him to get his attention. "So…Chloe? What's her story?"

"What do you mean?" Michael spins back around.

"You know what I mean?"

"Why? You interested?" Michael gives Liam a quizzical look.

"No, not me. You guys have been making eyes at each other all day."

"That's not true. Anyway, as if she'd be interested."

"So, are you into her?"

"It would be too complicated."

"So, you've already thought about it?"

"No, I haven't. Just answering the question. She isn't my type anyway. She's…"

"Out of your league?" Beth chimes in with a laugh.

"Gee, thanks!"

They join in with the rest of the beach goers, dancing for the rest of the night until the party quietens and the music comes to an end. At some point, Michael leaves to put Macy to bed and doesn't return. A few people remain swapping anecdotes.

Beth and Liam decide to call it a night and head back up to the house together, using the moonlight to guide them. They're both a little drunk, and Liam offers his hand to help Beth through the shrubs. They laugh as they both stumble a few times. They reach Beth's room first. She opens the doorway with a groan. "Oh no, this dumb bed."

"What's wrong with your bed?" Liam hangs in the doorway, amused.

"Look how little it is. I can't do single beds anymore; my feet hang off the end. And it's one of those really firm mattresses. You might as well be sleeping on the floor!"

Liam laughs. "Seems like you must have lost a bet or something. I have a king bed and my mattress is very soft."

"What? Typical. I have the worst luck."

"You know me. I'm always happy to share. That's the kind of guy I am."

"Yeah, yeah. Okay, Mr Nice Guy, I'm following you. But don't complain if I snore. I've had a little too much to drink."

"I promise I won't kick you out. And I'm pretty sure, I'm going to fall asleep pretty quickly anyway."

Beth grabs a few things and pushes him out of the doorway playfully. "Lead the way."

Liam reaches for her hand again in the dark hallway and leads her to his room.

He's slightly nervous as they enter, but he isn't sure why—Beth has already made it clear they're just friends. He excuses himself for the bathroom and returns to find Beth already changed and in his bed. There's just enough light in the room for him to make out the outline of her body.

The weather is still warm, so he strips down to his boxers and gets into bed next to her.

"Goodnight," Beth says quietly.

"Goodnight, Beth."

Liam lies there in the darkness, staring at the ceiling and thinking of how it felt to be so close to Beth while they were dancing. After what feel like an hour, he's still very much awake. He rolls over on his side to face her. She's facing away from him but then wriggles slowly back into his body. Liam instinctively puts his arm around her waist like he did before. But it feels different this time. He wants more.

*

In the morning, Beth is nestled into his side, her head on his shoulder, hand on his chest, and one of her legs is wrapped around him. The silk of her nightie is soft against his skin. The moment is even more intimate than last time, and he tries to ignore how much she's turning him on right now. His body throbs for her, but his heart is telling him to put up safety barriers.

Beth's hair tickles his face a little, and he gently brushes it away. She almost seems to purr as her body inches even closer to him. Heat builds. Before he can stop himself, he brushes the top of her shoulder and glides the back of his knuckles gently down her arm. She sucks a breathe in. Liam then slowly continues down to the curve of her waist to the top of her hip and rests his hand. He stops, waits. Beth responds, moving her hand ever so slowly up his chest. Each one of her fingers taunting him as it explores. His heart beats faster with each light stroke. He looks down at her, and she looks up with an inviting look in her eyes, her lips slightly parted. He leans in. Suddenly, a banging on the door startles them, and they spring apart.

"Hey! Liam, you up yet? Come on, we have a golf game on." Michael bangs on the door again. Liam sits up. The spell broken.

"Hang on." He jumps out of bed and grabs a towel to hide his arousal, pretending he's on his way to the bathroom.

Beth quickly darts off the bed and into bathroom, shutting the door.

"Come in."

Michael bursts in holding Macy in a pouch, a half-eaten pastry in his hand. "Sorry if I woke you, you're normally such an early riser."

"All good, I was awake. Your timing couldn't have been better."

"Great! There's coffee and pastries downstairs and eggs and fruit. I don't know where it all came from, but everything is delicious. I could get used to this." He takes another bite. "Sorry, I should have brought some up."

"You know you're dropping food all over the floor?" Liam says.

"Oops!" He sweeps some pastry flakes towards the wall with his sneaker.

"That'll do it," Liam jokes.

"Also, you must have left your phone downstairs last night." He reaches for his back pocket. "I couldn't help but notice you had a ton of missed calls, from Evelyn. Still interested, is she?" He hands him his phone, gleeful.

Liam stiffens. "Must be about work."

"Sure, heard that story before."

"It was nothing too serious. Between her and I." Liam says, mindful that Beth can hear their whole conversation.

"Whatever you say, Romeo. Anyway, seems she thinks it was. She must have fallen for you hard." Michael playfully shoves him in the shoulder. "You have time to call her back before we play golf, if you want. I'll meet you downstairs."

"Okay, sure." Michael leaves with Macy, and the room is uncomfortably quiet.

Liam knocks on the bathroom door. "Beth?"

"Yes?" She opens the door to face him.

"Just so you know, there's nothing happening with Evelyn and I," Liam says.

"You don't need to explain," she says casually.

"I just wanted you to know."

"Why would I need to know?" She seems so indifferent.

"I just thought...I just wanted you to know..." He sighs at the lost moment. "Don't worry about it then."

Beth steals his towel out his hand. "Since I'm here, I'm using your extra-large en suite too." She smiles cheekily. He tries to catch it back, but she quickly shuts the door.

*

Liam wants to reflect on what's just happened, but the car ride over to the golf course with Michael is a barrage of questions about Evelyn.

"Did you call her?" Michael says.

"Yeah, I tried," he lies.

"Would you consider seeing her again if she moved here?"

"Ah, maybe. I don't think so, though. Seems like a long time ago now. Plus, the more likely scenario is that I'd end up in Beijing again. I've been offered a management role back there."

"Damn. I just got you back! How long for this time?"

"Perhaps, indefinitely."

"Indefinitely!" Michael whistles. "I mean, that's great and all, but for selfish reasons, I hope it doesn't work out. What are going to do?"

"I don't know. I need to consider it. The company is pushing. But I'm not sure where I should be at the moment."

"That's a tough one, but this is what you've been working towards, right?"

"Yes, but I kind of thought the only travel I'd need to do at this point would be our New York office, LA, Toronto. Not this."

"Does it help that Evelyn is there?"

"No, that makes it worse. I don't want it to be part of the decision process."

"Why not? You don't think it will last between you two?"

"I'm just not sure about anything at the moment."

"Me neither, buddy." Michael slaps him on the shoulder sympathetically.

Liam tries to divert the conversation. "Everyone seems to be talking about you. Seems quite positive so far."

"Better than them saying what a low-life father I am."

"I haven't heard anyone saying that. Do most people know?"

"Yeah, I reckon so. No one has mentioned anything to me directly, but I do feel like I'm being assessed?"

"I'm calling it. You are doing an awesome job."

"Thanks, bud. But only because there's a nanny and a house filled with maids. How would I do this by myself?"

"I don't know. That's a tough one."

"How is your boss taking this all?" Liam asks.

"He's not."

"Maybe you just need to take a break."

"He won't give me any more time. If I don't pull a ground-breaking story out of thin air soon, it could be my job."

"Shit, Mikey, that's not good. I can't believe he isn't being more understanding of your situation."

"I never really elaborated what the situation is."

"Why not?"

"I don't know. I guess because I don't know myself what's happening. How do I say to him I need another month or two, or maybe five years? I feel like I don't really want to tell anyone else until I have this sorted."

"I get it."

"I just wish I was more motivated with my work, but I'm just not."

"A lot has happened to you. And the daily grind of work can be pretty soulless sometimes."

"What a softie you've turned into," Michael jokes.

"We're getting older, you know. We can't just keep working and drinking forever. Right? There has to be more to it than that."

"I think I came to that conclusion a while ago, but look how well that turned out."

"You'll meet the right woman soon enough."

"Perhaps. Speaking of not having a life outside of work, have you spoken to Beth much this weekend?" he asks.

"Umm, not really."

"When I asked her about the dinner the other night, she kind of shut down. Plus, she seems to be in a weird mood. She's normally so talkative about things, especially her work. I'm worried that maybe she isn't going to be offered the partnership. Did she say anything to you?"

Liam sighed. "It's nothing."

"Nothing? Doesn't sound like nothing."

"Okay, maybe she mentioned something. But I can't tell you."

"What? Even me?" Michael looks hurt.

"Especially you. She doesn't want you to worry because you have enough going on."

"But she's my sister."

"I'm aware of your connection."

Michael glowers.

"You'll have to ask her. I won't get in the middle of this."

"Come on."

"No way. She'll murder me."

"A risk I'm willing to take."

Liam sighs. "I'm not! Find her and ask her directly. That's all I'll say."

"I'm shocked you would take her side over mine."

"I'm not taking sides."

He can see that Michael is taken aback at his directness and takes a breath. "Sorry, bud. I'd tell you...but it's really not for me to say."

Chapter 19

Beth leans into Chloe and half whispers, "Do you know the rules for croquet?"

Chloe squints at the course of hoops set out on the grass. "I think it's just through the holes and out the other end."

Winnie has just done the rounds topping up ice and PIMM'S into their cucumber and orange-peel-filled glasses and saying to no one in particular, "Don't you love a ladies' day out?"

"All I know about croquet is from Alice in Wonderland, and that didn't end well, from memory," Beth says.

Chloe giggles, then coughs after sipping her drink. "Wow, this is quite the potent concoction Winnie has mixed up."

Beth laughs. "Let's hope she doesn't turn into a ruthless queen for the afternoon."

"We should be safe enough. She speaks her mind that's for sure, but she's sweet underneath."

"It's great that you're all so close."

"I don't see much of my parents these days—they're in Florida and don't like to travel as much now, so Winne and Harold are like my stand-in parents."

"What about you?"

"Me? Ah, oka...Michael and I were born and raised in Boston. Parents divorced, mum is forever on cruise ships, and we don't really stay in touch with dad."

"Hey, you're up," Chloe says. "I'll hold your drink." Beth takes a swing, and the ball goes off to the right, hitting the ground with a soft thud.

"Oops."

"At least you made contact with the ball," Chloe offers.

"True." Beth takes back her drink and rewards herself with a long sip. "So, what about you? There must be a bit of travel in your line of work?"

"Ah, yes, I do a bit. I was in New York the other month, East Asia before that, and we're scheduled for Eastern Europe, but…" She stares off into the distance.

Beth looks at her, unsure. "Everything okay?"

"I'm just…I'd almost forgotten that I'm taking a break at the moment. Anyway, it'll be good to just be in the city for a while. I can concentrate on something else for a change."

"Mayyybbee, you won't be having a break for too long. I hope you don't mind, but I posted a video last night of your performance, and it's almost gone viral. People love it."

"That's great!"

"Hey, I just had an idea. You should come and play at my work gala this week."

"Really?"

"Yes, you must. I have a team looking after it. I'll get them to arrange it with you. It'll be perfect. Some of our lawyer events can be a bit stiff and boring. I could really use your energy."

She laughs. "I can't say no now."

"Perfect!"

Beth looks over Chloe's shoulder to where a couple of women in the croquet game are talking closely and looking over at them. Chloe follows her gaze.

"Everyone in the neighbourhood loves to gossip. I've gotten used to just ignoring them."

"I just worry about Mikey. He's more sensitive than me. I kind of forget that sometimes."

"I think I've noticed that actually."

"I know you probably don't want to hear a speech from me right now, but I can honestly say, I'm lucky to have him as my brother. Everything he's telling you is the truth—he can't tell a lie to save his life. He's a terrible liar. The absolute worst."

Chloe grimaces. "It's not that I don't believe you, or him. But I just can't make sense of this."

"I understand. I'm sorry. I didn't mean to be a buzz kill."

"It's fine. Look…you all seem like genuine people, and I'm trying to be open-minded about this. I admit I wasn't so much before."

Beth touches her arm. "Thanks for listening to Mikey. I know he appreciates it."

"To be honest, he's probably done more of the listening. I don't think I've stopped unravelling to him this weekend."

Winnie yells out to them. "Chloe, your shot!" Chloe waves, then lines up her shot.

Beth laughs. "So, you didn't bring anyone with you to the Cape?"

"Umm no. My boyfriend…or ex-boyfriend. Let's just say we now live in different cities. He's in New York indefinitely." She whacks the ball, and it flies across the lawn knocking over a hoop.

"Wow, you've got a powerful swing!" Beth says "And sorry to hear about your ex."

"No, it's okay, honestly. I've been processing it over the weekend, and I'm still a little pissed off with him, but I actually feel okay about it."

Beth looks at her thoughtfully. "Look, you never know. Maybe you'll work things out. New York is close by."

"I just can't see that happening."

"It's pretty shitty timing for you."

"Completely." Chloe takes a long drink, then continues. "He was so focused on this new job opportunity. With everything going on in my head, I didn't see it coming. I knew he was going for meetings. Ignorance is bliss, right?"

"It's awful being blindsided like that."

Chloe shrugs. "I do understand though. It wasn't intentional; he had an opportunity. I know how hard it is to succeed in our world. He's a musician too. And trying to get a principal seat or first chair in one of the major orchestras is what you work towards. It's everything. You have to make sacrifices. He sacrificed me."

Beth rubs Chloe's shoulder.

"I'm sorry," Chloe says. "I shouldn't be burdening you with all my drama."

"No, please don't apologise."

"But I hardly know you."

"We're croquet partners for life," Beth jokes. "But seriously. It's good to talk about these things. So, keep going."

"Well, okay…the truth is, I don't think he was ever truly committed anyway. I'm so stupid for not reading into that more. But maybe I didn't care enough to demand more from him. It's weird right?"

"No, it's not that weird. I get it. It's so easy to fall into a routine with someone, and then that's all it becomes. The connection was initially there, but it's like someone put your relationship on mute, and the next day, it just fades out without you realising."

"So unromantic really, isn't it?" Chloe shakes her head in disbelief.

"Argh, romance. So hard to find."

"But you must have. How long have you and Liam been together?"

"What? Liam and me? No, no, no, we aren't together."

"Sorry…I just presumed you were."

"We're just…good friends."

"Ohh, I see. He seems like a really nice guy."

"Yeah, he is. One of the good ones. He's been friends with Mikey and I since college. More so Mikey, being roommates and all."

"But you've never dated each other?"

"No, definitely not."

"Why not? It seems like you guys have some chemistry there."

"You think we have chemistry?" She thinks back to the dance floor and to this morning. She was almost sure he was going to kiss her. And she would have let him. But where would that lead them?

"From what I saw—the two of you dancing—yes, you guys looked really happy."

"You saw that while performing?"

"Perks of the job." She shrugs.

"Oh…do you think Mikey saw?"

"Why do you care if he saw you?"

"I don't know. I guess…Liam is like his brother. It just might make things awkward for their friendship."

"You don't think he would like that?"

"I'm assuming not." She sighs. "When Mikey and Naomi, his ex-fiancée, split up, it was pretty shitty for everyone."

"Does sound hectic."

"Naomi also happens to one of my closest friends. She started seeing one of her clients while she and Michael were engaged. When he found out, it got ugly, naturally, and he broke it off."

"That must have been tough on him."

"It broke him, for a long time. I think that's why he's afraid to connect with someone new. They'd have to be someone pretty special for him to open up to them."

"Oh."

"Anyway, it wasn't a good time for anyone, and Naomi and I also didn't speak for a while. But I missed her so much, we reunited. And our ongoing friendship has caused problems between Mikey and I ever since. We're good now, but it's not quite like it was before, you know? He worries I tell Naomi everything."

"And do you?" Chloe asks.

"No, but I'm not sure if he believes that."

"Hmmm, sounds complicated. So, what about Liam? Has he said anything to you?"

"No, nothing."

"You sound disappointed. I think you really like him." Chloe winks at Beth.

"No! I don't know. I mean, even if there was, it's not worth the risk. Plus, I need to focus on making partner right now. I really shouldn't be getting distracted."

"Maybe in the future then."

"Maybe."

"What about pre-Liam? Any noteworthy relationships?"

"Hmmm…let's see. My last long-term relationship was well over four years ago now. Men don't seem to like playing second fiddle to my work."

Chloe sighs. "I hear you. I work most nights and not many people want to have first dates over their lunch break."

"Wow. I thought I had it tough."

"Ego is a problem too."

"Yes! I've had hundreds of dinners, balls, awards nights. Any date I ever bring, ends up getting frustrated I can't babysit them throughout the whole event."

"Ha! Try finding a man who's happy to listen to me play violin all the time and relentlessly discuss music. They think it's cute for a few weeks, then that's it."

"Arseholes! They should feel privileged to be in your presence. And can't they just buy some noise-cancelling headphones?"

Chloe laughs. "I guess our worlds aren't for everyone."

"I'd like to think that when you meet the right person, all these barriers just aren't there."

"You just need to find someone worthy...I wonder who that could be?" Chloe taps a finger on her chin in wonder and starts laughing.

"Stop it!" Beth shoos her away but joins in the laughing.

"Ladies, you've been chit-chatting for too long and are holding up the game," Winnie yells, waving her croquet mallet around.

Chloe calls back an apology and turns to Beth. "I think we're going to need our drinks topped up again."

"Great idea. I also better go and find my ball," Beth says, laughing.

*

At dinner, Beth makes an effort to talk to all the new acquaintances she's made. It's a perfect distraction from Liam, but she can't help noticing his light-blue shirt is open one extra buttonhole, showing off his bare chest and obvious muscle that she had her hands all over this morning. Who knew he would feel so good under her touch. It's a little humid tonight, and his skin glistens. She tries not to stare as he laughs along with the rest of the group that he's with—all listening to a local who's telling a rambling story with a few jokes intertwined.

The flickering candlelight reflects in Liam's welcoming olive-green eyes. The same eager ones that were staring down at her when they nearly kissed. He catches her gazing over at him and offers a sly smile. Beth bites her lip, trying to hold back her own smile, and looks away, re-joining the conversation closest to her. *Idiot, stop daydreaming about him.* She takes a big gulp of white wine to aid her dry mouth.

As soon as the guests start to thin out, she excuses herself, avoiding any awkward conversations with Liam, and heads for her room. The small bed is totally uninviting. She reluctantly changes into her nightclothes and crawls onto the firm mattress. Her mind immediately transports her back to this morning's happenings—Liam gliding his hand over her hip so delicately and with such intention. Anticipation builds in her core, desire flaring so intensely that she wants to jump out of bed and start banging on his door.

She can picture it. He answers, standing there in tight trunks, glasses, and a couple of loose pieces of hair falling around his face. She would reach up around his neck and bring him in, tasting his mouth, their tongues finding each other.

His hands would wrap around her quickly, pulling her close. Her skin would shiver in delight with every one of his touches. Then he would push her against the door. He would lay hungry kisses across her chest. Then he would tilt her head back so his mouth has access to the sensitive part of her neck. She would feel his hardness between her legs, making her body ready for him. Then he would hoarsely whisper in her ear, "I want you Beth."

Ugh, stop. Her mind snaps back to reality. She rolls over and pushes her face into the pillow, letting out a muffled frustrated scream. Why can't she stop thinking about him? And what about Evelyn, the phone calls from this morning? There's obviously something still going on there. Maybe, he's missing Evelyn, and she's the next best thing. Or maybe Liam just felt sorry for her and wanted to offer comfort. Too many unanswered questions and too risky to even delve into. It might ruin everything they have now, and Mikey would be upset. Plus, her partnership was hanging on by a thread.

This has to stop now.

Chapter 20

Michael sits, eyes closed, feeling extremely uncomfortable to be sitting cross-legged on a forest floor, sticks digging into his skin. He tries to breathe in and out slowly, as instructed, but loses concentration again when Liam elbows him in his side.

"Why did you say we'd come 'Forest Bathing'?" He whispers.

"I felt I had to! I said yes to everything on the email. I didn't think I was in a position to be selective."

Liam nods towards their Forest Bathing guide, a friendly weathered-looking man who'd introduced himself as 'Benny.' He's dressed in an old scruffy hat, curly grey hair sticking out from underneath the rim. "Is this guy really into meditation? He looks like a fisherman."

"He's one of Winnie's yoga friends."

Benny talks over the top of them. "Now, a gentle reminder that this process will be much more beneficial if you engage one hundred per cent in the process."

Michael nods politely, then looks back at Liam with wide eyes.

Liam pulls a face of annoyance, then closes his eyes.

Michael peers around the circle formation around him—Chloe, Beth, Winnie, plus a few other people he's seen down the beach. They all follow each word that Benny relays. He veers back to Chloe. She looks so picturesque sitting there, cross-legged too, arms delicately on her knees. Of course, she looks pretty damn cute in her matching Lycra top and bottom. She must have felt him peeking at her, as she's suddenly staring back at him. Michael grins, and she does her best to hide a smile as she closes her eyes again.

Benny coughs loudly and continues. "There are quite a few new faces here today, so I'll tell you a bit about myself. I'm a farmer by trade; we mainly grow apples here. Now, some people might think that you can't learn much from apples, but let me tell you—you can! Now, you can try and plant an apple seedling any old time, but you're not going to get the best results that way." He

133

takes his hat off, ruffles his hair, and replaces his hat with satisfaction. "If I planted a tree in spring, it would produce fruit, but it wouldn't have had time to grow the roots properly. But, if I planted the same tree in autumn, it would allow time for the roots to grow. It builds the foundation. Then comes springtime when the fruit comes, its perfect. And then it comes back again the next year. You see, I get more than one bite of the apple tree."

A few people shift in their seated positions.

"So, what am I saying? Obviously, 'don't rush.' But also, timing is key. All you need to figure out is when your autumn is. It's tricky, isn't it? No one knows what the right time for them is. But if you sit back and do nothing…nothing grows at all…but that's enough of that. Now where were we? Oh, yes! Welcome. Please, I want you all to keep your eyes closed. Take a deep breath in and out."

Benny stops talking and takes a few long breaths himself. The group mimics him. Michael shuts his eyes again and tries to re-engage with the activity.

"Now try and remember your breathing. Feel around you, the grass…the stones…the twigs…the soil, the earth. If you would like to, you can pick it up in your hands, smell it. What does it smell like? Can you smell minerals, oils, what's the aroma? Now listen. Listen to the trees. Ah! And before you laugh, have you ever tried before? Perhaps, like my apple tree, there's something trying to talk to you, and you're just not listening. Hmm? You're welcome to stay here with me, or soon you can leave and find a spot nearby that feels right for you. You might find a patch of grass and lie down, or maybe you want to keep walking, and that's okay too. I want you all to slow down and listen. Today, and what it should always be, is about connection. Connection with the life around you and connection with each other."

Benny quietens and Michael hears a few people shifting around him. He opens his eyes and watches them get up and look for another place to sit. Some walk further into the forest. Liam does the same, and Michael gets up to wander after him. When they're far enough away from Benny, they find a spot to sit and whisper.

"That was interesting," Michael says, eyebrows raised.

Liam bats away a gnat. "Sorry, I'm just not in the right frame of mind."

"You neither, huh? I want to know though, what happens when you're forced to plant an apple tree at the wrong time?"

Liam smirks. "So about growing those apples—you have done the paternity test, right?"

"Umm, no. I keep losing my nerve."

"Didn't think to do it sooner? Before you dragged us up here to sit in a forest with a bunch of insects?"

"Yeah, yeah, I know. Sorry," Michael says.

"I get that your nervous, but you need to get this done so you can know for sure. Then you can make your plans."

"It just seems final. Like I have to start doing more shit."

"And dealing with plenty of shit…sorry, I had to." Liam shrugs with a smirk.

"But…what happens if I'm not her father?"

"Then you aren't. Do I sense nervousness—that you *want* to be looking after Macy? Or am I wrong—you want to be off the hook and never see these people again?"

"Umm, good questions…I do like being with her."

"You feel a connection?"

"Yes, I guess I do, but that could be in my head. I also have a connection with my Barista, but that doesn't mean I want him to be part of my family."

Liam chuckles. "Just to clarify, are we talking about Macy or Chloe?"

Michael looks at him, shocked. "Macy!"

"Got it."

"Stay on topic."

Liam lightly pushes his shoulder. "Just wanted to check. Look, in all seriousness, stay positive. You'll know soon enough. Just do the test, for crying out loud."

"I will as soon as I get back."

"You've got this. You're going to be a great dad," he offers.

Footsteps alert them to approaching company. Benny. They quickly close their eyes and remain quiet for the next half hour. Michael thinks back on the riddle of the apple tree, about the timing. He reflects on the reason he's sitting here right now, in the middle of this forest. Was Macy meant to be a part of his life or not?

*

Later, lying in bed and frustrated by his ongoing internal monologue, Michael listens to the soothing beach noises in the still night, but nothing seems to aid his sleep. Admittedly, the weekend is working out better than anticipated, and having a baby right now doesn't seem that bad—when there were maids, cleaners, chefs—but back in the city, it would be different. As if on cue, Macy stirs and starts to cry. He knows Roberta will get up, but he wants to attend to Macy himself—it'll be a relief to have something to do.

He's walking down the hall, past one of the many bathrooms, when a door suddenly swings open and Chloe steps out. She stifles a scream as Michael nearly runs into her. He reaches to steady her, catching her arm, and her hand ends up on his bare chest.

"I'm so sorry," he says. "Are you okay?"

"Yes, I'm fine, thanks." Chloe drops her hand away, and her eyes drift down to his trunks.

"I'd have put on more clothes, but I wasn't expecting to run in to anyone."

She looks embarrassed to be caught out looking at his underwear.

"That's fine. You don't need to wear clothes…ah, that's not what I meant. You can wear whatever you like."

Michael smirks at her fumble of words.

The moonlight streaming in from the bathroom highlights her curves. Michael is about to make a witty remark but forgets what he was going to say when he notices her revealing singlet. He swallows hard. They're standing so close to each other—*Move away from her before you do anything stupid*—but his feet won't seem to obey. Macy's cries become louder. "Ah, I better check on her."

"Okay, yes, ah…goodnight then." Chloe quickly turns and walks off in the other direction.

Michael watches her disappear in the shadows down the hall. He breathes a big sigh of bewilderment. Every time they touch, it's like electricity. *Pull yourself together.*

*

Macy's crib is by an open window with a soft breeze. There's enough moonlight to show the tears on her face. Michael reaches in and pulls her onto his chest, making hushed, soothing noises that she seems to like. Macy seems to settle after a while, and he returns her to the crib without any fuss. He feels like high-fiving someone.

As he walks back towards his room, a familiar figure appears down the hall.

136

"Beth?"

"Hi, just needing a change of scenery. I couldn't sleep."

"Yes, it seems to be a running theme around here at the moment," he whispers. "Are you okay? We haven't spoken much this weekend."

"Yeah, I'm fine."

"Really? Because I hear that maybe things aren't great."

Beth looks at him and sighs. "I don't really want to talk about it right now."

"Fine, but don't have a go at me later for not caring, or asking…"

"Look, I don't have to tell you everything, okay?" She hisses.

Michael holds his hands up. "You used to tell me everything."

"That was a long time ago…"

"That's not true. It all changed after Naomi, and you know it."

"I'm not going to stand here in the hallway bickering with you all night like our parents did. I'm going to bed." She storms off.

Frustrated, Michael heads downstairs to calm down with a glass of water. Outside on the deck, next to the kitchen, he sees a figure and a puff of smoke. "Winnie?"

She seems startled to see him there and moves to put the cigarette out.

"Don't on my account."

"Do you smoke?" she asks him.

"No. I have on occasion, but it's not my thing."

Winnie nods. "Harold doesn't know. I gave up when I was pregnant with Ariane. But I keep a packet here at the house. It's a bit like my holiday treat."

"I won't say anything."

She offers him a cigarette from her packet. He shrugs, takes one and lights it with a lighter she passes to him. Neither of them says anything for a moment.

"You look annoyed," Winnie says.

Michael takes in a long drag and coughs a little. "Sisters."

"I see. Sometimes meditation can stir the pot a little. Makes you face your internal conversations."

"Didn't work in Beth's case."

"She might need more time than you. Did you enjoy the wilderness today?" she asks.

"I did actually. It was more insightful than I was expecting."

"Yes, he usually finds something."

"I take it, Harold isn't a fan?"

"No, certainly not, and I must admit I never was. But you know, as I get older, I think why not try these things?"

"Speaking of Harold, we had a conversation about Macy."

"I see." Winnie inhales from her cigarette.

"I know I have a bit to think about, and I have been…"

"Regardless of what you decide, you should know that Macy will remain a Hennigan."

"Excuse me?"

"She's Ariane's daughter foremost. We want her to keep the family name."

"I…I must admit I hadn't really thought about that part. Not yet anyway. Wow…umm."

"We already lost one daughter. I won't lose my granddaughter too."

"You wouldn't be losing her."

"What happens if you decide you want to move away?"

"That's crazy. I don't have any plans to do that."

Winnie breathes in more of her cigarette and continues. "You know, you could walk away before you get too emotionally attached. We could offer you some monetary compensation for your troubles so far. You could leave as if nothing had happened."

"You're offering me money to leave?" Michael asks.

"It's an idea that maybe you should consider."

"Don't you think I should be looking after my daughter?"

"Have you really thought about how much this will affect your life?" She replies.

"It already is affecting my life. But I don't think you're actually concerned about me, are you? I mean, of course not. You just don't think I'm good enough to be her father, do you? You were hoping I'd just leave on my own accord. But now that you see I may not, you need to find a way to get rid of me?"

"I'm not implying you aren't fit to be a parent. I'm just giving you an option, my dear. We'd rather you say something now. To not be a father who won't be there for her in a year, or five years' time, after she gets to know you. It wouldn't be fair on her, and we'd be left holding the pieces."

He's shocked. "I wouldn't do that."

"Really? Hmmm, apple doesn't fall far from the tree."

"What's that meant to mean? My parents are still a big part of my life. I speak to my mum all the time."

"And your father?"

"You can't suggest I'm anything like him, and you don't know anything about him or my mother, or about our situation. I came here to try and prove to everyone that my version of the story was the correct one. I've been desperate to show you I have morals, but now I feel like it's been a waste of time. You were never going to accept me."

"It's not about us accepting you. We're trying to keep Macy's best interests at heart. You're young. What happens when you meet someone? A woman who wants a baby of her own?"

"So, that happens all the time. There are happy blended families all over the world!"

"Perhaps. Please just have a think about what I'm saying. There's no shame in taking the easy path."

Michael stamps out the cigarette. "Maybe that's how you do things in this family, but easy isn't my style."

Chapter 21

Liam scrolls through the early morning news on his phone while he walks back to the house. He tries not to think about work or Beth too much. She'd disappeared quickly after dinner last night, which had hurt him more than he wanted to admit. He'd been stupidly hoping that she might come knock on his door. He'd lain in bed awake, waiting, just in case. She never came.

Since the encounter with Benny, he's been thinking about what it means for him and Beth. Has timing always been their problem? In college, she seemed so much more mature than him and completely uninterested. Admittedly, he'd always felt an underlying connection but never acted on it. That self-doubt had stayed with him as they got older.

Maybe, now isn't the right time either, he thinks—Beth has her partnership in the air, and he has his Beijing offer. Maybe he could try again with Evelyn. Perhaps, leaving town was the right course of action.

He heads to the shower to cool off on all fronts, but his phone buzzes as he's taking his shirt off. Evelyn on a video call. He can't avoid her forever, even though he didn't have any answers yet. Her pretty face appears before him.

"Hey, what's up?"

"*What's up?*" She looks annoyed. "Am I one of your buddies now?"

"Sorry, no…I just wasn't thinking. I've been for a run, and I'm super worn out."

"You haven't been answering my calls."

"I know, sorry. I'm away at the moment, helping Mikey deal with a few important things."

"I still don't know why you can't take any time out to talk to me."

"Evelyn, I've been busy."

"I guess I can talk you into taking this Beijing job when I see you in the flesh next week."

"Right. Of course, the gala. I hope I've made a decision by then. Look, I'm sorry too about the dinner the other week. I know you wanted answers about us. I was caught off guard. Let's talk later, okay?"

"We can talk later, but how about we play now?"

"Evelyn." Liam grimaces and rubs his face.

"Don't you miss me?"

"I...I do, but..."

"Don't you want me?"

"Now isn't a good time."

"Are you alone? Where are you?"

"I was just about to take a shower."

"So, you're alone! Take me with you to get wet," she coos.

Evelyn whips off her top revealing a white lacy bra.

"E-v-v-v-e-lyn," Liam groans.

She wriggles her skirt off her hips and turns around, showing her thong to the camera.

Liam closes his eyes and shakes his head. "I can't." He opens his eyes again.

She looks upset. "Why not?" She takes off her bra and throws it at the camera phone.

"Argh, okay." Perhaps, it'll take his mind off Beth.

Her turns on the shower, strips off the remainder of his clothing and steps into the running water. He props up the phone in the shower niche. Evelyn takes off her thong slowly, then starts touching herself and moaning, but he can barely hear her over the water pouring over him.

He closes his eyes, but all he sees is Beth—in bed, looking sultry, just like the other morning, but this time, they aren't interrupted. He reaches for her face and kisses her slowly on her soft full lips. She kisses him back with equal amounts of surprise and pleasure. He pulls away slightly, and she leans in for more. He playfully ignores her request and moves to the side of her neck. One of her hands grips his shoulder, the other pulling him close. The more he touches her, the more she gasps with delight.

The straps fall off her shoulders, and he kisses her across the collar bone. He pulls her nightie further down, revealing parts of her body he hasn't been privileged to see before. There hands all over each other. His mouth nibbles across her breasts, down her stomach to her sweet spot. Her hands tug at his hair with satisfaction. He wants to give her everything she wants. She lets out a moan and calls out his name. His body explodes with pleasure as the phone slips and smacks onto the shower floor.

*

Liam sits at the kitchen breakfast counter, eating toast and feeling remorseful. He knows now, without a doubt, it's not Evelyn he wants. As he's pondering what to do about this, Michael walks in with Macy in the baby carrier, alerting him to the real reason he's here.

"It's weird to keep seeing you walk into a room with a baby," Liam says.

"I must admit, when I see myself in a mirror carrying her, I do a double-take. She's not my usual accessory." Michael looks around. "Beth not awake?"

"Nooo, not yet." He tries to push away the awkwardness that bubbles up at the mention of her name.

"I guess she's taking the opportunity to sleep in for once. Or who knows, she might have met someone on the trip."

Liam coughs, almost choking.

"You okay?"

"Yep, I'm good. Dry toast." He takes a sip of juice.

"I know I've been focused on other things this trip, and you've been stuck with Beth quite a lot. Sorry about that. I know she can be a pain sometimes."

"Things you do, hey?" Liam swallows down his guilt with another gulp of juice.

"I need to talk to you guys, but I'll wait till she's here."

"Sounds serious."

"Ah, a long and slightly complicated story. I'll tell you both after breakfast."

"Sure, okay."

"Have you made any work decisions yet? Evelyn?" Michael asks.

"Hmmm, work no...I'm pretty sure I know how I feel about Evelyn."

"That was fast."

"She's an amazing woman...buuut, I don't think she's the one for me."

"Really? Wow. You sorted that one out quick. What happened? Did you meet someone new already?"

Liam runs a hand through his hair. "Ah...no."

Michael reaches over and punches him on the shoulder. "You, sly dog, you. Already moving in on the local turf, hey? Who's the lucky lady?"

142

"There isn't anyone."

"Talking about me?"

They both turn at the sound of Beth's voice.

"Wouldn't dare," Michael says.

"Morning," Liam chimes.

"Did everyone sleep well?" She looks over at Liam.

"Not particularly, so I decided on a quick run this morning might help clear the mind and liver." He can't hold her gaze without feeling as if she'll catch him out on where his mind went earlier. "What about you, bed comfortable?"

"Yes. Wasn't that bad after all." She shrugs looking indifferent.

"Good to know," Liam says.

Winnie enters the room, and they all sing out a morning greeting. Michael makes silent motions for them to leave.

"Shall we have a game of tennis before we hit the road?" Beth springs into action grabbing an apple and heading for the door.

"Shit," Liam adds, "not you two on the tennis court. I better come and supervise, so it doesn't end in a fight."

"We aren't that bad," Michael says.

"Sure, sure."

"Meet you at the courts in fifteen," Michael says.

Liam follows Beth down the hall, towards their rooms. Beth is quiet and Liam is in agony over the awkwardness between them again.

"Liam, maybe we should talk before we go back downstairs?" She says as soon as they reach her door.

"Talk? Sure."

She opens the door.

"Do you want to sit?"

Liam sits nervously on the bed as she paces the room.

"This bed is really shit. This was your preferred option?"

"About that. This…" She motions her hand to herself and back to him.

"The fact that we…or maybe it was I who nearly kissed you?" He tries to read her face, but she keeps looking away.

"I'm okay about it."

"Really? You don't seem okay."

She turns to him. "I'm sorry. It's probably me who needs to apologise. Maybe, I've been relying on you too much. Since that incident. I probably shouldn't have involved you."

"You shouldn't apologise for that."

"True…I guess that's what friends do, right?"

Liam feels as if someone has punched him in the stomach. This possibility had always been coming, but it doesn't make the blow any easier.

He shakes his head in disbelief. "Friends, right. Of course. That's what we are." *What was I thinking? She's never been interested in me.* He takes a deep breath and tries to sound upbeat. "This is good. You've solved a question I needed answering."

"What question?"

"It's nothing. Nothing that would worry you."

Chapter 22

Michael takes a moment to rehydrate on the side of the well-kept grass tennis court.

"I can't believe Winnie said that to you!" Beth says as she runs to join him for a drink of water. "What did you say?"

"I was caught a bit off guard. Harold was more diplomatic about it, whereas with Winnie, she offered me the money to walk away. I was so pissed off; I could barely speak."

"She thinks they can buy you off?" Liam says.

Michael shrugs. "I know. What a family."

"What are you going to do now?" Beth asks.

"Obviously, not take the money…you know that right?"

"Of course," Liam and Beth mutter.

He looks at them both and shakes his head. "Honestly, you thought I'd take the money?"

"No, of course not!" Beth says, then pauses. "But I'm curious to know how much Winnie would have paid."

"Lawyers." Michael shakes his head.

"Winnie isn't wrong though; it's a massive commitment," Liam adds. "You're so busy trying to prove yourself to everyone else, but what do *you* really want for yourself?"

"He can't just walk away," Beth says.

Liam glances at her sideways. "Really? I thought you would be open to that."

"What is that meant to be mean?" She snaps.

"Seems to be your thing."

"My thing?"

"I just think you should try something before saying no. Who knows? It might actually make you happy," Liam says.

"I try new things all the time!"

"Really?"

"And what would you know about what makes me happy? You haven't been here for two years!"

"Maybe, I'll just go away again for another two years!"

Michael waves his hands in a time out. "Woah! What's wrong with you two?"

"Nothing," Beth mutters.

"Sorry," Liam says quietly.

"Anyway," Michael says. "What I was saying is that I know what my answer is now, despite any curveballs Winne wants to throw at me. I want to do this. Be a dad. As much as I'm absolutely shit scared about this, I can't turn my back on her. That would be like being the dad I never wanted to be." He looks at Beth.

Beth frowns. "You aren't anything like him."

"But what if Harold and Winnie are right? What if I do become him, and one day I just decide to leave?"

"That's not you. It never will be. You care about people too much."

"I agree. I wouldn't be your best friend otherwise," Liam offers.

"Thanks…well…okay then. So, are you all with me on this?"

"I'm in," Beth says.

Liam slaps his shoulder. "Me too."

Beth smiles at Michael. "She's very cute. And worth fighting for if we have to. We're all quite attached to her now."

"Great, then it's settled," Michael says. "Come on, I have a game to win!"

*

As Beth is serving for the last set, Chloe appears on the side-line next to Liam. She looks relaxed in espadrilles, jeans and a white button-up shirt that scoops low, showing off her shoulders. Michael averts his attention back to Beth's serve, but he's a few seconds too late and swings and misses. It's an ace, and Beth does a small celebratory dance. Michael tries to focus on the next serve, but Chloe is giggling at something Liam says, and he ends up losing the game, which makes Beth jump up and down with glee.

The day has started to heat up, and Michael needs to change out of his sweaty shirt. He rips it off and excuses himself, making a quick dash down to the beach for a dip. On his return, he's saddened to see Chloe has already left. He consoles himself with the thought of her riding back to the city with him. He spots Liam relaxing under a tree and heads over.

"How's the water?" Liam asks.

"Brilliant."

"Where are the ladies?"

"Packing."

Michael grabs a bottle of water and pulls up a chair next to Liam.

"What was going on between you and Beth before?"

"How do you mean?"

"There are some weird vibes going on between you guys at the moment. You seem all chatty, but the next minute, you both seem shitty with each other. I'm assuming it's all to do with what neither of you will talk to me about."

"Ah…yep you could say that."

"Great!"

"Change the subject."

"Okay fine…sooo, what were you and Chloe talking about?"

Liam smirks. "It wasn't about you."

"I know that. I was just wandering."

"Nothing really, but if it makes you feel any better, I think Chloe had to run off and cool down."

"What do you mean?"

"I think you made her a bit hot and bothered. She seemed interested in what was under your shirt. That's all I'm saying."

Michael raises his eyebrows. "Really?"

"So, still nothing going on there?"

"No way. You know I can't go there."

"Why not?"

"You know why not."

"So, you've thought about it over the weekend then?"

"I'm just stating the obvious. It's a massive complication. And weird, right?"

"No, I don't think so. I mean people meet at funerals all the time, don't they? It's sort of like that."

"Yeah, but you know there's more than that. I slept with her best friend."

"But that happens too. And that's old news."

147

"But normally, those are all separate things. This is all of these issues combined into one mess. Plus, I'm also the father of her best friend's baby. Imagine explaining to people how we met."

"You can always lie."

"But everyone knows who I am already. Anyway, can't happen, and I'm sure, she would never let it happen."

"Whatever you say. I'll be watching this space."

Chapter 23

Chloe is glad to be hitting the road again, comfortable enough now with Michael that she doesn't feel the need to fill all the quiet moments. She's enjoying watching the silver maple trees flash past her window, the afternoon light flickering through their green leaves. She sighs, content. The feeling surprises her, it's been a while. And then a sign for Boston.

"Oh, no. A sign for reality."

"What?" Michael asks, glancing at her before turning his attention back to the road.

"I was just enjoying the last few moments of the weekend. But then seeing a sign for the city…it's just that, when I get back, I need to start over, in literally every aspect of my life. I don't know if I'm ready for that."

"Does sound like a lot on your plate. But who knows? Maybe this is a really good opportunity. Now you get to spend time figuring out what it is you want."

"But what if I don't know what that is?"

"Then I hate to say it, but you'll be stuck with me in this car forever." Michael takes a hand off the wheel, grabs some leftover petrol station popcorn they'd been sharing earlier and throws it at her. She squeals with laughter and throws bits back at him.

"Sorry, I couldn't help it." He grins.

"You know, at the moment, being stuck in this car doesn't sound too bad."

"Maybe the weekend doesn't have to end after all."

"How's that?" she asks.

"I'm in noooo hurry to go back to the city either. As you know, I have a lot of stuff to sort out too, and I'm not ready for that…hey, I know the perfect place where we can go for a few hours to forget all about our adult responsibilities. Interested?"

"Sounds good to me."

Michael takes the next turn off and heads towards a sign: 'King Richard's Faire.'

*

"What is this place?" Chloe asks as they park near a grand set of black metal gates. Gold-painted cherubs sit along its top, and colourful flags fly either side.

"I just knew you wouldn't have been her before," Michael jokes.

A man dressed in armour clanks past them, and two men begin jousting nearby.

"You're correct," Chloe says. "I'm not sure if I even want to get out of the car!"

"Let's go." Michael hurries around to her side to open the car door. He holds out his hand and bows. "M'lady."

She momentarily hesitates before taking his hand and allowing him to lead her through the entrance and into a crowd filled with horses, knights, acrobats, and magicians. Lively music fills the air, and Chloe holds tight to Michael as they head into a tent labelled 'The Dragon's Tavern.'

"I'm going to get us something to eat. Do you want to mind a spot at this table, and I'll be back?" He winks as he lets go of her hand. She misses the contact immediately but nods, still awed by her surroundings. A short while later, Michael returns triumphantly with two turkey legs, loaded waffle fries and beers.

"I take it, you've never had a giant spit-roasted turkey leg before either?" Michael asks.

"No, absolutely not."

He laughs. "I can tell by the look on you face."

"What look?"

"You're so outside of your comfort zone."

"I am not!"

"You are," he teases. "I guess most guys would also never bring you to something like this." His face grows serious. "Can I ask you something?"

"Sure."

"What about this guy you're seeing? Francis. What's the real reason he isn't here?"

"Well...we actually broke up. He took a job in New York."

"I see. Sorry."

Chloe sighs. "It's okay. I think, him moving to New York just sped up the inevitable. I think our relationship was dormant, and I was too blind to not see that."

"Are you okay?"

Chloe picks up a fry and dips it in the gravy. "Yes, I am, actually. I can see now that we didn't have that spark. Know what I mean?"

"Connection is important."

He looks at her, and Chloe holds his gaze momentarily. "It is."

"I hope you'll be happy."

"I think I already am."

"You looked like you were the other night."

"When?"

"When you played on the beach."

"Really?" She pauses to reflect. "It was such a great experience."

"You even looked different—your hair all out. You looked...relaxed."

She reaches up and pulls her hair out of its bun and shakes it, making her curls extra fluffy.

Michael nods an approval. "Mind you, I think it kinda looks good any way you have it," he says.

Chloe blushes.

"Maybe you could play gigs like that for a change of pace."

"Funny you say that. Beth mentioned she'd like me to play at the gala."

"You should do it!"

"I think I will...and will you be there?"

"I'll be a discreet participant. I turn up more to be supportive. Also, my ex's agency is running the event. So, I won't feel comfortable being there, if I'm honest."

"I see...Is there still something there between you two?"

"No, it's not like that. I just don't enjoy her company that much anymore. It never would have worked out, regardless of what Naomi did. She was never the right person for me."

"That's great you've come to that realisation."

"Yeah, took a while, I'll admit. But it's very far from my mind now."

Chloe holds up her glass. "Here's to starting again."

Michael lifts his beer. "To both of our next chapters."

A moment later, Chloe squeals as a fire breather lets out a large flame, close to where they're seated. Michael puts a protective arm around her as she ducks, almost knocking over their drinks. She laughs into his chest, catching his mesmerising earthy cologne, then spots one of his tattoos peeking out onto his collar bone. It's just as enticing as it was the other night when she'd bumped into him in the corridor. That moment, when she touched his chest, had made her body tingle with anticipation. Then, this morning at the tennis court, she'd tried not to gawk as he took his shirt off in front of her.

The fire breather moves on, and Chloe feels a little disappointed when Michael drops his arm away. He notices her looking at him, so she asks, "I was just wondering how many tattoos do you have?" She peels away his T-shirt collar so she can see more of his chest—the drinks have given her boldness.

"What? So, you've been checking me out then?" He jokes, playfully swatting her fingers away.

"No! You just seem to keep parading your body in front of me." She drops her hands back into her lap, trying to look innocent.

"So, do you like what you see then?"

"Hmmm, I'm still thinking on that."

Michael laughs. "I'll have to work harder to get your attention it seems. But to answer your question, I have nine tattoos. I may get more, but that's it for now. You?"

"You'll have to wait and see," she blurts.

Michael's eyes widen. "Ohh, near a pleasure zone, is it?"

Heat rises in Chloe's face. "I mean...I didn't mean that...you and I."

Michael laughs and holds up his hands in defence. "That's okay. I know you'd never be interested in someone like me."

"Why would you say that?"

"Come on...I'm not really your type."

"So, what is my type then? I'm curious to know what you think."

"I guess...someone similar to you. Probably, someone who comes from a good family, and is one of those highly educated music types," he says.

"You think I'm a snob, don't you?"

"I didn't say that."

"Be honest," she pleads.

"Okay, fine. I *did* presume you were a bit of a snob. But every time we've been together, I…I've…liked hanging out with you. You've kinda grown on me."

"You make me sound like a noxious weed!"

He smirks. "Maybe I could've phrased that better…I was wrong about you…you keep surprising me."

"So, that's a good thing?"

"Yes, it's a good thing,"

She playfully nudges him with her elbow. "So…what's your opinion of me now?"

"Hmmm, you challenge me, which I like. And I feel as if you have this stage personality with this tough exterior, but really, that's not you. Underneath, you're so different. You're gentle and sweet. I kind of want to find out more."

Chloe's heart skips a beat. It seems to do that around him.

"What about me?" he asks.

"Well, since it's confession time. I was wrong about you too. And I'm sorry for being a bit of a bitch to you."

"A *bit* of a bitch?" He teases.

"Fair enough." She smiles. "Anyway, what I was trying to say is that you seem totally opposite to what I thought. I think you're very loyal, noble, you care a lot for the people in your life, and you're…kind of funny. I feel like you don't hide from anything, and you unashamedly wear your heart on your sleeve."

"So, am I worthy of your presence then?" He jokes.

"Yes, but my one criticism is that perhaps next time, you take a woman on a date, you don't bring them here." She laughs.

"Sooo, is this a date?" he asks flirtatiously.

Chloe blushes. Why did she say they were on a date? So awkward.

Luckily, Michael swiftly moves on and keeps the mood light. "Come on, 'Juliet,' let's get a goblet of wine."

They spend the rest of the late afternoon being tourists among the festival crowd—dancing, singing, and for the whole time, she's happy. It feels good to let go and forget about everything for a while. She likes being in Michael's presence, even though a small voice keeps trying to tell her it isn't right. Michael declines another drink, but Chloe doesn't want the night to end and convinces him to keep drinking with her.

As the night quickly escapes from them, they find themselves joining a group of festival staff who are staying overnight in the camp grounds, so they're having a few vodkas after work. A friendly juggler offers them a spare tent, and they gladly accept. They crawl inside, giggling like school children on a camp. Under a shared blanket, they're shoulder to shoulder on the bedroll. The top of the tent has a window for star gazing. Michael reaches up to unzip it so they can look out.

Chloe gasps. "Wow, look at all the stars. It's so amazing."

"Isn't it?"

"Thank you for bringing me here. I've had a really good time."

Michael sighs. "Yeah, me too. I was a bit apprehensive about this weekend, but it turned out better than I anticipated."

"Yeah? What were the highlights?"

"Hmm, let's see. The Fourth of July beach party was pretty good, watching you play Bob Dylan, all our conversations over the weekend, being here right now...and..." He props himself up on an elbow.

Chloe rolls over to face him. "And?"

"I think I've found my common denominator."

"What's that?"

"It's you." Michael reaches out and lifts her chin, pulling her towards him, and gently kisses her on the lips. Chloe holds her breath in surprise, but is swept away in the moment. She kisses him back. She can't stop. He matches her growing intensity. Her mind is hazy from the drinks, and all her reasons for stopping retreat to the back of her mind. Her hands find the sides of his face, travel down to his shoulders and body—the muscles under his T-shirt flex with her touch. Her desire to have her hands all over his body is undeniable.

Michael gently pushes her onto her back and manoeuvres himself on top of her. A groan of delight escapes her at the sensation of feeling him pressed against her. He breathes in her air. They kiss again, tongues searching in need. The pace increasing. Chloe holds on tightly around his neck, then her fingers rummage through his hair. Adrenaline pumps through her body. Michael's hand movements become urgent, trying to find a way into her top. She pushes him off and onto his back. He seems a little surprised by her boldness, then groans as she straddles him. She bites her bottom lip and slowly unbuttons her top. His hands glide over her upper thighs, and up her waist. She reveals her black and gold lacy bra, and he seems to stare up at her in awe. Chloe grows impatient, wanting to touch his bare chest again, and edges up his T-shirt. He helps to lift it up and over his head. His arms hit the side of the tent, making it shudder, and they both giggle, having momentarily forgotten where they are. He reaches up and pulls her down on top of him, his mouth searching for hers, his bulge hardening. She wants him, all of him. This was the point of no return.

"Chloe?" he says huskily into her ear.

"Yes?" She breathes heavily.

She pauses and looks down at him. He takes one of her hands and places it with his on his chest. She can feel his heart beating rapidly.

"Before we go any further. I need to ask…is this what you want? I don't want you to wake up and regret this."

"What makes you think I'll regret this?"

"We've been drinking a lot today and…I like you, and I feel like we have something. Something more than just one night."

Chloe rolls off him with a heavy sigh and sits up. "I know, you're right. I haven't been thinking about Macy."

"Chloe, you know I'm only saying this for you. I want you. Unbelievably, so much right now…and not just physically. I just…argh…sometimes I don't know why I open my mouth." He sits up next to her and gently strokes her back. "I don't want this to be the first and last time."

She offers a weak smile. "I want to do the right thing too. Maybe we should think about this some more." Suddenly, she feels cold and hunts for the blanket, glad of a distraction to hide how disappointed she is.

"Chloe, are you okay?"

"Yes of course…fine," she lies.

"At least I got to see your tattoo after all—a dragonfly." Michael touches her lower back.

Relieved at the light-hearted change of subject, she says, "You found it. I put it there thinking my parents wouldn't see it. They didn't for a few years."

"I like it—it suits you."

"Thank you."

With the blanket in hand, Chloe lies on her back. Michael reclines next to her, offering his arm under her head and shoulders. She accepts, feeling angelic about agreeing to show restraint—she deserves some closeness with Michael. She curls into his body, their faces close.

"I suspect your tattoo must have a good story?" he says.

"I like to think it does. We used to go to Barbados a lot when I was younger, before my grandmother passed. I used to play violin in her garden. There were always dragonflies. I thought they were magical. And my mum said that watching them fly was like watching me play music—they had grace, calmness, yet assertiveness. My grandmother said there were always more in the garden when I was there, and that they came to watch me play."

"I like that. And I think that's a perfect analogy. When I watch you play, that's what I see as well."

"Really?"

"Totally. You have a gift. You make people feel emotion. That's powerful stuff."

Chloe looks up at him. "Thanks. What about your tattoos? What's their story?"

"Mine? Nah, I just like them. Never any stories. Maybe that's why I don't have objects, just shapes, lines and patterns."

Chloe props herself up and traces the outlines of his tattoos. His body tenses at her touch, but then she feels him surrender.

"Some people find them too much," he says.

"I like them."

"Really?"

"Yeah. They remind me of sheet music in a way. And they do have a story. You just have to know how to read them."

"Hadn't thought of it like that before. Thanks."

She lies back on his chest again.

"Hey," he says, "you know what a dragonfly can symbolise?"

"What?"

"Change. Self-realisation, like you're being re-born."

"I never knew that."

"Maybe your dragonfly is ready to take another flight?"

"Maybe."

He kisses her head, and after a while, she drifts off with Michael mumbling something sweet in her ear.

*

156

Chloe awakens with a throbbing headache, unsure if she should be relieved or embarrassed at being half-dressed in her bra and jeans. Flashbacks snap her out of her morning haze. She rolls over, but Michael isn't there. *Ugh, thank goodness, my breath is disgusting. What the heck was I thinking last night? This cannot happen...no matter how good it felt.* She runs her fingers through her unruly curls, then reaches for her top as footsteps approach the tent.

Michael pokes his head through the entry flap, greeting her with a wide grin. "Morning. Coffee?" He's holding two cups.

"Ah, good morning." Chloe quickly pulls her top down, feeling sheepish. "You seem rather chirpy considering how much we drank last night."

"Yep, that's true. Guess I'm just more upbeat than usual this morning."

His look says he's hoping for a clue from her, but she doesn't know how to respond yet. He hands her a cup.

"Had to barter for this—you may need to play at a birthday party next week in Salem, but I knew you would want this really bad."

"I do. I'll do anything." She nods keenly, and he chuckles.

"Sooo...are we just going to pretend nothing happened last night?" he asks.

"Yep."

"Thought that might be the road we're on. Do you need a moment?"

She nods.

"Okay then...I'll meet you at the car when you're ready."

*

On the way back to town, Chloe still doesn't know what to say. Her nerves are as distressing as if she were about to audition for her chair at the symphony. She's grateful that they're back at her apartment sooner than she anticipated.

"Are you sure I can't carry this up for you?" Michael offers as he pulls her last bag from the trunk.

"No, honestly, I'll be fine."

"Okay." He holds up his hands in a mocking defensive manner. "I can tell you're dying to leave my side as soon as possible."

"No, I'm not. I'm just really tired."

"Are you sure? Because you still haven't looked at me this morning."

"That's not true!" She takes off her sunglasses, tucks them into her shirt and meets his gaze. Her body wants to lunge for him as he stares back at her with those dreamy eyes of his. His regrowth, she once thought was him being lazy and messy, is now really sexy. *Damn him!*

"We can talk about it another time if you want," he offers.

"Okay. I better go. Thanks for everything…and as weird as that festival was…I actually had a good time."

"Good…wait, *all* of it?"

"You said you weren't going to ask."

He winks. "I didn't say I wouldn't try."

Chloe looks around nervously, although no one walking the street is in earshot. "I need to say thank you. For stopping…last night. You were right; I wouldn't have felt right about it today."

He nods. Then after a few moments says, "Can I ask you one thing though?"

"What?"

"Is it me…or because I'm Macy's dad?"

Chloe breathes in, stares at the pavement. "I…I don't know."

"Okay."

She lifts her head. Michael has lowered his gaze and looks as if she's wounded him. She leans in and kisses him on the cheek. His mouth so near to hers. Eyes closed savouring the moment. The faint smell of forest and dirt fills her nose.

Don't think about last night. Just walk away.

"Goodbye, Michael," she whispers, stepping back to escape the clutches of desire pulling at her. She keeps her head down, fumbling with her bags until she reaches the bottom of her apartment steps, then sighs with relief, but also despair. She senses a figure in front of her and looks up the flight of stairs to the main door. "Francis? What are you doing here?"

"I've been waiting for you." Francis rushes down the stairs, grabs the bags out of her hands and places them on the ground next to her. He gets down on one knee and grasps her hands. "Chloe, I'm sorry I didn't do this sooner."

Stunned, Chloe watches as Francis reaches into his jacket pocket and brings out a box. He opens it to reveal a diamond ring.

"Chloe, will you marry me?"

Chloe gasps as Michael appears beside her.

He looks as shocked as she feels. "You…you left a bag behind. I…I'm sorry…I shouldn't be here."

He awkwardly rushes off, leaving her standing before Francis, who's still on one knee.

Chapter 24

Michael looks down at the sound of a gurgle. He's almost forgotten he's sitting in the park with Macy in her carrier—the anxiety of the paternity results has been playing on his mind, that and the short movie clip of Francis proposing to Chloe. She's probably engaged now. How could he have been so idiotic to fall for her? He keeps remembering snippets of what happened between them in the tent, but the engagement reel keeps stealing away the highlight of his weekend. Still, he can't shake his feelings for Chloe. But what's the point of any of this? It's too complicated.

His phone buzzes with a work calendar reminder. "Oh shit!" He calls Beth. "Beth, I really need your help. I have a meeting with my editor, and I need someone to look after Macy right now. It would be one hour. I can't take her back to Harold and Winnie's as this is the sort of thing, they're expecting me to do. I just can't!"

Macy looks unsettled. Michael picks her up and pats her back as she rests her head against his shoulder.

"What about Chloe?"

"Ah," he pauses, unsure of how to explain he hasn't had the nerve to return her calls the past couple of days, "she can't."

"I want to do this, I do…shit…I want to, but I can't help. I'm so sorry. But I know someone who was a Nanny in London for a while. She might be able to help…"

Macy coughs and vomits up excess milk down Michael's chest and onto his favourite sneakers.

"Shit!"

"What now?"

"I've got to go."

An hour later, Michael is outside a back-door entry of the Longwood State Room where tonight's gala will be held. The door swings open.

Michael forces a smile. "Hi, Naomi."

"Hi. So, you need my help?"

Michael sighs. "Yeah."

Naomi wrinkles her nose. "You don't smell very good."

"Nice to see you too."

"I'm just telling you because you can't go to a meeting like that."

"This is why I'm in a rush and don't have time to chat. So, please. Can you look after her? I won't be long."

"Is she going to vomit on me?"

"How do I know? Look, can you do this or not?"

"I got it...I suppose, it's nice to be asked."

"Well, I didn't have much choice in the matter."

Naomi places a hand on her hip, her chin pointed at him. "Charming. I have a thousand things to do this morning to set up for Beth's event, and having a baby strapped to my chest while I instruct the lighting guys isn't something I have on my running sheet. So, can you lose the attitude?"

"Okay, fine. I'm sorry. I know you're helping me out." Michael passes Macy to Naomi. Naomi eyes her curiously as Michael unclips the baby carrier. "She's had a bottle, obviously, as half of it is on me. She has her favourite toys in this bag here, also..."

"Michael, I got this. It's only for an hour."

He nods. "Okay, sure." He kisses Macy on the head and passes over the baby bag. A second later, he's sprinting for his life back to his apartment to change. Cleaned up, he jumps in a taxi to get to his office.

His boss is walking out of a lift as he arrives. "Michael, we had a meeting."

Michael walks with him as he heads out the front turnstiles, "Please let me explain."

"That meeting ended, and I have another one to go to." McMillan picks up the pace.

"I'll wait till you get back."

McMillan turns to him, "I wouldn't bother. My afternoon now looks even busier since I need to interview another business reporter."

"But...you can't fire me. I...I really need this job."

"And I really need someone who can deliver me news. Michael, it's over for you here. I'm sorry it has to end like this, but you've left me no choice."

Michael lowers his head, "I'm sorry to let you down. I never wanted my time here to finish like this."

"I know."

McMillan walks off, shoulders slumped, vape in hand.

Michael trudges back to the Longwood. He finds Naomi behind a stage being set up with tech equipment. Macy is strapped to the front of her, taking in all the excitement.

"Hey, I'm back."

"You weren't as long as I thought you'd be."

He shrugs. "How was Macy?" He reaches for her hand and she gurgles at him.

"No problems at all. I think there was enough going on to keep her distracted."

"Thanks again for taking her. I really appreciate it."

"You're welcome. How did your meeting go?"

Michael rubs his jaw. "Umm, realistically, I guess as well as could be expected."

"That good, hey?"

"Pretty much. Anyway, we better let you get back to it."

"Of course." She passes Macy to Michael but then struggles with the buckles.

"Here, you hold Macy, I'll get the carrier off you."

Naomi holds Macy as Michael's hands move around her waist and reach behind her upper back. They are close. Macy squirms in between them.

Michael steps back and gets set up and gets Macy settled. "Thanks...especially with everything happening today."

"That's okay."

Michael glances around. "It looks good in here. Beth will be happy...hey...can I ask? How is she?"

"What do you mean?"

"I've been trying to talk to her. I know something is up, but she says she doesn't want to worry me...I just need to know—is she okay?"

Naomi brushes him off with a hand wave. "Ah, she will be. You know what she's like. She's a trooper."

"She won't talk to me...so, I'm glad she has you to talk to."

Naomi smiles. "Me too, and she'll talk to you. She just needs more time."

"Okay. Thanks for saying so."

Michael meets her gaze. "It's weird. You standing there, a baby here...I always thought this would happen, just not like this."

"I know you did. Maybe, I wasn't ready yet, for any of it." Naomi looks down at Macy.

"I don't think I am either, to be honest. But here I am, a father...well, I'll know for certain soon enough."

"What?"

"I um...I'm waiting to find out if she's actually mine. I mean, I'm pretty confident she is, but for legal reasons, I need the paperwork."

"Wow. I just assumed you knew already."

"I know it's dumb. It was complicated at the beginning."

"I see...I'm sure, it'll turn out how you want it to."

She offers a comforting smile and untwists a carrier strap around Michael's shoulder. Her hand pauses around his shoulders and her fingers trace down his chest. Her eyes lock with his and he knows what she wants. She leans in to kiss him, but he springs away.

"Naomi."

"I'm sorry. That was my fault. Hard to break habits."

"I know. I used to think about it every time I saw you."

"Why didn't you let it happen?"

"You know I couldn't."

"We could've tried again."

"I just couldn't trust you."

She pouts. "What about now? Don't you still want to kiss me now?"

"I'm in a good place now."

"You didn't say no." She tilts her head.

"It's a no. Can't you see? We weren't right for each other."

Naomi sighs. "Maybe."

He reaches out for her hand. "Also, I'm sorry I've made things hard for you, and between you and Beth."

"Thank you for saying that."

"I'll see you around."

He kisses her on the cheek and walks off.

Chapter 25

The State Room is adorned with black drapes, candle-style chandeliers, and pedestals lined the room showcasing floral arrangements. From the rooms large scale windows, the city lights below sparkled—a show for all the who's who of the city, along with Beth's firm's most important clients.

"What are you doing?" Naomi asks.

Beth spins around. "What?"

"You've been hiding behind the curtains for a while now."

"I have? Shit? How long?"

"It doesn't matter."

"I just needed a minute."

"And you've had it. Now, it's time for you to be on the floor. You're my queen, so go out there and show everyone else what you've got."

"Naomi. You're the best. Also, this place looks unbelievable. You did this!"

They share a quick embrace.

"Okay. Ready." Beth strides across the floor with Naomi, then whispers, "I shouldn't have worn this red dress. It's too much." She tugs at the hem, hoping to make the dress seem longer and less figure hugging.

"Are you kidding?" Naomi says. "I love that dress—it makes me so happy. Plus, I think the big sleeves balance out the short length of the dress. If you put all the material together…it's basically a full-length dress."

Beth smirks. "Thanks, but my partners are freaking out."

"Wait until they sign off on the bill for this party." Naomi says quietly.

"What?"

"Nothing. Anyway, I can see that they're just checking out your booty."

"Keep it down, they might hear you."

"They will not. Half of them haven't turned their hearing aids on yet."

Beth spots someone familiar entering the room. "Isn't that Logan? As in Logan, the ice hockey player?"

"Yes! Can you believe he was in town and available? Apparently, he's friends with Kent Carindale. The pair of them are just drool worthy."

Beth frowns. "He's also Ari's ex-boyfriend."

"Who?"

"Macy's mother. You know."

"Oh, right."

"Shhh, he's coming over."

Logan grins as he approaches. "Haven't I met you before? It's Naomi, isn't it?"

Beth smirks as Naomi almost melts to the floor. "Yes! We have met before. A few club openings."

"Thought so."

Beth quickly offers her hand. "Thank you so much for coming and supporting the fund."

He looks at her now. "Hi. I'm Logan."

"Yes, I know. I'm Beth, Michael's sister. You know, Macy's father?"

"Right. Got it."

"Well, depending on the test," Naomi mutters.

Beth turns abruptly. "How do you know about that?"

"He told me."

"Really?"

"What test?" Logan asks.

"Ah…" is all Beth can say.

"Are you saying Michael isn't sure if he's the father?" Logan asks.

"I'm sorry!" Naomi covers her mouth with her hand.

"It's a personal matter," Beth replies.

Logan is quiet for a moment. "Right…I see." He looks rattled.

"No!" Naomi is touching her earpiece and her face has paled. Beth grabs her wrist. "What is it?"

"Umm, the surprise celebrity speaker, who shall remain nameless now, is currently throwing up in the bathroom."

"What?"

Naomi laughs nervously. "The flu. So original."

"No, no, no! What are we going to do?"

"What was this guest speaker meant to talk about?" Logan asks.

"Ah, the charity," Naomi says. "That we hope to raise a lot of money tonight, and a thank you to Beth's company for hosting, then Kent's introduction. All the normal stuff, you know."

Logan shrugs. "Easy. I can do it."

"Really?" Beth and Naomi say in unison.

He smirks. "Why not? I'm here anyway. I don't like to put on a suit for no reason."

"But I can't afford you," Namoi says.

"This is charity, not work."

"Wow. That would actually be amazing."

Naomi nudges Beth.

"Yes," Beth says, breathlessly. "Thank you. We'd love to have you speak."

"Awesome."

"Amazing! You're on in twenty minutes, but we'll need to get you mic'd up. See over there," she points to the left of the stage. "I'll have Glen, the stage manager get you ready."

"You got it." Logan heads over.

Naomi talks to Glen through her headpiece. He nods, then welcomes Logan.

"What a lifesaver," Naomi says, looking back at Beth. "And can I just say, he's even just as hot from the back."

Beth holds up her hands. "Please don't even go there."

"I wasn't going to. Just appreciating that big chunk of man right in front of me." Naomi flicks her hair and smiles.

Beth groans as she looks over Naomi's shoulder.

Naomi turns to follow her gaze. "Oh my! When did Liam get so hot? Was he always like that? How did I not notice this? And…who's that smoking hot woman with him? Is that Evelyn holding onto his arm?"

Beth feels as if she's been slapped in the face. "*That* is Evelyn. I'd forgotten she'd RSVP'd."

"Oh, yeah, you're right. She looks pretty amazing, doesn't she?"

"Yep." Beth switches sides with Naomi to avoid seeing them.

"She just radiates presence. She's basically glowing. What sort of amazing face cream does she use?…Wait! We're spotted. They're heading over." Naomi waves, then murmurs, "Even with his apparent ex on his arm, he's checking you out. And not like a friend, but a woman he wants to…"

"Shhh!"

Naomi shrugs. "Just saying." She looks at Liam and Evelyn. "Hi!"

Beth bolsters herself, then spins around. "Oh, hi. So good to see you again, Evelyn."

"Likewise." Evelyn smiles demurely.

"Liam, thank you for coming." Beth smiles hard, trying not to look as deflated as she feels.

"Beth." He politely kisses her on the cheek, then rests his hand on her waist for a moment. A message maybe? She isn't sure. Somehow, Liam saying very little is making him even more alluring. Tonight, he's in a tuxedo, and it makes her weak at the knees. He says nothing else. Unreadable.

"Everything looks great," Evelyn chimes in.

Beth focuses back on the situation. "Evelyn, this is Naomi, the mastermind behind all this setup."

"Incredible job."

Evelyn offers her hand and Naomi accepts it. "Thank you. I love it too. We're lucky we get to work with great clients." She winks at Beth.

They all stand awkwardly for a moment before Naomi excuses herself to rush backstage and Evelyn heads off to find the powder room.

"I'd almost forgotten Evelyn was coming," Liam says.

"Me too," is all Beth can muster.

"I thought she should still come…I mean, why not, right?"

Beth plays it cool, though she's hurting inside. "Always doing the honourable thing, aren't you?"

"Should I not be?"

"Whatever. And don't worry, I won't tell your girlfriend that we've been sharing beds."

"She isn't my girlfriend."

Beth raises her eyebrows. "She looks like your girlfriend to me."

"Tonight, could've played out another way."

"No, it couldn't," she almost hisses.

Liam rubs his jar. "Are you angry with me? I'm confused, as you made it pretty clear what you wanted. Or didn't want, I should say. But now, you seem jealous."

"I'm *not* jealous."

"Fine, Beth. But I can't keep doing this with you. You open up to me, and I feel this connection, then you shut me out again. I understand if you want to be just friends, but I don't know how to do that at the moment."

"Okay, fine. I guess we don't have to be friends at all then. Are you happy now?"

"No. I'm not happy!" he almost yells back.

Beth sees Evelyn walking back over and uses it as an excuse to rush off to find her personal assistant.

"Jordan, please remind me to breathe," Beth says.

"I can do that." Jordan smiles as he sweeps his hand through his slicked-back hair. Not one part of him is out of place. "Who's the guy you were talking to?"

Beth turns to see Liam talking to Evelyn again. Liam looks over to her, but she spins back around. "No one."

"Hmmm. Really? He seemed interested in you. But then…he looked a little pissed off at the end."

"Fuck," she mutters. "I keep messing things up between us."

"I don't think, he'll stay annoyed for too long."

"I don't know about that."

"Please, I know when a man is infatuated."

"Even if he was, I'm pretty sure that was the end of a relationship that hadn't even started yet—a new one for me!" she jokes.

Jordan holds out his champagne to Beth. "I'm sure you can salvage it."

Beth takes a large gulp and hands the glass back. "Thanks. Argh, I just don't even know anymore. I mean, look at me—I'm a mess. Who'd be interested in a self-absorbed, work-addicted woman like me?"

"Come on, Beth. There's always a million guys lining up to be with you. But I don't think you ever stop long enough to notice. I'd line up too if I wasn't so into my new boyfriend…and if you weren't my boss."

"Really? And boyfriend?"

"Ah, yes. My flatmate, the designer. He kind of turned into my boyfriend. But you know, I'm bi, right? So, my previous comment it totally legit," he grins. Beth blushes, as he continues. "And so, what if you work a lot? That doesn't make you a bad person, and you aren't self-absorbed; you've just had a lot going on. And that guy over there doesn't seem to be fazed about any of that. So maybe…give this one a chance?"

"Maybe you're right…Thanks, Jordan." Beth throws her arms around him in a warm embrace.

"Hey!" Naomi yells, rushing over to Beth. "As much as I'm enjoying this work-husband and wife moment, I need you on stage, Beth. Showtime."

*

Waiting in wings backstage with Logan, Beth parts a side curtain and peeks out at the crowd and the firm's partners. She thinks about how hard she's been fighting for this promotion. Even if she were made partner, would that be enough now? It always was before. But now, she can't get Liam out of her mind, and here, he is slipping between her fingers. What if she lost both opportunities? Then what would she do? At least then, she could press charges against Mr Williams.

Naomi appears by her side. "You're on in two."

Beth waits for her cue, then walks out into the spotlight. The background music stops, and guests turn from their chatter to watch her.

In a matter of minutes, it's all over, and she hasn't missed a word, or fumbled, or fallen over on stage. The partners and guests loved the unexpected arrival of Logan, and now are all enthralled, listening to Kent's misfortune on the ski slope and his journey from depression to bravery, courage and conquering fears. She too now understands real fear. Mr Williams has introduced her to that, and it's still debilitating for her. So far, all she's done is ignore it.

A loud applause erupts at the end of all the speeches. The crowd is buzzing.

Beth spots Kent still backstage and thanks him.

"I can tell you want to ask me something, Beth?"

"Just…what you said on stage. You believe you will walk again, despite the odds. How do you stay so determined and positive?"

"This can be taken literally or figuratively, but if someone pushed you over, what would you do? Would you just stay on the ground?"

"No, I'd get up."

"Right, and then what if it happened again?"

"I'd get up again."

"That's right. So, despite what people tell me is impossible, or the shit days that might get you down, or the obstacles in your way…you fight. I fight to stand up again."

"Thank you. You are…"

"Go on, say it." He smirks. "Not just a party-boy womaniser." He winks.

Beth widens her eyes. "I wasn't going to say that!"

Kent chuckles. "That's okay. I quite like it. I know the reputation Logan and I have. But I prefer that than people feeling sorry for me. So, just remember, it's all up to you, Beth." Kent winks at her.

The word 'courage' is still circulating in her mind as she walks across the room to find a drink. The crowd is even thicker than before. A plethora of dark suits, plus the dim lighting, creates more shadows. As she weaves her way through a hopeful small gap, she catches a man's elbow. "Sorry."

He responds in kind, and they turn to face each other. It's Mr Williams.

"Bethany, it's been too long." He trawls a look up and down her body.

She shivers, trying to remember her new mantra, but her heart races, her breaths become shorter and her hands tremble. She needs to hold on to something. But then someone places a warm hand between her shoulder blades and a familiar voice sound behind her. Liam.

"Augustine Williams. Is that right?" He offers his hand.

"Why, yes. I'm sorry, have we met before?"

"No, we haven't. I'm Liam Andrews, Beth's friend."

"The lovely, Bethany. Isn't she something?"

Beth wants to interject, but she's still trying to regain her breath.

"She certainly is," Liam responds.

"A pleasure to meet you, Mr Andrews."

"Wish I could say the same to you, Williams."

Beth holds her breath. Horrified.

"I'm sorry? What did you say?" Williams tilts his head towards Liam, as if he hasn't heard correctly.

Liam leans in. "You heard me. This is an official warning. Stay away from Beth, or I'll report you to the cops myself."

"I don't know what lies this woman has told you, but I can assure you it's all fabricated. I suggest you watch your step, son. I'm a powerful man around this city, and you look like you're hanging on at the bottom of the ladder. I can kick you off."

"I don't give a shit who you are or what city we're in. You can try and intimidate me all you want, but you'll not come anywhere near Beth again. Do you understand me?"

Williams leans in, his voice stern. "I don't think that's possible. She needs me. Don't you, Beth?" He points a finger in her face. "And if you say anything about any of this, I'll have you fired and sued for defamation."

"Wow, Beth." Liam looks at her. "And this is the sort of client you want to have your firm take on?"

Beth remains speechless.

Williams raises his voice. "Leave this alone. I'm warning you."

"You, arsehole," Liam yells. "You think that's it? That you can get away with treating women the way you do?"

"Look at her. Dressed like that. Everyone in this city can tell she's a slut!" Williams fires back.

Liam swings and punches Williams squarely in the face. He stumbles back onto the floor, knocking guests' drinks from their hands. Liam stands over him. "Don't you ever call her a slut again." He grabs Williams by the lapels and lifts his chest. "And if you *ever* go near her again or touch her in any way, I'll come after you," he says through gritted teeth, then lets him drop.

"You'll pay for this," Mr Williams screams, shoving away people trying to help him up.

Security is rushing over, and Liam seems to realise how much of a scene he's created. Everyone is watching the commotion. Beth and Liam lock eyes. "I'm so sorry, Beth." He escapes just before security gets to him.

Beth stands there in shock as waiters rush around, cleaning up the mess as discreetly as possible. Williams dusts himself off and closes in on Beth, whispering, "Tell your friend I'll be pressing charges."

Beth swallows, shaken, her words escaping without thought. "I'd say sorry about that, but I'm not."

"I don't know what lies you told him…"

"I told him what happened."

"Nothing happened."

"*What*? I suppose you're going to say you were too drunk to remember?"

"I barely touched you. Wasn't you that was perhaps drunk?"

Beth scoffs. "I knew you were going to say that. I could write your lines for you." She shakes her head in disbelief as her anger flares. "Even if we end up with your account, you're never going to step foot inside my office, period. You will never touch me again. Got it?" She stalks off just as James comes her way. Could this night get any worse?

"So, I see your boyfriend really got stuck into Mr Williams. I guess what I saw was true then?"

"What are you talking about?"

"You know I saw you and Mr Williams together in the bathroom at the farewell dinner. So, it seems your boyfriend just found out about your slip up."

"Shut up, James! You don't know what you're talking about."

"Oh, but I do. See, I've finally worked out why you've been getting ahead in this race. It's not because you work hard; you just sleep your way to the top. I looked your boyfriend up too. I see he's a new player in town. At least I know now how you're getting new business. And who knows, maybe you'll try and seduce me too?!"

Beth slaps him across the face. "You idiot!" She steams off, ignoring the gaping bystanders.

"You won't win now," he yells.

Chapter 26

Michael has been desperately trying to forget that Chloe is performing tonight at the gala event. He's intentionally turned up late and arrived in the middle of a song. He tries not to watch her, but he loves the way she moves around the stage, playing with such energy and grace. She's wearing a shimmery gold dress with a high collar but a short hem. *Does she have to be so goddam sexy?* His hands feel deprived from not reaching out and touching her body. His mind transports him back to the tent. The heat between them as their kisses intensified. Her legs around him as he lay on his back. Chloe was this exciting concoction of provocative, elegance, fire and calm. She's everything. Everything he wants. *Damn it, how did this happen?*

Chloe sees him, and for a moment, they're connected. He isn't sure if she's happy to see him or not. Her stage face reveals nothing. He looks around to see where Francis is. Probably backstage. A woman standing next to him leans in and says, "Pretty talented woman. I noticed her looking at you. Is she your girlfriend or wife?"

Michael shakes his head. 'In another life,' he wants to say. He takes two drinks from a waiter and gulps them down one after the other. He messages Beth, announcing his arrival, then tries calling Liam.

"Where are you?" He yells down the phone over the crowd noise.

"I left," Liam responds.

"Already?"

"Drop by when you're done. I'll explain."

He looks up at Chloe again. She's between songs and seems to be smiling at someone off stage.

"I'm done. I'll be there soon." He turns abruptly and leaves.

*

A short Uber drive brings him to Liam's apartment.

"You left early?" He says, as Liam opens the door.

Liam nods. "You too? Beer?" They head to the kitchen.

"And a whiskey too. One for every problem I have." He pulls out a stool at the bench.

"That bad, hey? Everything okay?"

Liam pulls out a beer and slides it down the counter to Michael, pours two generous whiskeys and hands him one.

"Where do you want me to start?" Michael says.

"The beginning?"

"Chloe."

"Ah, see, I knew this conversation would reappear."

"Yeah, alright. I was waiting for that," he says, a little frustrated.

"You, okay? I didn't think you'd be this sensitive about it."

"Sorry. I just feel like an idiot. I thought I'd made a connection with her. I was obviously wrong." He sighs and picks up the whiskey. "Thanks." They clink glasses.

Liam sits next to him at the bench. "Walk me through it."

Michael takes a long drink. "We sort of fooled around a little the other night. I know we were both drunk, but she seemed interested. There was chemistry between us, a moment and…I feel like I'm meant to be with her."

"So, what happened?"

"I stopped it."

"You stopped it? Why?"

"I had this stupid voice that popped into my head telling me not to do it. I knew she would probably regret it in the morning." Michael rubs a hand over his face.

"How did you know that?"

"I just did."

"So, what has she said since then?"

"Ahh…nothing, she went cold on me the next day."

"Maybe she felt rejected?"

"But she said thank you for stopping it."

"And then?"

"When I dropped her home…I saw who I can only assume is her ex, proposing!"

"Shiiiit!"

"I've been ghosting her since." Michael sighs heavily.

"Do you know if she said yes?"

"I'm not sure."

"So, you're just going to ignore her and not find out what happened?"

"That's been my game plan so far."

Liam throws his hands up. "Your game plan sucks. Sorry, bud. You know what I'm going to say—you need to talk to her."

Michael finishes his whiskey and starts on his beer. "I know…I just feel like she's going to tell me what I already know—that she's getting back with her ex. She told me she wasn't interested in him anymore, but you know people say that, then get back together again. And things with me—it's complicated, right? So, I'm just back in the friend zone."

"Geez, I hope not. I know that's not a good area to be in if you like this woman. I know that from experience."

"I've never known you to want to date a friend."

"Umm, sure I have. Before I met you." Liam takes several gulps of his beer.

Michael pauses to study Liam for a moment. *Is he acting cagey?* "Okay. Anyway, it can't work. But then, why does it feel like this? Just doesn't seem logical."

"I get it. More than you realise."

"Hey, do you know what else happened today? I lost my job!"

"What? Can I just say, you're having a really shit day?"

"The worst."

"What happened?"

"I guess my editor knew I wasn't getting out of this brain fog in a hurry. Or more like I'm in a tunnel, and I keep running towards the darkness instead of the light."

"Did you explain what's been going on?"

"No. But I'll reach out after this all calms down. Make amends."

"Man, what a crazy day."

Michael notices the fresh bruise on Liam's knuckles. "Whoa! Hang on, what happened to you?"

"I kind of hit someone."

"You hit someone? I don't think I've ever seen you lay a finger on anybody. Wait, was this at the gala? Is that why you're here and not there?"

"Yeah. I think Beth now officially hates me, and she may not only have lost the running to be partner, but quite possibly, we may all be looking for jobs at the same time. The guy is probably going to get me fired as well."

"Ohhh. Holy shit! That's big. Who was the guy?"

"That potential new big client of Beth's. He was in my face, which I could sort of deal with, but then he threatened Beth, and I snapped. The guy really pissed me off."

"He threatened her?"

"It's a long story. Beth can fill you in, but he deserved it. I probably shouldn't have done it at the gala, but truthfully, I don't regret it, and I'd do it again."

"Well, you saved me from having to do it. How did he fair?"

"On the floor."

"Shit! That's impressive. How did Beth react?"

"I left straight away." Liam sighs. "I think Beth will have a hard time forgiving me. I created a bit of a scene."

"Was it good though?"

"Was what good?"

"Punching him in the face?"

Liam chuckles. "Yeah, it was pretty good." They clink drinks again.

"Didn't know you had it in you."

"No, me neither, but he really got under my skin."

"And what happened to Evelyn? I thought she was there?"

"I kind of forgot she was with me and had to send her a message to say sorry for leaving her there."

Michael pulls a face. "Gee, I thought I was in for a rough next twenty-four hours."

Liam's intercom buzzes, and Evelyn's face appears on the security screen. Liam looks a little panicky and torn.

Michael gets off his stool. "You should talk to her and I should head off anyway. I've had about five drinks in ten minutes. I'm going to walk home and pass out and pretend this day never happened."

"Are you sure? I can't imagine she'll want to stay around for long."

"You never know. But I'm better now that I have a few things off my chest." Michael heads to the door and buzzes Evelyn in before Liam can stop him.

"I have a car waiting," Evelyn says over the intercom.

Liam looks at Michael and shrugs. "Looks like I'm coming down with you."

"Just so you know, I'm not stopping for a chat. I don't need to be involved in this."

"Thanks, Mikey. Appreciate that."

"That's what friends are for." Michael grins and pats him on the shoulder as they walk out. "But honestly, good to talk to you, buddy."

"You too. Hey, Mikey. It'll be okay," Liam promises.

"I hope so."

Evelyn is waiting on the front step. Michael offers a polite greeting before sauntering off down the road. The easterly wind has picked up, cooling the night air and he ducks his head a little to shelter himself. He passes a few strangers, when suddenly one stops and grabs his arm.

"Beth! You scared the shit out of me."

"Sorry, I just saw you."

She looks distraught, and Michael puts a hand on her shoulder. "Are you okay?"

She hugs him. "Sorry, I'm just having an emotional night."

He's a bit shocked by her hugging him so hard. "You, okay?"

"I'm okay now. I'm glad I bumped into you."

"Me too. Liam told me what happened tonight. Or half of what happened. I want to know what's going on."

"I'm sorry, I haven't told you sooner. It's just that you have so much going on with Macy."

"I get it, but I'll always have time for you. No matter how many children happen to turn up on my doorstep."

Beth chuckles a little, and they huddle on a nearby bench while she reveals her story.

"I'm not only shocked by this, and really angry, but now I want to hug Liam even more for punching that guy in the face. I know I've got a lot going on, but you still should have come to me."

She sighs. "I didn't want to tell anyone, to be honest."

"I understand." He nods. "But it's not just this—I feel so shut out of your life lately. When mum and dad split, we always had each other's back."

"I know, but things haven't been the same…"

"Since Naomi?"

"Yes, since that."

"I'm sorry," he says. "That's my fault. I know you weren't taking sides, but it hurt me so much that you stayed friends with her. But I get it; she's your best friend."

Beth nods. "I still feel terrible about it."

"I've moved on. I really have. I want to put this all behind us. Can we start over again, like how it used to be?"

"I would love that."

Michael pulls her in for a big bear hug and kisses her forehead.

"So, how come I didn't see you at the gala?" Beth says.

"Sorry. I got there late. I had a bad day."

"Want to talk about it?"

"Hmmm, let's talk tomorrow. I'm tired, and drunk, and need to go to bed. I might actually finally sleep tonight. And you? What will you do?"

"I need to quickly drop in on Liam."

Michael shakes his head. "I've never known him to hit anyone before."

"You sound proud of him."

"I am, actually. I know you always like to do things your way, but I'm glad, he was there when I couldn't be."

Beth smiles "Me too. And I'm feeling better about things. More empowered."

"That's great. What worked?"

"I think I found something to fight for."

"Something or someone?"

"Both."

"You know, you're more important than that job. You know that, right?"

"I think, I finally do."

Chapter 27

Liam thought Evelyn would be furious, but instead, she just looks tired. Her face dipping to her chest.

"Why don't you come in for a drink!" he suggests.

"I'm not staying." She looks over at the hire car with its engine running.

"I'm sorry about what happened. And for leaving you there."

"That was quite the performance you put on…I saw how angry that man made you, the one who was being rude to Beth. You weren't just being polite and sticking up for her; you were being protective."

"Of course. I'd do that for any of my friends."

"A friend? Maybe you can't see it, but I can."

"See what?"

She pins him with her eyes. "The way you two look at each other."

Liam blinks, wondering what to say. He can't deny it.

Evelyn sighs, grabs hold of Liam's hands. "What we had was special to me. But I can see where your heart is now."

"I'm so sorry. I've only just realised it myself, and I…but that aside, I wanted to tell you how I was feeling, in person."

"I guessed as much," she says, squeezing his hands. "That's why I booked a flight for tonight. So, this is goodbye."

Liam gently pulls her hands up to his mouth and kisses them.

"I had a good time, Evelyn."

"Me too." She smiles sweetly, then climbs into the back of the car. And then she's gone.

He turns to go back inside and sees Beth walking towards him. He looks up at the sky, sighs as he waits for her, then follows her up the stairs to his apartment. They're silent until they're inside, where Beth picks out a glass from the cupboard and pours herself a drink from the open whiskey bottle on the bench. She downs it quickly.

"Beth, before you say anything…"

She walks over to him, grabs his hand and looks at the bruising across his knuckles. "Does it hurt?"

"Not so much."

She presses it and he winces.

"Liar," she says. "You should put ice on it."

"Yeah, I should, but I had a drink instead. My head needed that more."

She walks over to his freezer and looks for what she needs, then grabs a tea towel and comes over to him. "Sit down," she commands, pointing at the lounge. He follows her orders.

Beth remains standing, looks around. "Why did Evelyn leave?"

"She only came to say goodbye."

She grabs his hand and inspects it before applying the tea towel wrapped ice. "I see. I thought maybe you were…reconnecting."

"No. It was nothing like that. It was very much an official goodbye."

She finishes wrapping his hand but doesn't move away.

He looks up into her face. "I'm so sorry about tonight; I know how important it was for you. You were so incredible on stage, and I'd hate to think I may have jeopardised your dream opportunity."

"At least the partners were excited about all the other 'scheduled' events, so I'm hoping it'll be enough. Anyway, there isn't much I can do about it now."

"I really am sorry." Liam reaches for her hands.

Beth hesitates. "I was horrified about what you did tonight in front of all those people…but at the same time, I feel really honoured that you did that. I want to be mad at you, but…I can't. I'm glad that I have you."

She looks down at him with those eyes, the ones he can't stop thinking about, and he desperately wants to reach up and kiss her, but he resists. "Beth, you'll always have me."

"You promise?"

Liam stands. "I promise." He looks down at her and brushes a strand of hair off her face.

"Beth."

"Yes?" Her lips seem to beckon him.

"You were incredible on stage tonight, and you look so goddam beautiful." Liam edges closer, testing, feeling her breath.

"You looked pretty good yourself."

"Beth, I can't hold back anymore. Tell me no and I'll walk away for good."

She doesn't say anything. He pauses his breathing for a moment, then cups her face and leans in. Kisses her.

She moves a hand to his back and the other to his neck, pulling him in. Their kisses grow more urgent, but then he feels her hesitate.

He pulls away. "Are you okay?" He says, breathing heavily.

"I'm okay, I just, I don't know. Should we talk about this?" Beth's eyes glistening, looking to him for answers.

"Probably. But I don't feel like talking at the moment."

Beth grins, and Liam can't help what he assumes is a goofy smile right back at her. Their lips meet again. His hand is still bound with the ice bandage, limiting his actions, so he unravels it to the sound of Beth's disapproval, which quickly turns to delight as he leads her to his bedroom. He gently lowers her onto the bed, then moves on top of her, ever so slowly. He places gentle kisses below her earlobe then up to her mouth before making his way down her breasts. He ignores the ache of his bruised knuckles and explores every inch of her. Beth runs her hands though his hair and over his shoulder blades as he heads further down her body. Her dress now bunched around her hips. She arches her back and unzips her dress for him. He glides the fabric over her hips onto the floor. She isn't wearing any underwear. He groans in approval.

"Liam," Beth purrs.

"I need you to tell me. Tell me you want this," he asks.

"I want this. I want you."

*

In the morning, they stir. A sheet covers most of their bodies. Last night's clothes and extra pillows are scattered all over the floor. Liam has Beth pulled tightly against his body, and he kisses her on the neck to see if she's awake. She makes soft purring sounds. He smiles.

"You know we never spoke about this," he says.

"This?" Beth says coyly.

"Us." He pulls her closer. "Where should we start?"

"I don't know. But I've a lot I want to tell you." She moves out of his embrace and rolls over to face him.

He tries to hide just how exhilarated he is, waking up with her like this. "I feel like we're in dangerous territory that we may never come back from." He looks at her for clues.

"I know," she agrees. "So, what do we do? We have a lot of history here, and I don't want to ruin anything."

"Might already be too late for that." He runs a hand over her hip and leaves it there.

"Probably."

"As long as you're not about to say that you see me as a brother."

She pushes him in the chest playfully. "Gross. No, that's not what I was going to say. But I thought you always saw me as the sister you never had?"

"I've never thought of you that way. But I did think about you—about us—in the past, but you never seemed interested."

"How do you know that? You never said anything."

"What would you have said?"

"I don't know."

"See? I obviously didn't make a good enough impression back then," he jokes.

"Stop it. I always liked you…but I always saw you tied to Mikey's hip. And plus, we were always dating other people—not very successfully, might I add. Then you left."

"So, indulge me. What changed?"

"I…I think it happened as soon as you got back. It made me realise how much I missed you."

"So, you *did* miss me?"

"Maybe a little." She grins sheepishly. "I guess it made me think about *why* I missed you. Then the more I saw you…I started wondering why nothing had ever happened between us, and all of a sudden, I couldn't stop thinking about you. It was like trying to put a popped champagne cork back into a bottle…perhaps seeing you with Evelyn didn't help."

Liam smirks. "I see."

"I did get a bit jealous of seeing her on your arm."

"Did you now? Well, I'm glad she turned up then."

She pushes him lightly on the arm.

"So, what about you? I've just told you all of my secrets. Spill."

"Hmm…things did seem to shift between us when I got back. Maybe I felt you starting to see me differently, and I think it ignited some old feelings I might have had."

"I can't believe you used to have feelings for me!"

He smiles slyly. "I might have. That's not confirmed."

"Sure." She laughs as she pushes him on his back and rolls on top of him, kissing him. Liam pulls her close. Her body is intoxicating, and he wants her all over again.

*

Sometime later that morning, while Liam showers, he reflects on last night and how everything has changed with his relationship with Beth. He can't stop grinning. As he finishes up his morning routine, he hears her pottering around the apartment. He could get used to this.

He pokes his head around the corner. "Hey, I was wondering where you got to."

Beth is in the middle of the lounge holding his phone, staring at it. She looks up with dismay. "I just saw your phone on the coffee table. I wasn't trying to snoop, but…when were you going to tell me you had taken a job in Beijing?"

"It's not what you think. I haven't agreed to anything…"

"Really?" Beth drops the phone with a thud and pushes past him to grab her clothes from the bedroom.

"Wait, where are you going?"

"Where am I going? I'm certainly not running off to Beijing! I can't believe you slept with me knowing this whole time you were going to leave."

"Please just stop and listen to me…"

"I trusted you, and the next instant…" She brushes past him and out of the bedroom.

"I was still working out the details. I haven't said yes." He reaches for her hand.

She turns to face him. "Why didn't you even tell me about it?"

"It wasn't that long ago that you made it clear you didn't want to be that involved in my life at all."

"I was lying about that."

"I know that *now*." He squeezes her hand.

"So why haven't you said yes then?"

"I was hoping…I wanted to see if something might happen between us. And then it didn't, but I still couldn't say yes."

Beth stays silent for a moment. "I know how important your career is to you, and you know how important mine is. We'd never jeopardise that for each other."

"Maybe we should! What's the point to any of this if we just wind up alone?"

"You might find someone in Beijing. Or rekindle things with Evelyn."

"So, I settle with someone out of convenience?"

"I'm just saying…"

Liam huffs. "I want you. You know that now."

"But you've been working so hard to get to this point in your career. I can't let you make me be part of this decision."

"You don't want to be?"

"No, I can't…it's not fair."

"You tell me then," he says. "If your company offered you a partnership, but you had to leave Boston. What would you do?"

Beth pauses for thought. "But this is your dream, not mine. I don't want to be the one standing in your way." She turns and heads to the front door.

Liam grabs her arm. "Wait. But what if I want you to?"

"I'm sorry, Liam, I…I can't do this right now. You have a lot going on, and so do I. Maybe this was all a mistake."

"Please, don't say that."

Beth withdraws her arm and walks away.

"Beth, don't do this."

Liam watches her open the door and leave. She doesn't look back.

Chapter 28

Chloe pauses for a quick reflection. Could this be a moment that defines her career? Or potentially a moment that seals the end of it? She pushes the last thought out of her mind and knocks on the wall.

"You may enter," a familiar voice calls out.

Chloe walks into the room.

The maestro looks up from his desk. "Ah, the lovely, Miss Chloe. We have missed you."

Chloe's smiles. She's missed being here too. In a way, this has felt more of a home to her than her apartment. "Thank you for taking the meeting."

"Of course. How could I not?"

"I wanted to talk to you about my future."

"If this is about Europe…"

"I don't mean immediate future, more long term."

"I see."

"I've been thinking. You're right about not sending me to Europe. I haven't been quite myself, and I'm not playing with the same passion. I didn't realise, and I'm sorry to have let you down. I know things were made worse with losing my best friend and then Francis."

"Ah, yes, Francis. Sorry that we lost him to New York, and you did too."

"Thank you. But he isn't the reason behind this…I've made a decision. I need to do something for me, just for me."

"Is this because of the friend? You're having some sort of awakening? Do you need to go bungee jump, or run with the bulls and feel alive?"

"I think it's just made me realise how much every day has been the same. I need a break."

The maestro eyes her suspiciously. "How much time do you need to…find yourself?"

"I'd like a year off."

He shakes his head in disgust. "There's no way you'll be in shape to play after twelve months."

"But I'll still be playing. May I?" She walks around to his side of the table and opens her laptop. Googling her name, she scrolls past all the normal entries until she gets to a clip of her performance at the gala, then plays it for him.

He watches, saying nothing until it ends. "Interesting. So, you want to take time off for this?"

"Yes, but not just this. I think I want to also spend more time on composing. I want to bring some fresh ideas back with me, for the orchestra. I know we're already working on collaborations and working with different genres. But I want to see how far I can take it. I also want to go out to dinner, go to a birthday party. Just live for a while, with no rules and no restrictions."

He nods. "I see. You know, by breaking your contract, it means I can't hold your seat. You worked so hard for that position, Miss Chloe. It's unheard of to give it up when in the prime of your career."

"I know, but I think, I need to take this step back so I can move forward again."

"Are you sure this is what you really want to do? You'll miss it."

"Yes, but I want to see what else is out there."

"When you come back. You'll need to re-audition."

"I understand."

"It's a big risk, Miss Chloe."

"I need to do this."

Maestro nods. "I'll have someone send you the paperwork." He motions for her to leave.

"Thank you, Maestro." Chloe quickly heads for the doorway in case he changes his mind.

"It's not bad," he calls out as she's leaving the room.

She stops, turns around. "What's not bad?"

"That music. I don't mind it." He shrugs and then offers her a sly smile.

*

It's almost dinner time as Chloe walks home, and people are filling up the bars and cafes on the sidewalk. She loves the energy of this city, the anticipation of what the evening might hold. But for her, tonight she's looking forward to staying home with a wine and pizza, at a normal, regular dinner time.

As soon as she arrives, she heads for the couch and puts her feet up with a contented sigh. She's free! But the person she really wants to share this news with won't call her back. Michael is still ghosting her. He couldn't possibly think she'd accepted the proposal, could he? Not after everything she'd told him about Francis—and he still seemed interested in her when he dropped her home, but perhaps now he's had more time to think about it? Maybe Michael is relieved they never slept together and doesn't want to have to reject her all over again. And of course, he's still Macy's dad. It's probably for the best she stops reliving that moment in the tent where he touched her face and brought his lips to hers. It makes her body tingle every time she thinks about it.

She startles as her phone vibrates next to her. It's Logan calling on video. She groans but answers.

His face looks tired, drawn. "Hi."

"Hi. Big night last night?"

"Just a lot going on." He frowns.

"So, why are you calling me?"

"Are we ever going to have a civil conversation?"

"I don't see why we need to have a conversation at all. I've said already we have nothing that connects us anymore."

"About that, what you said, about us being connected..." Logan sighs, and his big shoulders drop a little. "Since we met up, I've had some time to think. And I may not have been honest with you."

"What do you mean?" Chloe narrows her eyes.

"I...I'm not sure but, I'm worried...not sure if that's the right word."

"Spit it out, for goodness' sake!"

"I overheard that Michael isn't sure if the baby is his."

"And?"

"And, I guess, you could say that things happened between Ariane and me." Logan's face twists in anguish. "We were sleeping together again."

Chloe tenses. "You *what*? Logan, after everything you..."

"Just wait. I need to finish."

She bites her lip and breathes deeply, trying her best to keep calm, but rage is building.

"One day, she told me she was pregnant. We had a really big flight. I accused her of planning it, to finally get me to commit to her. She yelled at me and told me that she had wasted her life. I told her I didn't want anything to do with her or the baby." Logan looks pained.

Chloe gasps. "How could you say that?"

"I thought she was trying to manipulate me!"

She doesn't want to believe him, but her heart is telling her it's true. "Then what happened?"

"She called me roughly a week later and told me it wasn't my baby, that I didn't have to worry anymore, and we never had to see each other again."

"And you just assumed she was telling you the truth?"

"Yes, because I thought she was trying to trap me from the beginning. Plus, I didn't really want a baby. The thought terrified me, so I never questioned her. She said I was the reason she could never move on and why she never dated anyone else. That was the last time we spoke."

Chloe is momentarily lost for words. She swallows, holding down her fury. "Do you know how much pain this is going to cause someone else?" She growls. "Michael's life has been turned upside down. What if you're the actual father?"

"I didn't mean to…I obviously never expected any of this to happen."

"But if you had just been honest with me from the beginning!" she yells.

"If you were more approachable, I probably would have," he yells back.

"How dare you blame me? You're unbelievable. I really hope Macy doesn't belong to you, because I don't want to have to talk to you ever again. And she deserves…someone like Michael."

Chapter 29

Michael's phone wakes him from his morning slumber, but he ignores it. He gazes around his bedroom, head throbbing. An empty bottle of whiskey and a half bottle of gin sit on his dresser, and his laptop is open. Last night's shock hits him again, and he's suddenly awake. Hoping it was a bad dream, he rushes over to his screen and reads the email again. It's there. The result. He re-reads it to be sure, even though he read it over twenty times last night. There's no mistake. He isn't Macy's father, after all.

The phone rings again. He picks it up this time. "Winnie?" Ugh, his throat feels as dry as paper.

"I'm so sorry to call, but there's a bit of an emergency." She sounds rushed.

"Is it Macy? What's happened?" All of a sudden, he feels sober and alert.

"Macy is fine. It's Harold. We had to call an ambulance. And we're at the hospital now."

"Oh, no. I'm so sorry. Is it his heart?"

"Looks that way. I had to bring Macy with me; Roberta can't get here for another two hours, and I've tried everyone I can think of…I just need someone to be with Macy in case I can go in and see Harold, someone to walk her around the halls…"

"I'll jump in an Uber. I can be there in fifteen minutes."

"Oh, thank you!"

*

Michael spots Winnie in the emergency waiting room. She looks unusually dishevelled and her face blotchy. She has a tissue in her hand, which she quickly puts away in her handbag.

"Thank you for coming," she says.

Macy is asleep next to her in the pram. He takes a peek, and his heart aches when he sees her face.

"She just fell asleep."

He nods and sits next to Winnie, awkward because he knows he probably smells like a bar. "You know he'll be okay. He's as tough as they come."

"Thank you for saying so." She nods and continues. "Since Macy is asleep and I'm waiting for the doctor to come out, we might as well talk about the elephant in the room. I got your message, about Macy…and you not being her biological father."

"Oh god, I emailed you?"

"Yes, and not just me, a group email."

"Great." Michael rests his elbows on his knees and props his chin up with his hands.

"I'm truly sorry."

"I'm sorry too." He looks over at the pram again.

Winnie sniffs. "With Harold…I haven't had much time to let this sink in."

"Me neither." He leans back and shakes his head. "I sort of just woke up."

"I tried calling everyone. I don't have the right to contact you now, but I didn't know what to do. It's just that she knows you now."

"It's okay. Honestly."

Winnie looks at him. "You could have said no."

"I wouldn't do that."

"I was wrong about you." She fusses with her skirt. "And I'm sorry for the other night. How we left things. I've been so worried about losing contact with Macy, especially after losing Ariane."

"I would have never taken her away from you."

"I shouldn't have compared you to your father. I'm embarrassed about that."

"I get a little sensitive around comments made about my dad. I want Macy to have a better relationship with her dad than I have with mine."

"I understand…you will be a wonderful father someday."

"Thank you."

Winnie looks back at him. "I think Chloe will be quite upset about this news too."

"Really?" Michael looks up.

Winnie has a slight smile. "I don't think Macy was the only one enjoying your company."

"I'm sure, she'll get by, now that she has Francis back in the picture." He hopes he doesn't sound like a jealous ex-boyfriend.

"Francis? I don't believe so…but maybe you should ask her?"

She looks over his shoulder, and Michael turns to see Chloe walking down the hall towards them. She runs over when she spots them and embraces Winnie. "I'm so sorry. I had my phone off, and I just saw all your missed calls. I feel so terrible."

Chloe looks over at Michael as she lets go of Winnie.

He doesn't know what to say. *Did I drunk call her, leave thirty voice messages, was she on the group email?* A nurse comes over, requesting paperwork be filled out, and Winnie follows her to the desk, leaving them both standing there like awkward teenagers.

"How are you?" she asks.

"Okay. Had a bit of a rough night."

"Uh…you kind of smell like you did."

Michael tries to smell himself and wrinkles his nose. "Winnie sounded pretty distressed…"

"Thanks for coming. I wasn't sure if I'd see you again. I got your email. It was brief, but I guess you didn't need to elaborate."

"Oh…right."

"Michael, I'm so sorry."

"I'm not having a good season, it turns out."

"I've been trying to call you."

"I've been busy."

"I need to talk to you about Logan."

"What about Logan?"

"You want to talk here?"

"Why not?"

"Okay then…let me say, that I've been such an idiot. I let my attitude get in the way of the truth."

"The truth about what?" Michael frowns.

They both turn at the sound of heavy footsteps—Logan is walking towards them.

"What are you doing here?" Chloe asks.

"My mum got a call from Winnie, but they live too far out of town to help and my hotel is around the corner, so she sent me. Also, I had a feeling the two of you would be down here."

Macy stirs in the pram, and they all look at her.

Michael looks back at Logan. "You're her father, aren't you?" He narrows his eyes.

"Yes."

Michael clenches his fists, his heart thumping loudly, chest tight.

"This is unbelievable," Chloe says, aghast.

Michael looks at her. "You said there was no one else?"

Chloe crosses her arms and looks back at Michael. "I should have listened to you from the beginning. I'm sorry."

Logan looks to Michael. "Look, I'm sorry this got so out of hand. It's just that women play me all the time. They're always after money or fame or both."

"Yeah, I know the stories. It's a weak excuse," Michael says, glaring.

Logan's shoulders seemed to sag in defeat. "I was just getting sick of feeling pressured, lied to and often bullied into situations I didn't want to be in. I just couldn't see how it could work between us. I enjoyed my life as it was." He shrugs. "Then I heard you were the dad, so I just assumed it was a closed case. But at the gala, I heard a comment that you weren't sure. I just had this feeling that maybe Ari had lied to me. I've lied to her plenty of times…so I got tested and…Macy *is* my daughter."

The alcohol in Michael's stomach is threatening to make him vomit. He rubs his chest and winces.

Logan continues. "I'm not a good guy, Michael. And you seem like you are. If Macy ever went looking for her dad one day, Ari would have wanted her to find someone like you."

"So…do you think she knew Michael wasn't the father?" Chloe asks.

"Maybe not." He thinks for a moment. "She was so pissed off with me. Maybe she thought if she just *believed* the baby wasn't mine, then it wouldn't be, you know? I guess she didn't want to find out for sure, didn't want to have it confirmed."

"This is fucking crazy," Michael says as he rubs his face. "I can't believe I ended up in the middle of this chaos."

Winnie appears from around the corner. "What's all the commotion? Logan?"

"Maybe sit down, Winnie," Chloe suggests.

Chapter 30

Beth tries calling Michael again. Still no answer. She sits in the boardroom, nervous. The partners have already made her wait over twenty minutes. She presses her suit pants and jacket with her hands to ensure there isn't one crease. Finally, the door opens, and they all walk in. Beth jumps from her seat and smiles, nodding to each partner as they acknowledge her.

Mr Bourke speaks first. "Please sit. The board and I have been discussing the incident that occurred at the gala. I understand that our client was assaulted, but we've spoken to him, and he won't be pressing any charges. He's also agreed to keep it out of the press, which is a big relief for us. The gala was hugely successful, but it was also very embarrassing for this firm. This man who was involved, I believe he's a friend of yours?"

"Yes, sir. He is."

"I see. And is there something that this board needs to know?"

"Needs to know?"

He sighs. "Beth, you know the importance of making partner. The people we associate with reflect on this firm."

One of the other board members chimes in. "Will you be associating with this man again?"

"I'm not really sure, sir."

"You aren't sure? Can I make a suggestion here that you do not? The board and I have been favouring you to be partner, but in light of this event, it certainly changes the landscape. We simply cannot have our clients being assaulted by staff's friends, partners or otherwise."

"I understand, sir."

"Good."

"Is there anything else we should know?"

Beth fidgets with her hands. "There's something I wish to bring up."

"Yes, and what's that?"

"Umm…how should I put this? Mr Williams was…"

"Was what?"

"He made inappropriate advances towards me," she blurts.

Mr Bourke leans forwards across the table almost standing. "Inappropriate advances?"

"Yes, that's correct."

"When did this happen?"

"He followed me into the women's bathrooms at Neil's farewell dinner."

The boardroom fills with murmurs from the board members. One of them turns to her. "These are serious allegations you're making. Do you understand that?"

"Yes, sir. But it's the truth. And I need to say something to protect other female colleagues. I don't want him near me or any other female staff members. I've decided that I'll be pressing formal charges against him."

"I see, well this certainly changes things," Mr Bourke says.

"I know the timing isn't ideal. But obviously this wasn't something I was in control of."

"Of course. We suggest you take a leave of absence. With our support."

"Yes, sir. Thank you."

"All decisions regarding the partnership will be postponed until this matter is settled. That will be all. We'll let you know when we're ready to discuss it with you again."

"Thank you for your time," adds another partner.

"And, Beth, all business aside, do take care of yourself. There are services available here at the firm."

"Thank you."

She leaves the room and finds Jordan outside, pacing the hallway. He falls into step with her down the hall.

"So, what happened?"

"Nothing yet."

"Did you say anything about Mr Williams?"

"Yes."

"Good on you, Beth. That was a tough decision. So, what now?"

"We wait and see. A lot will be dependent on what he says."

"He'll lie though."

"I know. That's the problem. It'll be my word against his."

"Okay, just remember, I'm here."

"What would I do without you?" She smiles and gives him a hug. "I'll go and pack up a few things from my desk, then I'll call it a day."

*

Arms full of her belongings, Beth enters the lift. When it reaches the ground floor, the doors open to reveal Mr Williams. She gulps and tries to walk past him without saying anything. He grabs her arm, stopping her.

"I thought we had an understanding. You don't talk, and you and your friend keep your jobs. But you couldn't keep your mouth shut. Could you?" He seethes. "They said you were pressing charges against me. So, now I'll have to tell them my version of events, of what you did to me."

"What I did?"

"You came on to me. I rejected you because it was inappropriate. You're just some young, naive lawyer who thinks they can climb their way to the top using any means necessary."

Beth's fear turns to rage. "How dare you! You know I'd never come on to you. The thought of it makes me sick."

"I will not lose my reputation because of you. I'll tell everyone what a liar you are, and when I'm finished telling everyone about you, I'll destroy you and your boyfriend's career. He can forget about that job in Beijing."

Her hackles rise further at the mention of Liam. "I will not hide away from this. Nobody else will be intimated, feel threatened or be touched by you without their permission!"

"Who do you think they'll believe? You or me? Do you know how much money I'm worth, how much I'm also worth to this firm? You're finished at this company, and by the time I'm finished with you, no law firm in this city will employ you!" He steps into an open lift and pushes aggressively on the buttons. He glares at her as the lift door shuts.

Beth reaches for something to steady herself but misses the wall and crumbles to the floor. Her belongings spill onto the ground and she starts to cry. Footsteps hurry towards her, then James is standing over her, reaching out a hand to help her up.

She knocks his hand away. "How long have you been standing there?" When he hesitates, she pushes herself off the ground. "I suppose, you'll be happy now?"

"I…"

She bends to gather her things, then stands to face him again. "The partnership is yours. You won, James." He looks stunned. Before he can answer, she takes off in a hurry, refusing to let him see her cry further.

"Beth, wait!"

She rushes to the public bathroom, dumps her belongings on the floor, then sits sobbing on a toilet. "Screw them. Screw them all." Eventually, she loses track of time, lost in her misery until her phone buzzes. "What now?"

It's Jordan and he sounds panicked. "Where are you? The partners want to see you."

"Really? Now? Okay, I need a few minutes."

She splashes water on her face and drinks some, trying to regain some sort of calmness and professionalism.

Back upstairs, she knocks on the large oak doors to the boardroom. She walks in and James is sitting there. *What's he doing here? Are they going to fire me in front of James? Is James already partner? Will he fire me? Shit!*

"Please sit, Bethany," Mr Bourke says.

Beth fumbles as she places her things on the table. She looks up and offers an apologetic smile. The partners faces are unreadable. She takes the seat next to James. He doesn't look at her. She feels like she's on trial. *My heart is going to explode.*

Mr Bourke begins. "After speaking with James, I believe we won't need to hold up proceedings on the partnership."

"No?" She inhales, anticipating the inevitable.

"We've also spoken with Mr Williams."

Even his name makes her skin crawl.

"He's told us you've been harassing him. So, you see, this would have created a difficult situation while we waited for an outcome. But none of this matters now, because James witnessed Mr Williams threatening you just now, and we also have the incident on our security cameras, of course. We must say that we're appalled by his behaviour. We'll be ceasing all future business dealings with him."

Beth looks from James back to the partners. "I don't know what to say."

Mr Bourke continues. "We will support you, and it won't affect your position here."

Beth nods her thanks. "That really means a lot to me. I've been working so hard for the partnership…"

"Yes, indeed. This brings me to my point of discussion. We know the quality of work, the countless hours, expertise and energy both you and James have been contributing to this company. We've tried to not let these recent events cloud our judgement on the outcome."

Beth swallows hard, sits forwards in her seat.

"We only ever planned on taking one of you forwards…Bethany, we've seen your dedication to this firm, and we know that you want to take this firm into its next growth period. The gala event, although dramatic in some parts"—Beth cringes—"was a success in terms of publicity for the firm, attracting lucrative new business and raising money for such a great cause."

Beth relaxes and smiles her appreciation.

"However, James has certain qualities that we feel cannot be overlooked. He also has great vision for the future of this firm, and it would be a shame to not have him here. The situation is that, together, you make the perfect duo to ensure the survival of this firm. Therefore, we are offering you both partnerships."

Beth and James each sigh heavily, then look at each other, beaming. James gets up to shake her hand. "Congratulations."

Beth stands. Holy shit! I can't believe this.

The other partners all move out from the table to congratulate them. Beth responds her thanks, her heart still racing. She walks out of the meeting room, grinning from ear to ear.

"Who would have thought?" Beth says as James follows her out of the room.

"I know, right? I thought for sure they were going to offer it to you."

"I thought after everything that happened…" Beth shakes her head. "There's just no way I could've imagined this outcome, James. What you did. Coming forward to tell the board what you overheard. I can't ever thank you enough."

"After I heard what he said to you in the hall…I was embarrassed to have misjudged you. That man is the biggest piece of scum walking around. I can't wait to see him get what he deserves." He shakes his head. "I wish I had known sooner."

"You spoke the truth as soon as you knew, so you don't need to apologise. I owe you one."

"As much as I shouldn't take it, I'm going to cherish an IOU from you. It could come in handy." He grins.

"Oh, no." Beth chuckles to herself. "Also, I need to say sorry for slapping you."

"That's right. That happened." He rubs his cheek, as if remembering the blow. "You sure deliver with conviction."

"I'm so sorry!"

"Hey, I deserved it anyway. I'm sure I've been pissing you off enough."

"That's true." She laughs.

"You run a mean race, Beth. I can't believe it's actually over."

"Is it over? I think it's just beginning."

He grins. "You're right. Hey, should we grab a drink to celebrate?"

"Sure. Let's get out of here. I've had enough of the boardroom for one day."

In the lobby, a receptionist calls Beth over and hands her a large box with a bow.

"Hmm, looks like news travels fast around here," James jokes.

She opens the lid, and inside she finds a bunch of blue cornflowers with a note:

I remember that you were always desperately waiting for someone to give you blue flowers...I should have bought you these a long time ago.

Liam.

"I'm so sorry, James, but there's somewhere I need to be. I really do want to get that drink though."

"Okay, sure. But now you have to buy the first two rounds," he jokes.

"Fine." She pretends to look annoyed. "Wait. One more thing...I need to ask..."

"Ask what?"

"You're always killing it in this role, its infuriating, but there must be something you're not good at. A weakness? Please, I need to know."

"That's an interesting question." He smirks. "I'm surprised you haven't worked it out yet."

"Enlighten me."

"It was you, Beth. I couldn't work out how to beat you. That was my weakness."

"Huh...don't you want to know mine?"

"I already know yours."

"Oh yeah? What's that?"

"Me, of course. You couldn't work out how to beat me either." He throws his head back with laugher as he walks off. "See you in the office, partner."

Chapter 31

Liam is sitting at Malcolm's desk, the late afternoon light making him squint as looks at his boss, who's standing and staring out of the floor-to-ceiling windows.

"We're very disappointed, but we understand you'd like to stay local. I'm a little taken aback though."

"I understand that, sir, but I'm not in a position to leave Boston at the moment."

"Why would you want to stay here? Traffic is terrible. Look at it down there. Chaos."

"Well you know the traffic is worse in Beijing."

Malcom sighs and returns to sit at his desk. "I'm giving you an opportunity of a lifetime here." He looks at Liam for an answer.

"It's complicated."

Malcom frowns. "Complicated? If you can un-complicate it in twenty-four hours, can you let me know?"

"I actually wanted to pitch another idea to you."

"What's the summary?"

"I've been working here since I graduated. You know I'm extremely loyal to this company, and I plan to stay here for many years to come. I also don't like to pass up opportunities, so I have a proposal I'd like to present to management. It'll show how I can run the operation from Boston with an assistant in Beijing. They can micro-manage the day-to-day operations, and the rest of the time, I can be do conference video meetings. I'm approximating I'll need to fly over for meetings once a month, or for anything else major. Adam says he'd be interested in the assistant's job—he's the perfect candidate—if it went ahead."

"Hmm, I see. If I'm honest, Liam, I don't really want to give this job to someone else. And it would be good to keep you here. Fine. I'll set up another meeting."

"Thank you, sir. You won't regret it."

"Make sure that I don't," he says with a sly smile, "Does this have something to do with a woman by chance?"

"She might have something to do with it."

"Hmmm, I see. Well, I hope she is worth it."

"I believe she is, sir."

Liam self- congratulates as he leaves the office, then checks his phone for missed calls. There's only one he's really waiting on. But still nothing.

*

At home, Liam works on his presentation until a knock at his front door interrupts his concentration.

"Hello?" He calls out.

"It's me…it's Beth."

"I know your voice, Beth." Liam opens the door to see her standing there, looking guilty, a pizza box in hand.

"It was open downstairs, so I just came up. Hungry?"

Liam looks inside the box. "Wait, I thought you said Reggio's was closed?"

Beth looks pleased with herself. "I found out that Mr Reggio opened another pizzeria across town, and I got him to make this pizza just for you. It's probably cold, but it'll still be as you remembered."

"Okay, you can come in." He leads her through to the kitchen. "I see you got the flowers." He nods to the cornflowers Beth places on the bench next to her handbag.

"I don't know how you remembered that."

"You're hard to forget, Beth."

"My choice of words sometimes isn't so memorable. I'm sorry about what I said."

Liam looks at her, wary. "About this being a mistake?"

Beth fidgets. "Yeah, that."

"So did you mean it?"

"No…of course, I didn't mean it. What's happened between us, it's incredible…" She sighs. "I got so upset because of the thought of you leaving…"

Liam moves closer. "Beth", he sighs, "I had mentioned to a colleague in Beijing that I might take the position. I needed time to explain…but you took off so quickly." He takes her hands.

"I panicked. I shouldn't expect to know everything happening in your life. But here it is. I'm going to be selfish and say I don't want you to leave. Not before we see where this takes us. But I also know it's a great opportunity for you, and I want you to be happy. So, I'm really torn about how to handle this and what I should be saying to you."

"Beth."

"Wait, I just need to say one more thing. It's taken me a long time to work out what I want and what type of person I want in my life. It frustrated me that I couldn't articulate it. But I know now…it's you. It's always been you."

Liam drags her body to his and kisses her intensely.

He pulls back for a moment. "I'm glad you said that because I've already decided. I'm not leaving."

"You're not?" She looks back wide-eyed.

"I'm pitching another role where I head up the Beijing team, but I just go monthly for any meetings we can't do remotely. I'll still work across the Asian market but from right here in Boston."

"And they'll let you do this?"

"I'm pretty confident they will."

"Oh, Liam." Beth places her hands on his shoulders and jumps up and down. "So that's it? You're staying?"

"Yes. I mean, if I had nothing important keeping me here, I probably would have considered it. But I can't leave, not now."

"Why?" she asks with a coy smile.

"Because of the pizza of course. Reggio's is back."

She playfully pushes him in the chest.

"You want me to say it, don't you?" He says.

"Of course."

"Beth, I can't watch you walk away from me ever again. That's why I know this is the right decision."

She wraps her hands around his neck for another kiss, then abruptly pulls away. "I have news too!"

"What's that?"

"I made partner and so did James!"

"Woah! That's incredible news. Wait, I can't believe you didn't tell me this as soon as you walked in. Congratulations!"

"I needed to make things right with you first."

"I knew you would do it." Liam lifts her up and spins her around the room. "But…what about Mr Williams? I hate to bring it up, but will you be working with him?"

"No. I've told the firm I'll be pressing charges, and they've given me their full support. I hope this doesn't jeopardise your job offer."

"He can try if he wants to, but don't worry about that. As long as you're going to be okay."

"I will." Beth embraces him.

"I have a question I've been wanting to ask you for a long time."

"What's that?"

Liam pulls a serious face. "I've been waiting a long time to ask you this…do you think I can take you out on a date?"

Beth beams. "Yes! I thought you would never ask."

"But first I want to eat this pizza."

Chapter 32

Michael waits for Liam to open his front door. "You, okay? You look flustered."

"Yep. All good."

Michael looks past him to Beth on the couch. "Hey, I didn't know you were here."

"Umm, yeah, I just dropped by," Beth says with coffee in hand.

"I didn't know you guys hung out without me."

"Umm, sometimes," she says.

Michael eyes them suspiciously.

"We do sometimes," Liam agrees.

"You guys are acting weird again. Anyway, you're both here, so that works." He sits himself at the dining table.

Liam follows suit. "I'm sorry again about Macy. I still can't believe Logan was the father the whole time."

"Yep, it's going to take a while. It's still messing with my mind."

"So does everyone know now?" Beth asks from the couch.

"Yes, except Harold. They're just waiting until he's a little more stable."

"I don't know what else to say, Mikey. About all of this," Beth says.

"So much changed so quickly, and now that it's all gone…I think I was enjoying it, as weird as that sounds."

"That's not weird," Beth says.

"I'm sorry to you guys, too. I've dragged you through this mess with me."

Liam pats his shoulder. "Can't think of anywhere else I'd rather be."

"Thanks." Michael tries to smile.

"And what about Chloe?" Beth asks. "What does she think about all of this?"

"Ah, I know she was pretty shocked by it all."

"And?" Beth presses.

"I don't know the rest."

"What? So, you aren't talking to her anymore?"

"No, it's not like that…it's complicated."

"I thought you and Chloe seemed, you know…friendly?" Beth says.

Michael looks over at Liam. He obviously hasn't gone into details with Beth.

"We're…I'm not really sure. Probably nothing now." He scratches the back of his neck, confused. "We don't have anything tying us together anymore."

"Isn't that a good thing though? It makes things less complicated," Liam offers.

Beth gasps. "You *like* her?"

Michael sighs. "Maybe. Anyway, doesn't matter."

"This is so, so good!" Beth says.

"Just call her," Liam demands.

"I don't think I can."

"You know, one day you're going to have trust someone again to not break your heart," Beth says.

Michael huffs. "It isn't that."

"I agree with Beth on this. You haven't dated anyone seriously since Naomi."

"I told you already—I don't think she'd be interested in me."

"You've used that excuse on me already."

"They aren't excuses."

"Don't just do nothing," Beth says.

"Yeah, yeah." Michael stands to get a drink, then looks at Beth and her bare feet. "Hey, Beth?" he asks.

"Yeah?"

"Don't you own a pair of high heels with balls that look like a sculptures as the heels? I always thought they were odd."

"What about them?"

"They just look oddly familiar to the ones over in the doorway to Liam's room."

Beth stares blankly.

"I knew it!" he says, pointing a finger from one to the other. "I knew there was something odd going on between you two."

Liam stands now, too. "It's not what you think, Mikey."

"I'm pretty sure it is. You're sleeping with my sister!"

"Okay, so it's exactly that. But…" He looks at Beth for help.

Beth holds up a hand. "Mikey, look, this is all new, and we haven't had a lot of time to talk about it." She looks back at Liam. "We're as surprised as you are, but we know we have feelings for each other."

"You," he points at Liam, "if you ever," he hesitates, then turns to Beth "if you break my buddy's heart, you'll dishonour our family."

"Me? Why would I break his heart?"

"Liam has already punched a guy out for you. He has well and truly proven himself."

Liam laughs. "Buddy, I'm so glad you aren't mad at me. I was worried you'd hate me, or hit me in the face, or both."

"This doesn't mean we're cool. And I still might punch you in the face. Sorry, but I think I need to walk around the block or something." Michael heads for the front door.

"Wait! Are you going to be okay?" Beth calls.

"Yeah, I will be." He shakes his head. "I just can't look at either of you two at the moment. It's weirding me out. My life's too full of surprises at the moment."

"So sorry, Mikey. I'm sorry about the timing…" Beth offers.

"Yeah, I get it—that goddam apple tree."

Chapter 33

Michael steals the last dumpling off Beth's plate.

"Hey!"

"What?"

"You're going to keep making me pay for this aren't you?"

"I better top up everyone's champagne," Liam says. He jumps up, grabs the bottle and pours some into Beth's glass. She looks up at him, and he kisses her on the lips.

"See?" Michael says. "This is why you owe me the last dumpling. If we weren't celebrating your partnership and Liam staying in town, I'd have to leave."

"Shut up." Beth pushes his arm. "Anyway, you can't leave. It's your apartment."

Liam reaches to top up Michael's glass. "Sorry. I know it's only been a few days for you to take this in. I'll try to remember not to kiss your sister in front of you."

"Thanks. That would be helpful. Even though I know you're full of shit, and you won't try at all."

Liam smirks. "True."

"Changing the subject for you, Mikey. Your place is looking pretty decent," Beth says, waving her chopstick around the room for effect.

"Why, thank you. I might have actually listened to you for once; I painted, bought some new artwork and furniture. Then threw out some really old mouldy, disgusting things."

"Gross!" Beth says, screwing up her nose.

"I've even thinking of turning my second bedroom into a proper podcast studio."

"That sounds great!" Beth says. "Maybe I can help find you some sponsors or something."

The doorbell rings.

"Want me to see?" Liam asks.

"Sure."

Liam walks over to the intercom. "Hey."

"Hi, can we come up?"

Michael knows that voice. He turns to look at Liam.

Liam looks puzzled. "It's Chloe…and Logan." He presses the buzzer to let them in.

"How does Chloe know where I live?"

"I might have told her," Beth says, nonchalant.

"Ahh, I see."

Beth shrugs and sips her champagne. "She told me she wanted to see you, since you won't call her back."

"I thought you wanted to speak to her?" Liam says to Michael.

"I do. I just don't know what to say or how to say it."

"How about, 'since I'm not Macy's father, do you think we can hang out now'?" Beth says.

Michael falters. "So much has happened…"

"How about *because* of what's happened?" Beth suggests. "Maybe you were never meant to get Macy."

"True," Liam agrees. "What if it was always about the girl?"

They all turn when they hear the knock at the door.

"Do you know why Logan is here?" Michael whispers to Beth.

"No, she didn't tell me that part."

"Great," he mutters.

"Just remember not to start a brawl with him, because you won't win. And you just redecorated."

"Thanks," Michael says flatly.

In a few minutes, they're all sitting around the table. Michael stares at the empty dumpling containers, trying not to look at Chloe.

Logan clears his throat. "I know you've done a lot for Macy, and for Harold and Winnie. Hell, you've been there when I should have been. I can't thank you enough for that. We turned your life upside down. So, on behalf of Ari and myself, I want to try and do something for you…Chloe told me you lost your job recently."

Michael looks up at Chloe. "How did you know?"

"When you didn't call me back…" She looks over at Beth, who's trying to look all innocent.

"Seriously?" Michel says. He looks back at Logan. "Yes, I did lose my job. What's it to you?"

"So, you've heard of NESN?"

Michael nods. "New England Sports Network."

"That's the one," Logan says. "They need a new sports reporter. I said I knew a guy and they want you to come in."

"But I'm a business reporter…well, I was."

"Come on, I've heard you're an expert on all the games. And Chloe sent me a link to your podcast. She told me it was really good, and she's right."

"Did she now?" He glances at Chloe, who shrugs.

"Mikey, this would be a dream for you," Beth says. "Plus, it might take me a while to find you some sponsors for your podcast."

"There's one more thing," Logan adds. "I also said that you would have this season's biggest scandal as an exclusive."

"It's not my field; my contacts aren't in sport. As if I can just magically pull a…"

"You can interview me. I'm breaking my contract, and I'm coming back to my home team where I started. Training is local, and the home games are here. Macy is my daughter now. I can at least try to be a decent sort of a father."

Michael is speechless, trying to process everything.

"So, is it a yes?"

Michael looks at Beth, who's nodding enthusiastically, then Liam.

"Bud, go for it," Liam says.

Michael breathes out, runs his hands through his hair. "I guess it's a yes." He thuds his fists on the table. "Yes!"

"Great. Oh, and one more thing?" Logan says.

"There's something else?" Michel eyes him, wary.

"I want you to know that you can see Macy anytime. I don't want you to be a stranger. Plus, I don't know what I'm doing and could really use your help."

"My help?" Michael chuckles. "I don't know if I'd be very useful, but I'd definitely like to see Macy."

Logan looks at Chloe now. "Do you want to tell him?"

Chloe looks up, a little nervous. "Ah, yes. We've all spoken—Logan, Winne, Harold and I—and we'd like you to be Macy's godfather. That is, if you accept."

"Godfather? Wow! Yes. I…that means a lot. I'm almost speechless."

"And Chloe?" Logan continues.

"Yes?"

"I hope this means we can start over? Especially since I've let you keep your godmother status."

Chloe almost snorts. "Ha! So noble of you."

Godmother? So, I will see her, Michael thinks.

Chloe sighs and looks Logan in the eye. "No more lies, okay?"

"You got it." Logan smiles and moves to embrace her, but she holds up a hand.

"I don't need a hug, thank you."

Logan rolls his eyes while Chloe tries to hide a smile.

Another bottle of champagne later, Logan, Beth and Liam make an obvious departure, leaving Chloe lingering. She picks up her handbag to leave. "I should probably get going too."

Michael follows her to the door. "Okay…I guess, I'll see you at Macy's birthday or something I suppose."

"Right, of course." She looks away, then moves to open the door.

Michael's heart beats faster.

"Goodbye, Michael."

He pauses. Is that sadness in her eyes? Or am I self-reflecting?

The door closes and she disappears. His heart sinks. "It's now or never," he says to himself. He flings the door open. "Wait, Chloe!" he yells down the hallway.

She quickly turns around.

"I just need to know…did you really listen to my podcast?"

Chloe's eyes are wide. "Is that really the question you're going to ask me?"

Michael looks down at his feet trying to hide a grin.

"Yes, Michael I did…is there anything else?"

"Okay, that wasn't what I really wanted to ask…I was just building up to it. It's killing me not knowing…are you engaged to Francis?" Michael's heart seems to pause awaiting her response.

"No, I'm not."

Michael breathes a huge sigh of relief. "So, you aren't getting married?"

"No, definitely not."

"I see…so, are you okay about that decision?"

Chloe tilts her head. "Yes, totally okay."

"I wish I could say I'm sorry."

"No need. He isn't the person I want anymore." Chloe takes a big breath, then releases it. "I don't want to talk about Francis anymore." She walks up to him and stands close.

"I can agree to that."

"I'm sorry this all happened to you. You didn't deserve this."

"Look, the outcome isn't all bad. I would never have met Macy, and I still get to be a part of her life. And then…there's you."

"But…you've been avoiding me."

Michael averts his gaze. "Okay, yeah, that's true. Sorry about that. I…I assumed the worst and I buried my head in the sand. And you were sort of cold to me the day after…you know after what happened between us. I took that as an indication where you were at with things."

Chloe looks down and fidgets with her hands. "I needed some time. I didn't know how to deal with the situation the day after. And you being Macy's dad…or *when* you were Macy's dad."

"It was awkward. I get that."

Chloe looks up at him. "But things are certainly less complicated now."

"Are they?" Michael raises his eyebrows with interest. "Look, I think you must already know how I feel about you. I was being honest with you. You know that right? That night at the festival? It was so hard for me to slow things down. Really, really goddam hard."

"I know. You've never lied to me…but I did lie to you."

"Really?" Michael gulps.

"When I said I couldn't be with you, it was never because of who you are. I was trying to do what I thought was right. I had to pretend—mainly to myself— that I hadn't fallen for you. But the truth is, I already had."

Michael closes the distance between them, brings her face to his and presses his mouth to hers. An intense feeing of pleasure spreads through his body. He pulls back quickly. "That's music to my ears!"

Chloe smiles up at him. "Been saving that line, have you?"

He chuckles. "Not my fault. These dad jokes are really lingering."

"Ha, of course."

He leans in and kisses her again, then pauses. "You know as much as I love this hallway, we could go inside?"

"Perhaps, we could pick up from where we left off?" Chloe grins cheekily.

Michael leads her back inside the apartment as their kissing heats up and gasps intertwine. They move past the kitchen and lounge, eagerly removing each other's tops until they reach the base of the bed. Chloe wriggles out of her skirt and pushes him down onto the bed, straddling him like she did in the tent.

Seeing her in black lingerie makes his body instantly ache for her. Her eyes eager, loose curls dancing playfully around her face, her breath more urgent. She bites her lower lip and begins exploring his chest once again, fingers gliding over his tattooed abdomen.

He closes his eyes, enjoying the sensation, barely holding himself back. She unbuttons his jeans painfully slowly. A low growl of anticipation escapes him. He feels her hesitate. He leans up on his elbows and looks at her.

Her fingers tease below his abdomen. "I have a question."

"Got me right where you wanted me, didn't you?" He smirks.

"Exactly…I want to know what you said to me in the tent before we fell to sleep that night?"

"Ohhh…I…I don't remember that." His jaw twitches and he looks away.

Chloe shakes her head in amusement. "Your sister was right; you're a terrible liar."

"She said that? Unbelievable." Michael scoffs.

"So, are you going to tell me?"

"Hmm, I don't think you'd be interested." He pulls her gently down on to his chest.

"I think I would be. It sounded meaningful." Their eyes meet.

"How do you know?"

"Because of your tone and the way you held me."

"Hmmm."

"Tell me"

Michael lifts a hand and brushes her cheek. "I said…I don't want to ever let you go."

"That's what I was hoping you said." Her lips curve into a wide smile.

With that, Michael pulls her close and doesn't let her go.

End